WITHDRAWN
UTSA LIBRARIES

The High Spirits

Also by David Huddle

A Dream with No Stump Roots in It
STORIES

Only the Little Bone
STORIES

Paper Boy
POEMS

Stopping by Home
POEMS

The High Spirits

STORIES OF MEN AND WOMEN

David Huddle

DAVID R. GODINE, PUBLISHER ✦ BOSTON

Thanks to the National Endowment for the Arts, the Virginia Center for the Creative Arts, Lindsey Huddle, Charles Huddle, Lyn Tisdale, Barbara Murphy, Ghita Orth, Allen Shepherd, Frances Smith, John Engels, Marisha Chamberlain, and Margot Livesey.

First published in 1989 by
David R. Godine, Publisher, Inc.
Horticultural Hall
300 Massachusetts Avenue
Boston, Massachusetts 02115

Copyright © 1989 by David Huddle

All rights reserved. No part of this book may be used or reproduced in any manner whatsoever without written permission, except in the case of brief quotations embodied in critical articles or reviews.

In slightly different form, "Apache" and "The Gorge" appeared in *Denver Quarterly*, "Sketching Hannah" in *The Hudson Review*, "Underwater Spring" in *Triquarterly*, "Playing" in *Quarterly West*, "In the Mean Mud Season" in *Yankee*, "The Crossing" in *Prairie Schooner*, and "The Deacon" in *Epoch*. "Apache" also appeared in *The Breadloaf Anthology of Contemporary American Short Stories*, edited by Robert Pack and Jay Parini, University Press of New England, 1987.

Library of Congress Cataloging in Publication Data
Huddle, David, 1942–
The high spirits.
I. Title.
PS 35558.U287H5 1989 813'.54 87-46298
ISBN 0-87923-735-X HC 0-87923-817-8 SC

First Edition
Printed in the United States of America

Library
University of Texas
at San Antonio

for Bess

Contents

The High Spirits

Underwater Spring

June

THE FIRST HOT DAY in June she took her son down to the water so that they could talk. Old man Blair's flat-bottomed boat was just where she thought it would be, and she showed James the secret place where the pushing pole and the paddle were always hidden. They sat down together to take off their shoes. Then she had him get in the front of the boat, while she unhitched it and pushed it out a little way before stepping in herself. She told him to hold still, stood up carefully, balanced, and began poling the boat. At first she was awkward, laughing at herself when the boy looked back at her, but then she got steadier. She told James that old man Blair was just about dead and that when he died Aunt Bernice and Aunt Alicia would have the boat taken off their property. James didn't ask why his great-aunts would do that. She knew it was because he was almost ten, old enough now to understand for himself.

They got out to where the water was too deep for poling, and she sat down. She stuck the heavy end of the pole down in under her feet, letting it rest on the seat beside the boy. Then she took up the paddle and worked without talking. She was tired when they got out to the big rock; sweat was coming out of her hair, down her forehead and around her ears. When she finished tying the boat up the way Mr. Blair had showed her how to do it years ago, she helped James get out and up onto the sitting place of the rock. She explained to him about the spring, the strong pressure of pure fresh water coming out of a crevice in the rock, how far down she didn't know. She heard herself telling him the same things Mr. Blair had told her when she was a child: the pond got low and stagnant late in the summer, but here it was always deep enough and the water was always cold. She asked him if he wanted to go for a swim, but he said no, he guessed not. She knew he was waiting for her to tell him what was on her mind, and so she went ahead and told him: she expected it wouldn't be long before she left.

"With Mr. Shumate?" James asked. She nodded once, keeping her head down, keeping her thick brown hair between her eyes and the boy.

"He doesn't want me to come along?"

This time she made herself look at him. "He likes you, but he doesn't want you to come with us."

"You think he'll stay with you?" James asked it in a soft voice; it was a way he had of letting her know that he knew her better than anybody else.

"For a while. He'll stay with me for a while," she said. She knew what he was about to ask next. She waited for it.

"Then will you come back?"

"I don't know," she said. "It'll be hard."

"Because of Aunt Bernice and Aunt Alicia," the boy said. She could see how he was thinking of them, widows who wore sweaters even in the summertime, who said grace over every meal, turned off the radio, and went to bed at nine o'clock.

"They'll be kind to you. They'll learn how to talk to you. They'll learn how you are." She didn't touch him then, though she wanted to, wanted just to take his thin arm with her hand.

"Like they learned with you," James said.

"No, better than that. Better than that," she said it again to try to make it sound right. It didn't.

James stood up on the shelf of rock to take his clothes off, using her shoulder when he needed it to balance himself. She watched him the whole time; she was tickled at the sight of his skinny little butt and spindly ribs, but she kept herself from smiling. He dived off the rock and came up sputtering, shouting that it was cold, that she should have told him how cold it was. "You didn't ask," she shouted back at him. He swam over to where she was dangling her feet.

"Lean down here, please. I want to tell you something," he said. She looked at him. "Come on, I'm serious," he said.

When she leaned down he caught her arm and pulled her in, clothes and all. She tried to grab him, to push him under, but he was too quick for her, got away, and swam out some distance from her. She knew her clothes made her too heavy to be able to catch him, and so she swam over to where the spring roiled up the water. She could feel a constant, cold rippling that pushed against her whole body. The boy swam over to her; they stayed steady there with the spring washing up between them, the water moving their arms and legs in a kind of slow dance. They began giggling at each other. Then she could tell that the boy's laughing had turned into something else. His voice was too loud and hoarse. She caught his arm and pulled him with her back to the rock, helped him up, and followed him. James coughed and snorted, as though he'd had water go up his nose. She sat beside him, shivering.

When they came up to the house, they decided to try the back door, hoping the aunts would be in the parlor. They were wrong. Aunt Bernice was sitting at the kitchen table reading aloud from the obituary column, while Aunt Alicia stood with her back to them, looking out the window. Aunt Bernice finished the listing of survivors and looked over her glasses at James and his mother. "Carolyn, you're wet," she said.

"Yes, I am, Aunt Bernice. I fell in."

"You have the worst luck, don't you, dear?"

"No, I don't," the boy's mother said. "I just fell in. It wasn't bad."

Aunt Alicia turned around and looked at them. Her eyes were still good; she needed no glasses. She had been watching them come up the hill toward the house. "I wish you hadn't taken the boy down there." Neither James nor his mother said anything. "Maybe James will get your bath water for you," Aunt Alicia said. She moved the big teakettle over to the hot part of the stove. Then she went out of the kitchen. Aunt Bernice trailed along behind carrying the paper with her.

James fixed his mother a tub of bathwater in the kitchen, while she was upstairs finding dry clothes for herself. Then he went into the parlor and sat with Aunt Bernice and Aunt Alicia. Soon his mother came in, smelling like soap, looking pretty and fresh in her clean clothes. Later that afternoon, Mr. Shumate came to visit, wearing a royal blue tie that he loosened almost as soon as he had sat down. Aunt Alicia fixed iced tea with fresh mint leaves for them all. James and his mother carried on a cheerful conversation, but it was hard for them to get Aunt Bernice or Aunt Alicia or Mr. Shumate, who was sweating, to say very much.

July

James knew she was going that day when he saw her coming down the steps in her yellow dress and carrying a suitcase. She asked him to take the suitcase and go wait for her outside on the front porch. It wasn't very heavy. The air outside was cool; the day smelled damp and new. He put the suitcase down at the top of the steps but decided not to sit on the glider, which would squeak even if he sat still. Instead, he stood with his hands in his pockets, watching the trucks pass by on the little road that ran no more than seven good paces from Aunt Bernice and Aunt Alicia's house. Later in the day heat would come up in shimmering waves off the road, which would become slick with patches of melted tar. James guessed his mother was in the kitchen talking to them now, but he couldn't hear any voices through the screen door. They would talk about it quietly, he knew that; they wouldn't raise their voices.

The trucks made a lot of noise; they shook the house when they went by, but they had done that for as long as he could remember. He was used to it. When he'd been a little boy, he'd tried to make them stop by standing beside the road with his thumb out. Usually they'd just pass on by, the drivers lifting their hands to wave to him, or else one of them would toot its blatting air horn at him and make him jump with the noise. One day, though, he'd been standing there with his thumb out when a huge gray-and-red Purina truck had put on its brakes, shrieking and clattering to a stop. He'd been very scared, had run inside, found his mother in the kitchen and cried with his face in her lap. After he explained to her what had happened, he'd heard Aunt Bernice saying behind him, "Thumbing down trucks. Boy's got his father's blood," but his mother had winked at him.

Now he heard Aunt Alicia in the house, saying, "Carolyn, you come back here." Then his mother came out onto the porch, making herself smile at him. She bent, just a little because she wasn't much taller than he was; she kissed him on the mouth, so that he was stunned and couldn't think what to say or what to do. "Good-bye, James," she said, but he couldn't say anything back to her.

She picked up the suitcase and started down the steps. He went with her to the road. Then he asked her where Mr. Shumate was; it was all he could think of to say to her.

"He's waiting for me down at the post office," she said. "Say good-bye to me now, please."

"All right," he said. He swallowed; after a moment he said, "He should have waited for you here." It wasn't what he meant to tell her, but it was what came out of him.

She walked in the gray dust beside the road, down toward the post office, and he stood watching her. Two houses down, she lifted her hand. He heard her call out, "Hello, Mrs. Blair." He imagined he could see the toothless grinning old widow lady who had taken to sitting out on her front porch and asking everyone who walked by if they'd brought anything to give her. "No Ma'am," his mother shouted at Mrs. Blair the same as everybody did. "I don't have anything for you today." She walked on. A truck came by, too fast, like they all drove through here, like it wasn't even a town but just another mile of highway. The truck made a wind that blew her skirt against the suitcase. Then another truck came behind that one. The trucks passed him by the same as they had slammed past her. He watched her. He felt the waves of air hit him, knock him back, and sting his face with road dust.

August

At the breakfast table that morning, Aunt Bernice mentioned that the front window of her bedroom had begun to stick again. James watched Aunt Alicia open her mouth to say something but then close it again. He understood that she was about to mention Mr. Shumate, who'd fixed the window early in the summer. She'd caught herself in time, because they didn't talk about Mr. Shumate when the boy was around. He didn't say anything. After a while Aunt Alicia fixed his eggs and toast and set the plate in front of him. The great-aunts sat without eating. No one said anything. James ate as fast as he figured he could get by with. He stuffed the last of his toast in his mouth, excused himself, and walked outside. He headed directly toward where they had asked him not ever to go again, down the path through the rickety old grape arbor, past the red raspberry bushes and the outhouse, then down through the field where there was no path.

He came to the place where the boat used to be, where the silt-covered water began. There he undressed, folding his clothes and tucking them up into the branches of a half-dead cedar. He waded out into the stinking water. He had to go slowly; the bottom was mostly sucking mud, with stones here and there. Where he lifted his legs, his white skin streamed from the knees down with brownish-gray dirt. It took him a long time to get to where the water was up to his hips. He stood still there, catching his breath, willing himself to go on out farther. There were fewer trees growing up out of the water here. The sunlight came down in wide patches, making this ugly part of the pond sparkle. It was quiet and still.

He went on walking until the water reached his waist; then he let himself down into it and began swimming slowly. He could see now where he was going; it was so far away he wondered if he had the strength to get there. The water became clear and cold, much colder, as he went on. Now there were no trees. He swam under a hot August sun. Long before he reached the rock, he thought he could feel the force of the spring washing against him. Then he felt it directly beneath him, a strong surge of icy water that made him feel almost as though he was buoyed up at the top of a fountain spray. It was a giddy feeling, but he was tired; he kicked and made two more strokes with his arms to reach the rock, clinging to it for a long time before he was strong enough to pull himself up.

The stone shelf where he sat was not large enough for him to lie down or even to stretch himself out very much. He hugged his knees and shivered until the sun warmed him. He was in no hurry. He could see out across the water where it gradually turned from the clear gray-blue color into darker and darker shades of brown back in toward the trees. Without ever actually deciding to do it, he pushed himself off the rock, back into the water, dog-paddling until he was used to the cold again. He caught a huge gulp of air and flipped himself head down to dive, pulling hard with his arms and kicking with his legs. It was not very far beneath the surface that he wanted to go. Before he'd even opened his eyes, his hand touched and then caught the place where he wanted to hold on.

He caught another part of the smooth rock with his other

hand and pulled his whole body down, having to use all his strength to pull himself close to the powerful outward flowing of the spring. Finally his feet caught in the right places, and he clung, with his eyes closed, against the smooth stone, letting the cold water wash against him. He could hold this embrace for only a short while before the pressure of his lungs and the black dizziness forced him to let go and rise slowly to the surface. He dog-paddled again, until his head cleared and he'd caught another breath. When he went back down, he was able to hold himself against the spring's force a little longer. This second time, when he came to the surface, his head rang. He knew he couldn't go down again, and so he pulled himself back up onto the shelf of rock. He sat hugging himself, smelling his own wet skin, feeling his heart become calm as he dried in the sunlight. He stayed there on the rock until he was too uncomfortable to sit still. Then he stood up and dived off, out over the place where the spring roiled the water in front of the rock. He swam back toward the trees, pacing himself carefully, looking ahead only once or twice to adjust his direction.

He came into the thick brown water and put his feet down to test the depth. He found he'd swum in farther than he'd thought, but he was very tired. He half crawled and half dog-paddled until his knees began bumping the bottom. Finally he stood up, feeling sluggish and heavy, his body almost too much weight for him to move. He waded in toward the place where he knew his clothes were. Using swatches of broom sage, James cleaned himself off as best he could, while his skin was still wet. He knew he smelled bad now. Finally he took his undershirt and tried to scrub himself even cleaner. He thought he'd done a pretty good job with the dirt, but he knew he would still have the smell on him. He threw the undershirt away, dressed himself, and walked back through the field up toward the house.

Thinking they'd still be in the kitchen, James walked around to the front door to try to sneak upstairs without their seeing him. But they were waiting for him in the parlor. Aunt Bernice was working the crossword puzzle; Aunt Alicia was crocheting another doily. They called him in before he'd even gotten a foot on the stairs. He stood in the doorway while they considered him. Eventually Aunt Alicia turned her attention back to her crocheting and said, "I smell him, don't you?"

"Yes, I do," Aunt Bernice said. "I smelled him the minute the door opened." James stood at the parlor threshold watching the light shafting in through the window behind Aunt Bernice. He knew Aunt Alicia would think a long time before she told him what to do. He stood waiting until she said, "Go get the tub, son. Fill it up."

He went out onto the back porch for the big zinc tub, brought it into the kitchen, and set it on the floor. He put a full teakettle of water onto the stove to heat, then went back to the pump on the back porch to draw his bathwater. Using the white enamel bucket to haul in the water, he made five trips before he got enough for what his great-aunts would call a decent bath. When he was pouring in the hot water from the teakettle, they came into the kitchen and sat at opposite ends of the table. James hoped to delay the bath by staying out on the back porch for a long time, pretending to be looking for the washcloth and soap. When he came back in, they were still sitting there, waiting for him. "Go ahead, son," said Aunt Alicia.

With his back turned toward them, he took off his clothes, then stepped into the tub backward so as not to have to face them. Squatting down into it, he began washing himself. He made himself work very thoroughly so that they wouldn't give him directions. He knew they were watching. When he'd splashed the gray water over himself enough to rinse off the soap, he stood up, still with his back turned toward them, but he heard one of them getting up and coming toward him. It was Aunt Alicia, with a clean white towel. He took it from her. "Where's your undershirt?" she asked him.

"I didn't wear one this morning," James said. He felt Aunt Alicia staring at him. He knew she was determined to be kind to him.

"Go upstairs and get dressed," she told him after a while. "And then I think you should stay up there until suppertime."

"No," said Aunt Bernice. She sighed. "I don't think he should be up there by himself."

"All right," said Aunt Alicia. "When you've dressed, come downstairs. We'll find something for you to do." She smiled at him.

He walked upstairs naked, leaving the pile of his dirty clothes on the floor for them to deal with as they saw fit. He dressed very slowly. James combed his hair, and in the mirror he made the faces of a clown, an ape, a fish, and an idiot. Then he went downstairs. His great-aunts were watching for him in the parlor.

Sketching Hannah

NELSON IS OUT OF PLACE. His way is downhill, but even that does not excuse the speed of his pace or his odd carriage. He is bent forward, his hands are jammed into the pockets of his open trench coat, and his tie flaps out ahead of him. He seems almost to be butting the air with his head. The wind is chilly this bright November day; skirls of leaves fly in the empty streets and from lawn to lawn of the houses he passes. The lake at the foot of the hill shines now in the afternoon sunlight. If he cared to see the water, he could easily stop, catch his breath, savor a pretty view. But Nelson doesn't even slow down. His eyes function only to tell him whether or not the next ten feet or so of sidewalk are safe to travel. He lets the slope of the hill and the cold and wind carry him at a near run.

Hannah won't be home from work, and he knows it's foolish for him to get there so soon and then have to pass the time chatting with her roommates. Worse would be if he gets penned up in the kitchen with one or two of the scruffy young men whom the roommates introduce as friends and who bemusedly question him about his law practice. He can barely bring himself to recite the names of her roommates: Dawn, Michelle, and Heather.

Hannah is a lanky woman, but Nelson thinks she isn't remarkable-looking unless studied closely. In April she came to see him about back wages owed her by a former employer named Seaford. In a low voice, choosing her words carefully, she told Nelson that Seaford was a potter, that after dropping out of Mt. Holyoke she had apprenticed herself to him. Seaford owed her about $500 in wages and another $125 she had lent him. Seaford had left town two weeks ago, and neither Hannah nor anyone else knew where he had gone. Hannah was pretty sure he would head for Vancouver. Hannah had stayed at Seaford's shop until the morning a bank officer and various creditors came to haul away Seaford's pots, wheels, bags of clay, shelves, glazing materials, and even his kiln. Hannah told him she'd watched workmen disassemble Seaford's kiln with sledgehammers and then throw the worthless pieces onto the bed of a pick-up truck.

She takes care to dress plainly. That day in his office she sat across from Nelson in hiking boots, blue jeans, an old blue sweater; she wore a blue bandanna to cover most of her straight black hair. Ordinarily Nelson would have heard her out and then explained that he couldn't help her. The amount of money involved was small, the work complicated. But as she talked to him, Nelson saw her becoming more and more lovely. Her forehead was high, and she had wide cheekbones. She didn't appear at all uncomfortable, though Nelson imagined she'd never before sat in a lawyer's office. She was intelligent and even a little funny, laughing now and then when she described Seaford's peculiarities to him. She said that one afternoon back in January, when it was bitterly cold and the heat in the shop had broken down, Seaford became convinced his life had gone wrong. Shortly thereafter, the pots had begun to come out of the kiln cracked, pocked, and skewed. She said she missed Seaford. Then she smiled at Nelson and said softly, almost to herself, "I guess you didn't want to know that." Nelson assured her that he was very glad indeed to know it and that he found her frankness refreshing.

Until now Nelson hadn't located Seaford. For his efforts on Hannah's behalf, he could show only a report of Seaford's having received a speeding ticket in the vicinity of Minot, South Dakota. But today he has news for her, Seaford's address and phone number in Seattle. Nelson's attitude toward Seaford remains entirely dispassionate. He expects he won't get much money for Hannah, but he still plans to pursue the case conscientiously, knows he will hold on to it as long as it holds out any possibility.

Not so long ago, Nelson would have enjoyed looking carefully at the houses he passed. They were built back when this small northern city boomed with money from the lumber business. Nelson would have considered with sympathy the new families living here, husbands and wives trying in difficult times to raise decent children. But landscapes pain him now; almost anything he sees hurts. He knows if he goes slowly and looks out through the bare, waving branches of the oaks and maples toward the lake, he will be assaulted by the sight. The weather, the season, the hard objects of the world, all seem to him connected to his blood. This cold, windy sunlight projects every shape toward him too harshly, too vividly. He wants to fly toward whatever he sees, and he sees everything with terrific, agonizing clarity. He feels giddy, so alive he can hardly stand it.

Why Hannah sees him he isn't sure. "Why wouldn't I want you?" she asks in her wry way. "What's wrong with you?" They have long, complicated talks in which they evaluate themselves and each other. These talks seem dangerous to Nelson, as though one of them could easily say the cruel thing that would kill off what they feel for each other. They name this feeling as care: "I care for you," one of them will say, and the other must merely smile and not return the foolish, "I care for you, too." Walking now, with only a block or two more before he reaches the house, he puzzles over it, the name for what they are to each other. Hannah's body is beautiful and funny to him when he thinks of it not in her presence: her knees, of which she is ashamed because of their boniness; her arms, so thin and stringy-muscled he is always surprised at how strong she is. His consideration of her body and face is what he holds in his mind most often, the vision he cherishes, what he wants to fly toward now instead of these trees and houses and the stones of the high ledge here at the steepest part of the hill: the clean line of her hair past her forehead, behind her ear, halfway down her neck.

She has no shyness. "You should see how I do this. I'm sorry if you don't want to." That day in September she stood in the dark part of the room, near the bureau, with her back to him. He watched her thin shoulder blades moving as though they were about to become wings. Then she moved into the light, facing him. "So maybe you're a little older. You think that means you won't get me pregnant?" Now it has become ritual. With one foot on the bed and both her arms stretched downward across her breasts, she makes Nelson think of girls Degas painted. If he'd lived another sixty years, Degas would have found Hannah, Nelson is certain of it, and painted her this way—bending forward, awkward, the light on her hip, her foot on the bed turned outward.

Here at her house, the hill is so steep that Nelson's steps ring heavily on the sidewalk. He goes past the small front lawn that contains Hannah's miniature garden, past the walk that would take him to her front door. When he turns into the driveway below the house, he catches one glimpse of the sharp reflection of sunlight on the lake, a clear sweep of airy distance out across the water into vague blue-white nothingness. He doesn't want to see any of it. He goes to the basement door and pushes it open.

Both of them prefer this way of entering the house, coming up from beneath. In the dark silence, out of the wind, Nelson feels better. He doesn't even bother turning on the light. He knows the way here, knows even that Hannah's bicycle is standing just inside the door, knows and is comforted by the soft rumble of the furnace on the other side of the crude basement staircase. And when he has climbed the steps, not counting them but knowing anyway when he has taken the last one, and has come through the door into the light of the kitchen, he is immediately certain that he is alone in the house.

The basement door is never locked. A week ago he drove here at four in the morning, dousing the car's headlights just before turning into the driveway. He, Nelson, was a thief, coming up into the kitchen, feeling his way to the staircase to the second floor, walking softly so as not to wake the room-mates, opening Hannah's door so slowly and quietly he became almost dizzy with the blackness all around him. He closed the door behind him and stood at the foot of her bed. From the streetlights shining in through her windows, he could see her shape under the covers. He undressed, found the ashtray she kept for him on her desk, lit a cigarette, and sat down on the bed beside her. She spoke to him clearly; he didn't know how long she'd been awake: "I don't like you to come here like this."

"I can leave," he said. She was quiet, and soon he got in bed with her, put the ashtray on his stomach, and finished the cigarette. She let him curl himself against her back, run his hand over her shoulder and arm, her breasts, the sharp bones of her hip, her flank. He wanted to have her then, just to fly into her. And maybe he could have had it that way, but he thought he couldn't, thought she was having a difficult enough time getting used to his having violated her sleep and her bed. So he waited, listened to her breathing, thought it was all right if she went to sleep; he would be there with her when first light came into the room.

After a while she talked, and he knew she'd been thinking, not going to sleep at all. "Seaford came here like this once or twice. I'd wake up with him shoving me around, trying to pry my legs open." She laughed softly about Seaford; it was the way she usually ended whatever she had to say about him.

"I guess I wanted the same thing," Nelson said. "Was he very drunk?"

"No," she said. "He liked tea. Nothing with alcohol." She paused and then went on. "He just didn't care to say much. I never knew where I was with him. The best times we had were when we were both working on the wheels. That was the closest I was to him. When both our wheels were turning and making that soft noise, and the clay was taking whatever shape our hands were giving it, it was like I was living in both our bodies at the same time, same blood and everything. One day I tried to get him to talk with me about it, but he got mad and stomped out of the shop. He was gone a long time, and when he came back I wasn't even thinking about what I'd said to him. He came in and yelled at me, 'Listen, it's two pots. Any way you think about it, it's still two pots.' "

"What did you say?" Nelson asked.

"Nothing. I didn't say anything." Hannah sat up and put her feet on the floor. Nelson touched her back with the tips of his fingers, and after a while he felt her shivering. When she went to the bureau in the corner of the room, he could see the narrow strip of whiteness that was her back. He heard her opening the top drawer, and he imagined her hair falling forward around her face.

Nelson is at ease now, no longer in a hurry. He has never been here when the house was empty, when there wasn't music coming from Michelle's elaborate stereo system in the living room. He forgets even to take off his trench coat; he is absorbed in the extraordinary silence of the house. He walks slowly through the dining room, the living room, the downstairs bathroom. Then he goes upstairs and into each of the roommates' bedrooms; they are so cluttered and bizarrely decorated, it is difficult for him to distinguish between ornament and debris. He saves Hannah's room for last.

Her bed is made. The curtains are open at the bay window at the head of her bed. He can see the lake outside; and now he pauses a moment to look at it, finds the view pleasing, especially the sloping field of houses that curves down toward the water. Nelson thinks then of the city as having risen up out of the lake, housed and peopled, pleasant, busy, alive. Straight down from the window is the small circle of bricks where in May Hannah set out marigolds, pansies, nasturtiums, zinnias.

At this hour of the afternoon, the light here from this alcove of windows gives the room a quality of age and fragility. But Nelson knows it changes. Later today, when Hannah comes, the sun will fall directly on them, the trees will wave and move patterns of shadow over the bed. At that hour Nelson has imagined the two of them underwater, the room an aquarium. Occasionally Hannah likes sharing a cigarette with him; she will hold it in her teeth, "like a gun moll," she says, and lie on her stomach, letting the smoke roll up over her face. They no longer must remind each other to notice how the light is. Even on rainy days when it is muted and turns the room a soft tint of blue-gray, Nelson is grateful for it. Hannah lies sometimes with her hands behind her head, lifting one leg and then the other, pointing her toes toward the ceiling. Nelson pretends to drowse then, but usually he watches her through slitted eyelids.

He walks back away from the windows. He opens Hannah's closet, takes a blouse out, holds it to his face, puts it back. Then he undresses. He hangs up the trench coat, his suit and shirt; he puts his shoes and socks on the closet floor; on hooks inside the door he hangs his underwear and tie. He shuts the door and pats a light drum cadence with his hands on his belly, then stretches his arms up to the ceiling, stands on tiptoe for a moment. The cool air makes him shiver a little, but the feeling is pleasant to him, exhilarating, and he goes to Hannah's small mirror, standing first this way and then that to try to see as much of himself as he can. His chest and arms and belly are covered with hair the color of tin or ashes. But his muscles still hold enough form to allow Nelson a little pleasure in the sight of his body. He goes to her bed and gets into it. Hannah sometimes complains that the bed is too soft, but now it seems to him to be holding him up gently, as though he were floating on salt water. The covers, the sheets, the pillow are all full of her smell. He curls on his side and gazes at the picture.

The paper has been torn raggedly at the top edge; it is that of an ordinary sketch pad. The lines are sepia, and they appear to have been drawn deftly and quickly. Nelson picked up Hannah late one night after she finished posing for it. Sometimes she models for the students of a drawing class. Seaford suggested it to her as a way of picking up easy money. That night she'd been excited when she got into the car with Nelson. She tried to unroll the picture for him to see it, but there wasn't room enough, and in the dark he couldn't make it out anyway. "They let me keep it," she told him. She explained that she'd never been shy about standing in front of them, but she'd never had the courage to look at the sketches the students made of her. "They each make ten or twelve," she said, "and when they finish one, they throw it on the floor and begin another one. They keep only the best one or two." Hannah had picked this one up off the floor, but the girl who had drawn it was reluctant to let her have it because she thought it wasn't very good. Hannah had persuaded the girl, and when they got back to the house, she and Nelson went upstairs to her room where she showed it to him under the light at her desk. "I thought it was perfect. And she was going to throw it away," she said. She went downstairs and got Scotch tape. Together they put it up on the wall.

It is a good picture. It leaves out Hannah's face, one of her hands, both of her feet. But the lines that are set down on the paper suggest Hannah so precisely that Nelson marvels each time he sees it. "I have more affection for your body than anyone, but I couldn't draw even one line of it," he told her. Once when they lay spent and tangled, he saw her looking away from him and knew she was staring at the picture. When she turned back toward him, he told her, "Sometimes I want, without hurting you, to put my arms into your belly and up under your rib cage so that I can reach your heart and hold it in my two hands." She didn't say anything to him, but she held him closer and looked directly at him, her dark eyes intent and luminous.

He uncurls a little, still lying on his side so as to be able to see the picture better. He studies each of the lines. They are all familiar to him, and the bed is warm now. The art student, whose name he doesn't know and whom he has never seen, has rendered the thinness of Hannah's shoulders, the shape and weight of her breasts so that Nelson can very nearly feel her skin in the palms of his hands.

He remembers one night in August, after he'd cooked dinner for her, they went walking in Lakeside Park. They found a picnic table tucked away in the trees near the water and sat talking in murmurs for a long time. The night was cool after a hot, humid day. There were voices and laughter that came to them from people scattered all over the park, but they felt themselves secluded and invulnerable in the darkness. Hannah turned to look through the trees toward the black and silver water behind them; then she lay back flat out on the table. Nelson wanted to lie beside her, and she made room for him. He was an awkward fumbler, but he managed to unbutton her blouse and nuzzle her breasts. He tried to see her face; he thought she was smiling and looking up through the dark leaves of the trees. "That place where you live is like a motel room," she said. "It's like somewhere you'd forget the minute you walked out of it and shut the door behind you." Nelson wanted to ask her why she was talking that way, but he couldn't bring himself to say anything and so sat up on the edge of the table again and lit a cigarette. Hannah sat up beside him, not buttoning the blouse. "I was teasing," she said. She scooted closer to him. "If you're going to undress me, the least you could do is keep me warm." He put his arm around her, hugged her to him, but then felt her stiffen.

He saw it too, a small animal coming over the dirt path directly toward them. He knew it wasn't a cat or a small dog but a wild animal, and he started to stand up and shout at the thing. "Be still," Hannah told him, so softly he wasn't even certain she'd said it at all, but the creature had stopped when he'd moved. He saw the white stripe of its tail come up behind it. It faced them in the darkness, and Nelson held himself rigid. After a while the animal seemed to be backing away from them, and then it turned and shuffled back down the dirt path until they couldn't see it anymore. Nelson let his breath out.

Hannah stood up, buttoned her blouse, tucked it in. He put his mouth to her forehead, holding her shoulders lightly with his hands. But she was changed now, not so much stiff or resisting toward him, but indifferent, concerned with something else. When he asked her what was wrong, she become sharp with him. "Your beige walls, your stupid pictures," she said. "Little boys and girls with huge eyes."

"I don't plan to stay there," he told her. "It's just temporary."

"Are you going to find him?"

He had to think a minute to know what she meant. Then he said, "Yes, I'm going to find him. I write letters almost every day. I've made a lot of telephone calls."

She mumbled something; he understood only the repeated words, "letters, telephone calls." Then she went walking out away from him, into the shadows. "Those children are grotesque," she said. When Nelson remembered that night now, he changed what happened and what they said. He removed all unpleasantness. He made a logic that took them back to the table, naked, graceful, pleased with each other and the trees and the night all around them.

But in the room, in the bed, Nelson is free of yearning. He is aware only of brown lines on white paper. It is a sort of gift he is receiving, a likeness of Hannah that he is able to savor at the very center of what he feels for her. What he feels is something exact and nameless. He wants nothing more. He is suspended. He doesn't even have the memory of wanting.

He hears her footsteps coming down the hill toward the house. It is a quiet street, with cars passing only now and then, but even so, he would not have noticed the steps if they hadn't been hers, if he hadn't known she was coming toward him. He sits up to watch her through the windows. When he sees her, he wants to call out to her immediately, she should come inside, she isn't dressed warmly enough. She wears no coat; just a dark green sweater against the cold November wind. Her hair blows across her face, and she sweeps at it again and again with her hand, a child's gesture. She wears a denim skirt, and Nelson shivers to himself when he imagines the wind around her legs.

She cuts down into the small yard in front of the house, and Nelson must stand up and look almost straight down from the window to see her. He knows that she is tired, that she has been on her feet almost all day at work, and he is surprised that she goes so directly to the garden, the small circle of bricks that now holds only brown stems and shriveled leaves. She kneels beside it and begins picking out everything, flinging the stuff back onto the bank of thick ivy behind her. She is full of energy, extraordinarily alive. Once she loses her balance and catches herself with one hand against the brown grass, her wrist angled so sharply that Nelson shudders with his knowledge of its fragility. He can't see her face at all, just the top of her head, her hair blowing furiously in the wind. He clasps himself with both hands, and for a moment his face twists into a grimace that would frighten Hannah, were she to look up to the window and see him standing there. But she doesn't, and he goes to the closet for his clothes.

The Deacon

BECAUSE I HAD HAD NOTHING to do with the Episcopal Church for the past twenty years, Mariel made a strong impression on me. She wore a priest's white collar with a black gabardine cassock, finely tailored, close fitting around her arms and upper body, then loose from the waist down to the floor. She wore a plain gold ring, and her pale hands gestured over the prayer book as she explained various aspects of the service to us. Both her face and her hands had this clean-scrubbed look that I had always associated with nuns. Her hair was dark with plenty of gray in it, cut short, curled, clean.

My sculptor friend Marco Carter and his wife Emily were getting their son baptized at St. Paul's. Or rather Emily was getting the Tiger—Nathan, she called him—baptized, and Marco was coming along for the ride. Marco had enlightened parents who never had much to do with any kind of church.

Right then Marco was doing his best to overcome his condition of intense spiritual loathing.

Mariel's face had this all-encompassing honesty and generosity and concern for us, that radiance that the old painters of religious subjects tried to render in the faces of their Christs and Marys. And even though she was doing all the talking, it seemed like Mariel understood us all. She knew what a strain it was for Emily to be sitting there hoping Marco and I would behave ourselves, knew Marco was keeping a tight hold on himself until he could get out in the car and start screaming at the windshield and pounding the steering wheel, and knew I was reviewing a major portion of my childhood by way of those prayer book sentences she was explaining to us.

Mariel really was carrying out a project of astonishing complexity in her little talk with us around the table. Marco relaxed a little as she went on, though when Mariel mentioned that after the baptism she'd carry the kid around the church for the congregation to see, he held on to the Tiger like he was damned if the church was going get that kid even for a quick trip down the aisle and back.

All of us got up and trooped out of the little conference room into the main part of the church to find out just where we'd stand during which parts of the service. Mariel's back in that cassock had this stately straightness as she moved. The robe swished only slightly around her legs so that she appeared to float along ahead of us, looking back and speaking now and then, still gesturing with her pale hands.

When she finished telling us where to sit when the baptism was over, she escorted us back out into the nave. There Mariel said good-bye to us, looking into my eyes directly for a moment or two, and I had that old instinctive male-to-female response. It was just biology warping my perception, I knew that.

I didn't hang around to talk with Marco and Emily. In the natural course of time I'd see all I wanted to see of them, and I wasn't really in the mood to try to jolly old Marco up. He'd drop by the studio that night or the next day, and he'd have plenty to tell me about what the church was not going to get away with doing to the Tiger and how it was all a bunch of crazy shit anyway. I trotted off to my truck and got it onto Pearl Street without even decently warming it up. I love driving on snow-slick streets when there isn't much traffic. I fishtailed the truck all the way up the hill to my place. What I wanted to do right then was think about Mariel by myself for the afternoon—or however long it took to get her off my mind.

"Veteran of the sex wars" was what Marco called me. I didn't argue with him, but I wasn't proud of it. Biology had just asked more of me than it had of the average man.

And I was not without my defenses. I'd stripped myself of worldly possessions. I lived in my studio. I had a bed, some chairs, a table, what I needed to cook with, some books, an old black-and-white TV, a stereo, and some records and tapes. That was it, except for the truck, which had 82,000 miles on it, and the equipment and supplies I needed for my work—I didn't spare any expenses in that department. My stuff had been selling pretty well for a few years, and so I had a savings account that would have qualified me to be a respectable Republican. But I was determined not to spend my second forty years the way I did the first forty, being led through life like my brains were below my waist.

The first thing I did was get myself into my studio, alone, with the phone unplugged, the Stones on the stereo turned up as loud as I could stand it, a cold beer in my hand, and my sketch pad in my lap. Work was the secret. If the sketch pad didn't do it, then I didn't mind stretching a canvas and slapping some paint on it. If I couldn't get a lady priest out of my system, I figured I ought to declare myself sexual wimp of the decade.

The image of the cassock was what came first—came very quickly—and I had her hair so perfectly drawn you'd think I'd worked from a photograph. But between her collar and the bangs on her forehead, I didn't seem to be able to put a thing. It was a problem I wasn't accustomed to facing. I had what my critics called a real "facility" for representational imagery: if it was in the world I could set it down on paper or canvas or any kind of surface you could make an image on. My enemies liked to discourse on my lack of imagination and vision and so on, but nobody had ever accused me of having a failure of accurate memory. It wasn't even that—I did have her face clearly in my mind, but I couldn't make it come through my fingers. I wasted the afternoon and most of a new sketch pad.

Whadayagonnado? as Marco so succinctly liked to put it. Well, I'd spent a lot of time evading issues, lying to and hiding from women, running from situations I couldn't handle, and so on. I had sworn off of all that. I was committed to the direct approach. Face the difficulty head on, that was my motto. I called Mariel up and told her I wanted to talk with her. It was no help at all that she sounded glad to hear from me, glad to set an appointment for Wednesday afternoon.

Austerity sometimes has a pornographic effect on me. Her office was so squared away that if a mote of dust had snuck in and tried to settle on her desk, it would have gotten shy at the last minute and tried to float out the door. The lady's work space was immaculate. And her appearance was exactly the same as it was on Sunday, as if she'd never taken that cassock off for a minute—but also as if she'd found a way to keep it permanently cleaned and pressed, herself freshly showered and rested. She asked me if I'd rather we sat in the chairs by the window—actually a glass wall that looked out on the lake—or at the desk. "Your choice," she said, smiling at me, and went on, "You know, George, I didn't tell you this on Sunday, but I admire your work a great deal."

I had first pointed toward the desk, but as she spoke I changed my mind and pointed toward the chairs by the window; and so we executed a little dos-à-dos in the middle of her office. When I tried to laugh politely it came out a guffaw.

My explanation to her was that I was concerned about taking communion after the baptism. At some length I explained to Mariel my past history of a long-lapsed connection to the church. I told her that it would have been easier for me if I could have been more casual about taking the Eucharist—because I wanted to do everything possible to make the service meaningful for Marco and Emily and the Tiger—"Nathan," I corrected myself. Mariel nodded at me, a smile held off visibly in her facial muscles. "But I can't shake myself of this old concern for"—I searched for the words—"spiritual correctness, I guess."

This was not as much bullshit as you might imagine it to be. I would have worked the matter out for myself if it hadn't been for my need to see Mariel again. But that issue of the communion had been on my mind from the first time Emily had called me up to ask me to be the Tiger's godfather and I heard Marco laughing in the background until Emily hollered at him to shut his atheist mouth, I was going to do it and what did he think of that?

"Well, George," Mariel began, and now she really did have a smile for me, but it was an appropriate one, a sort of teacherly look of approval for a good student. "The church is not as it was when you were growing up. As individual human beings we know we undergo changes of various kinds, and we now understand the church must change and grow, just as we must, in order to stay spiritually vital."

It was a set speech, I knew. Nevertheless, it pleased me to hear her recite it for me. "At the time you were baptized, no one would have dared enter a church dressed as you are now." Now this observation of hers made me feel acutely self-conscious. I rarely paid attention to what I wore; I mean I put the same pair of jeans and work shirt and socks on every morning until I couldn't stand the smell; then I threw them in the corner of the studio and tried to find something clean. When the corner filled up, then I hauled it all to Suds City down on North Winooski Avenue and threw the whole pile of it into a row of washers. I'd gotten out of the habit of thinking about what I looked like, but all of a sudden I was able to see myself in Mariel's eyes as this bearded, skinny lout of a guy with his bare knees showing through the rips of his blue jeans, eighteen coats of paint-splatters on his cowboy boots, and a sweater that looked like he stole it off a dead Irish fisherman.

". . . less attention in general to such worldly matters," she went on, "and so you may not be aware of how much you and the church still have in common . . ."

By the time I was ready to leave I knew that she was familiar with the work of most of the artists around town and that she had a regard for me based on what she thought I was trying to do in my painting. She didn't have it quite right—nobody ever does—but that kind of effort to understand was so rare that I'd have had her on my mind even if she looked like a Soviet tank.

I remained blocked with my sketch pad. It wasn't that I couldn't make *any* face appear where hers should have been, it was just that the faces I drew weren't hers. My hand and arm moved just as fluidly as always, and it always felt like I was going to get it *this* time. But what I came up with was drastically wrong. In a way it wasn't such a bad thing since it had never happened to me before. I convinced myself to be grateful that Mariel had finally presented me with a problem of consequence.

The morning of the Tiger's baptism service was so sunny the church's glass walls were brilliant with this blue and white light. Looking out there, I almost forgot how my collar was choking me. St. Paul's has a kind of sprawling interior so it doesn't seem so much packed as "populated" when the congregation is there. Marco, Emily, the Tiger, and I all sat up in the balcony, looking down onto the tops of everybody's heads, until it was time to splash the Tiger. Then we went down and began our part of the service at the door at the rear of the nave.

As the prayers and responses went on, we made our way up toward the front, a parade of us with the acolytes, the deacons, the dean, and a couple of priests. Since Mariel was the one Emily had designated to actually do the work on the Tiger, she was at the center of all the choreography up there by the font. The rector poured water into the basin from a big stone jug, while Mariel stirred it around with a dish shaped like a seashell. I experienced this terrific welling of emotion in seeing her hands in the water like that. The Tiger was sound asleep on Marco's shoulder when Mariel lifted him away and carried him over to the font, but he never cried or made a sound, he just looked startled and a little indignant. Then when Mariel and the rector actually did douse the kid's head, I was the one who almost made a noise.

This very peculiar thing happened after Mariel had walked

the Tiger all the way around the congregation. He was still not crying at all; she had a lit candle that she carried along with him, and the Tiger hooked an arm around her shoulder and studied the flickering flame for the whole ride. Mariel was whispering to him, concentrating on keeping the kid calm as she came back to us. Then when she approached the four of us up there, apparently it was me she intended to hand the Tiger to. I was surprised, but I certainly wasn't going to refuse to take him. I had my hands lifted to him when Mariel realized her mistake. Such a blush came into her face that I couldn't keep myself from whispering to her, "It's all right." By then she'd already turned to Marco and was handing the kid into his father's arms, patting the Tiger on the back.

During communion Mariel regained her poise, seemed in fact transfigured in a low-key kind of way. I stood up front with Emily, Marco sitting in back of us with the Tiger in his arms and, I imagined, a disdainful expression on his face. The way I figured it, he was probably already thinking up what he'd say to me about "the temporary religious fervor of the veteran of the sex wars" and so on. But I didn't think it was so bad of me. To take the wafer, I put my hands up, palms open, left one on top, the way I was taught to do it in the old days when we knelt to take communion. The rector pushed the little white disk into my palm, and after a moment of staring at it, I took it into my mouth.

Mariel was the one serving the communicants from the cup of wine. For a few moments, as she stood in front of me murmuring Christ's words to his disciples, "Take this in remembrance of me . . . ," her hands holding the cup were about a foot from my eyes. Then she was holding it to my lips, tilting it for me to drink, taking it away, using a white linen napkin to wipe the rim of it where my lips had touched it. I didn't see her face during those moments, nor did I want to.

At the end of the service, when Marco and I were trying to convince Emily to hurry up and get out of that place, Mariel came up to us, speaking first of all to the parents, but then putting her hand on my arm and pushing slightly so that I was somewhat separated from them. "Can you forgive me for that?" she murmured, and I supposed she meant the part about almost handing me the Tiger. Her face was still filled with that energy I had seen in it during the communion; but there was another level of expression, too—hurt or concern or something—and I was again given over to a ridiculous gush of emotion. "Would you consider letting me sketch you?" I asked her.

Immediately I wished I hadn't. In that moment I imagined I could read the eight dozen thoughts that went in rapid sequence through Mariel's mind. Not until I'd blurted out my request did I remember that of course most of my work that people had seen and had written and talked about was female nudes. It wasn't that I hadn't done anything else, it was just that the nudes were what I'd sold mostly, what my reputation was based on. They were not even my best work, as far as I was concerned; I had done those pieces usually because I had had some woman hanging around the studio who wanted to be painted.

With what she must have had in mind, Mariel had every right to do what she did, turn away from me without responding. Though I couldn't see her face as she walked away, I was pretty sure she was blushing again, and I was sorry to have embarrassed her like that. Standing there among the cheerful parishioners, I felt like something down at the bottom of a compost pile. Sneaking out into the cold sunshine didn't help.

Marco and Emily had asked me over to their place to watch the NFC playoffs that afternoon, but they were just going to have to carry on without me. I drove to Montreal to see if a sordid evening on the street would improve my spirits and clear my mind.

It's a long, old story, with a lot of bars and smoke and loud music, but the point of it is that I didn't get back in town until Monday afternoon, and I didn't plug the phone back in until Tuesday around lunchtime. It was ringing almost immediately, and it was Mariel, telling me she was sorry. I was about to freak out and tell her she was crazy to be sorry, I was the one who was a sorry son of a bitch. I was a little hungover if the truth be told, not your most articulate telephone conversationalist. Before I knew it I'd agreed to meet Mariel at four o'clock.

From her office the light out across the lake at that time of day was the visual equivalent of the Vivaldi cello sonatas; it could break your heart just to catch a glimpse of it. There I was, remorseful and vulnerable, sitting two and a half yards away from Mariel by a window that every time I glanced out of it made me feel like I was going to float out into those beams of pale blue light over the water. I could hardly listen to what she was saying.

The gist of it was, she said, that her initial response had been conventional, non-Christian, middle-class, unaesthetic, and sexually-politically atavistic. I must forgive her. She recognized how in a generous spirit I had entered St. Paul's to be Nathan's godparent even though the Church had become alien to me. The courage required of me to do that had been immense compared to the courage it would take for her to allow me to sketch her.

I saw that she was taking the issue with a great deal of

seriousness. It would be easier for me to go ahead with sketching her than to try to talk her out of sitting for me. So finally I suggested that I bring my pad with me one afternoon that week and we do it there in her office. That seemed to me a decorous way of going about the project, but something was wrong with it for Mariel. She didn't respond for a moment; and even though the light in the room was very dim then, I could see that crimson blush of hers taking over her face.

"I'd rather come to your studio," she said, looking down at her hands. I agreed quickly. The whole thing had taken on more complication and significance than it ever had to. "Tomorrow morning?" she asked. "Around ten?" That was early for me, but I agreed to it anyway just to keep things simple. I'd hit the sack early that night and set the alarm for nine-thirty in the morning.

But Marco came over just about the time I was getting ready to straighten up the studio a little bit. He was pissed off because I hadn't shown up at their place after the baptism and he couldn't get in touch with me. He said he was still wound up from all that Episcopal mumbo-jumbo, and needed to talk it out of his system. He'd brought a couple of six-packs with him, and he had a lot to say. Around 3:00 A.M., when the last station went off the air, he and I were standing in the middle of the studio throwing cans and screaming at the TV. Then we decided to have a look at the last three or four pieces I'd done. I'd been working on these really austere landscapes—"Lake Sequence" I was calling the batch of them—just to see if I could depart that much from the fashion of the day. Marco was contemptuous of most of my ideas about painting, and I loved talking to him for just that reason. It was coming up daylight when he left the studio. I didn't set the alarm because I was just going to take a little nap before Mariel showed up.

I didn't know how long she'd been tapping at the door. There was a heavy snow coming down, and the wind seemed to push her right through the door when I finally got it open. She had on this black, hooded parka that went all the way down to the floor; her nose was red, her cheeks were pink, and she was out of breath. I was bleary-eyed, bad-breathed, and my beard was bent off at an angle from sleeping on it. While she was untying her hood, getting the parka and her boots off, she looked around the studio. Then she burst out laughing. "It's just as I imagined it," she said. "Except more so. Ah, George, to live this way!" She made a gesture around the room. "It's as if your life itself is a work of art."

I tried to explain to her about how I would have straightened the place up except that Marco came over last night and so on, but she wasn't listening to me. She had on dark slacks and a couple of sweaters. In her socks she was walking around the place, looking at everything. I shut my stupid mouth and went to the kitchen to make some coffee. While I was over in that corner of the studio, I tried to get my shirt tucked in and the knots finger-combed out of my hair. I didn't want to embarrass her by going over to the corner where the sink, mirror, and toilet were. I turned on the radio to see what Robert J. was playing.

"I'd have guessed rock and roll, George," she said when I brought a cup of coffee over to her.

"Wrong time of the day," I told her. I saw her wrinkle her nose at her first sip, and I was embarrassed to be serving instant coffee. "Dreadful stuff, I agree," I told her, but she shook her head and grinned. "Next time I'll make tea for you," I promised her. I went on to try to explain to her about what music I listened to—Robert J. if I was up in the morning, operas when I was working, country and western when I was in the truck, rock and roll if I was at a party and wanted to dance, and so on. "I don't know why I'm telling you this," I said.

She was examining my face intently. "You're a good man, George. I've known that from our first meeting."

How was I supposed to respond to an accusation like that? "You oughta talk to Marco," I told her, trying to turn it into a joke. Actually, with about two sentences, Marco could have straightened her right out.

"Perhaps Marco extends his own fantasy life into his perception of you."

She startled me with that remark. "Yeah, maybe so," I said.

"I think it's time, don't you?" Mariel said with this look of radiant sorrow on her face.

"Just a minute." I turned away to try to dig out my materials from the mess Marco and I had made last night. "Would you mind sitting over there?" I pointed to a stool at the far end of the studio, where even that day the twin skylights were letting in some grayish winter light.

It took me longer than I thought it would to find a decent sketch pad and some sepia pencils. While I was digging through my stuff, I could hear Mariel moving. I knew what she was doing. When I turned back toward that end of the studio, I didn't see her for a moment.

Then I did see her.

I know that if I hadn't anticipated it, I'd have shouted, "Please! Put your clothes back on!" But as it was I kept quiet and walked slowly toward where she sat, her body slightly angled away from me and her face, in profile, turned upward as if she could see right through the snow-covered skylight. Her skin was so rosy white I understood immediately that she had never had a suntan.

"Are you warm enough?" I asked her. Her response was the

slightest nod of her head, as if she were trying to hold some precarious balance. I didn't come too close to her, and she never changed her pose, never stopped looking up through the opaque skylight.

I set to work. And I had to do some hard, fast thinking. Mariel's breasts were small, her hips sizable, her thighs and calves were sturdy, she didn't shave her legs. It was a very likable, dowdy body. As my hand moved over the paper, I tried to imagine how she wished me to see her. If I cheated and gave her streamlined hips and legs, she'd know it in an instant's glance; if I was accurate in setting her figure down exactly as it was before me, I might really damage her perception of herself.

The decision had to come quickly because either I would rip the sketches out of the book and let them fall to the floor as I customarily worked, or else I would have to place them somewhere that would prevent her from seeing them. As it turned out, I had no choice but to set her down as I saw her—my hand wouldn't cheat for me though I suggested to it that perhaps it should. And I let the first sketch—just a roughing in of her torso—fall to the floor as I ordinarily would. That seemed to release me from further agonizing.

"You know, Mariel, what I do today is probably not going to be very satisfactory for either of us. Sketching like this does nothing to register how your skin takes this light."

Such a length of time passed before she responded that I thought she'd put herself into some kind of trance. Finally she did reply, softly and without moving her body at all. "I'll do what you want," she murmured.

What was perverse about this circumstance—I was on the third sketch then—was that her face was not coming to me much better than it had when I'd tried working from memory.

I walked around her and tried it from this angle and that one, and what I set down was probably close enough to keep her from being insulted by it. People usually don't know what they look like to others anyway. But I understood that what I was rendering with my hand was not what I was seeing with my eyes. Furthermore, every stroke I made for her torso, her arms, and her legs was accurate. I experienced this unnaturally fluid grace and precision in drawing Mariel's body, but could do no more justice to her face than some kid in his first high-school art class.

"I think that's enough for today, Mariel," I told her. Quickly I turned my back on her and walked to the other end of the studio so that she wouldn't think I was ogling her in a non-aesthetic way. I busied myself fixing the tea I had promised her, so that when she finished dressing and walked over to my side of the studio, I had a steaming cup to hand her. There were a couple more bar stools over there and a counter for us to set our cups on. Mariel sat quietly sipping her tea, but she had this intensely attentive manner about her, as if she were alert to the slightest gesture on my part. I asked her how she came to join the Episcopal priesthood.

"Oh, I'm not a priest," she told me with a smile, as if she thought I'd be happy to have that news, "though they say I could be one if I wanted to. I've done the work." She went on to explain that she was a deacon, or deaconess as they used to call it. She grew up a Catholic in New Orleans, and though she wanted a place in the church that was impossible for a Catholic woman, she had never actually wanted to be a priest. "It's a power with which I know I would be uneasy," she said, tightening her lips, then quickly smiling. "But instead of talking, I'd rather hear you tell me about your work," she said.

I promised her that tomorrow I would tell her whatever she

wanted to know. When she was putting her cloak on, tying the little string under her chin for the hood, I remembered that she hadn't mentioned the sketches. I didn't know if she'd looked at the ones on the floor or not. "Do you want to see how it's going so far?" I asked her.

Mariel gave this little shake of her head and a rueful sort of smile that could also have been a grimace. It was a touching moment. "You're not even tempted to look?" I asked her.

"Yes, George, of course I'm tempted," she told me; then she was out the door, in the snow and wind, waving to me, with her dark cloak flapping.

Marco dropped by before I got a chance to pick up the sketches. "Why don't you tell her about Ellen and Paula and Kathy and Susan and Mary B. and . . ." He was enjoying himself, carrying the sketches around and declaiming to the walls of my studio. "I tell you, George, you can educate this woman. You can teach her that taking off her clothes is just taking off her clothes . . ."

"She's not a priest," I reminded him.

"She baptized my kid," he said. "She's a priest. Or she will be until you get through with her." He was really pacing the floor with a vengeance now. "Maybe that's what you've got in mind, George. Maybe you ought to invite a bunch of us over when you defrock her. That's pretty good, isn't it? Defrock instead of . . ."

"Maybe you should take a walk, Marco," I told him. He wasn't the only one who had a temper.

"Yeah, you're right about that," he said. "Maybe I should." He picked up his coat and walked out, leaving the door open behind him so that if I didn't want a foot of snow in my studio I had to get up and close it fast.

When Mariel arrived the next morning I had heated the

studio for her, and I had water boiling ready to pour her cup of tea. I'd been up for a while, I had a canvas stretched, my materials organized and ready to go.

Mariel was quiet but cheerful; we were both very professional in our manners that morning. I had even moved an old theater screen over to a corner for her so that she could dress and undress the way they do in books and movies.

I didn't mind asking her to move around that morning, to try a couple of different poses. I tried to work quickly, making some very rough preliminary sketches on the pad, and then marking some even rougher shapes on the canvas. For Mariel to wear during our breaks, I'd found an old bathrobe my mom gave me for Christmas years ago; it gave us both a laugh the first time she tried it on. When I had my paints mixed and ready to go for the second sitting, we worked for almost an hour and a half without stopping.

"George, I think I'm turning into stone," Mariel suddenly blurted out after we'd had nothing but silence for long minutes.

While she was dressing behind the screen, I was so exhilarated from that morning's work that I bounced around the studio, chattering about Franz Hals and Vermeer and Corot and Matisse. But I couldn't stay away from my easel. "At this point you can't tell much from the canvas itself," I informed her, gazing at it, loving the look of it and hoping she'd glance that way. She kept her seat at the counter, warming her hands with her cup of tea.

"Can you tell me how you became a painter, George?" she asked when I walked back that way.

I launched myself into this tedious account of my training in college, feeling deprived because I couldn't paint while I was in the army, taking my MFA at Columbia, teaching at Putney and Windham, and so on. Mariel listened carefully and registered no disappointment. Maybe she hoped I'd get to the good part tomorrow.

That night I dreamed about the image. From the first time I had looked across the studio and understood what I was seeing, I'd known that it had to be this almost translucently rosy-white figure cast against these stark beams of grayish-blue light coming down from the skylight. In the dream I worked through a sequence of shades of color and through a sequence of very slight shifts in the figure's pose. When I woke up, I understood how I wanted to use Mariel's small breasts and her sturdy hips and legs. I knew how to prepare my palette and how to pose Mariel. And I knew in some final way how I needed to work in order to bring her face into the composition.

I didn't touch her, but I did move closer to her to point out exactly how she had to sit.

"And how should I hold my head?" she asked.

"Perfectly level," I told her, "as if you were gazing at a spot right over here." I walked over and slapped my hand on the wall to show her where I wanted her to look.

We had been working for maybe half an hour when she spoke. "I think it will feel more natural if I hold it up, if I look up like this." She turned to the skylight the way she did on the first day.

"What are you, a plant?" I asked her.

"Yes," she said, holding the pose, not smiling.

I worked a little longer, not really happy, but not entirely certain she was wrong. In every painting of mine that I've ever cared about, there is this turning point when it changes from being a burden that I'm trying to lift to being this force that actually lifts me and carries me through to the end. From the moment of my accepting Mariel's adjustment of the pose, the piece went so quickly that I was tempted to lie to her that I needed another day to finish it. I didn't, of course. I didn't really say anything at the end of that day's session because I wanted her to come again in the morning.

She did. When I let her in, she was full of chatter about the warm weather, the January thaw, the way it fooled her every year into thinking it was springtime. I'd hardly noticed the weather for that week we'd worked on the painting, and I was happy to listen to her, to imagine the world through her eyes. But when she put down her teacup and stood up to go undress, I had to tell her.

"Mariel, it's finished."

She looked steadily at me for a moment. "I'm sorry," she said. "I don't know why."

"I am, too, and I don't either," I said. "Come and see it."

Again she gave me that steady regard, as if whatever she saw in my face would tell her what she needed to know next. "Will your feelings be hurt if I don't?" she asked me.

Then I was the one who had to do the thinking and the staring. The truth was that I hadn't imagined past that morning when Mariel would see the painting. There was the rosy-white figure against the pale, blue light, just as I had conceived it and refined it in my dream. But there was also a way in which every element of that painting had cohered, including Mariel's upturned face, to make a picture that I knew was beyond my power to paint. I grinned at Mariel. "I need you to see it," I told her.

She knew I wasn't kidding, and so she walked over with me to stand in front of it. It took my breath away to look straight into it. Finally Mariel said, "The face."

"Yes?"

"That's who I am, isn't it?" The way she said it wasn't really a question.

"Yes, I think so."

And we turned away from it.

Back at the counter, with fresh cups of tea steaming in front of us, we were subdued. I wanted to cheer her up.

"I could give it to the church," I told her.

She didn't smile, didn't respond at all. I was sorry to have made a joke like that.

"I'm not sure what I'll do with it," I said.

She paused a moment, then seemed to make a decision. "I'd like to have it. How much do you want for it?" she asked.

"Mariel, I don't know. I haven't even thought about it."

"Then think about it," she said, smiling but definitely serious. She walked over to the other side of the studio and came back with the huge black-leather sack she used for a purse. "How much?" she asked, taking out her checkbook.

"It's not a god damn piece of merchandise!" I shouted at her. I was surprised at myself.

"I'm sorry," she said, and she put the checkbook away. "That was thoughtless of me." She had the good sense to let me sit there and calm down before she went on. "You see, I don't really know how to honor what you've done. I understand only that I want it. But if I had it, I wouldn't know what to do with it. I certainly can't hang it in my living room, can I?"

Then she didn't have anything else to say. I glanced up at her and she shrugged, then we both looked down again at our tea.

After a while I told her, "I'll bring it over to you this afternoon."

She nodded once.

While we sat there, there was this distancing that occurred. I could actually feel us departing from the intimate state we'd shared. When we said good-bye in the sunlight outside my studio, it was as if years ago we had been lovers.

That afternoon at her house she helped me carry the painting from my truck indoors and upstairs to her study. We set it against the wall in there, and we left it taped up in the sheets of plastic in which I'd wrapped it. I didn't accept her invitation to stay for tea or something to eat. Her house, with its Danish modern furniture, was not a place I wanted to hang around.

But nowadays I find myself drawn to the similarly modern interior spaces of St. Paul's. I know that before the Tiger's baptism I was powerfully affected by sitting up in that balcony and seeing out through the huge windows onto the frozen lake. And intense as it was that week of working on the painting with Mariel, my perception of our relationship now is that we have completed it, that we finished it when I delivered the painting to her house. What she did with it is a mystery she holds from me. We have little to say to each other on the Sundays when I attend, though when our eyes meet, a great deal passes between us. Whenever Mariel serves communion, I am there with my hands cupped and held up to her. But I aspire to nothing more than taking the wafer from her hands, the wine from the cup she offers me.

Apache

SHE WAS A BLUE-EYED BLONDE, her name was Apache, and if you didn't like it, you could kiss her ass. Worked at the Pussy Cat, not the Naked i Cabaret, which she and the other Pussy Cat girls considered tacky, though more than a few had worked there, too. Not Apache. When she came in from New York, she went straight to work for the Pussy Cat. Had the job before she even got there.

Up at the Naked i they had one of those peach-skinned girls with silicone tits and light-brown hair, and her name was Miss Cheyenne, but anybody could tell that was bullshit. Apache was called Apache because she had a temper. "I'll jerk a knot in your ass," Apache would say in a friendly voice to a clean-scrubbed M.I.T. sophomore if he ran a hand up her thigh. He would stop, too, because there was something back there, something that boy could tell from how she said it or looked.

Up on the bar Apache was damn sure no squaw. She started

out with what looked like one of those old-fashioned two-piece bathing suits, the kind that just barely showed your navel. The bottom had zippers at each hip, the top had a zipper that came up in the middle. Apache did the zips up to the top on her first pass up and back down the bar. By the end of "Nasty Girl," she was down to a pretty little white-crotched G-string. Blonde hair was one of her best features. Apache knew that, and she didn't care if some of the other girls thought she showed it maybe a little too soon. Apache was twenty-nine and said she was twenty-five, but she had some to spare. If you had style, you could work without resorting to implants.

But Apache knew that what got Lola and the Tucson Twister was the white peignoir and the bridal business. "I swear to God, girl, you look like a Barbie Doll up there," Tucson said; but Apache ignored her because her real name was Ida and God knew Apache didn't have to take anything from somebody named Ida.

"Barbie Doll that wants to fuck," murmured Lola, who was black and slinky as a hungry cat. Now that was true, but it didn't bother Apache because she had put some thought into looking kind of bride-like, even down to how she smiled when there was that long pause in the music and she opened the white peignoir and ran two fingers over her best feature.

Apache had been married and divorced three times, starting when she was sixteen, and for all she knew, she was married a fourth time, too. At least the Chinaman said she was. And she said she was sometimes, when one of the shitheads who bought her a drink asked her. "Yeah, I'm married to a Chinese man," she said, ruefully or hatefully, depending on how she felt and how much more the shithead was likely to spend on her. It didn't make a damn to her whether she was married or not, and the white peignoir struck her as funny.

"You feeding those little boys' dreams, honey. You jacking off twelve-year-olds," said Lola, and Apache turned on her.

"So what if I am?" said Apache, and she walked right up to Lola even though Lola was the one of all of them who scared her. Apache and Lola stared at each other, then Apache laughed and said, "I'm a jack off all ages." And Lola laughed, too, and said she was, too, and the Tucson Twister sniffed and went on out to find herself what she in her ignorance called "a sweet thing."

Apache met this real bullshit guy who said that he was an Indian of the Osage tribe. This was on a rainy Tuesday night in June when it looked like nobody and all nobody's cousins was going to come into the Zone. There were five girls for every man who came through the Pussy Cat's door, there were empty spaces around the bar, and Apache felt spooked by the place when it was that way. She figured she'd do her ten o'clock number and ask Paulie if she could go home. He'd say yes. Paulie liked her. Apache never complained about anything, even about the night that West Virginia girl, the Coalminer's Other Daughter, puked all over Apache's locker. And Paulie had caught Apache's number a couple of nights when she'd set that place on fire, had them stamping their feet and whistling. But on this particular night Apache was just sitting there having a vodka martini and telling Albert how she was going to leave early and go over and spend some time with the Chinaman, and Albert was telling her how maybe she ought to give the Chinaman a call first, when this guy with a ponytail and a poncho sat down beside her and started wiping the rain off his glasses.

The guy told Albert he wanted coffee, and Albert of course enjoyed telling him he wasn't going to get no god damn cup of coffee at the Pussy Cat, maybe he ought to try up the street at the Naked i. So the guy got his glasses on and ordered a Coke, for which Albert charged him three bucks. Apache saw him eyeing her through those gold-rimmed spectacles of his, his poncho still dripping on the floor and on the bar. What the hell, she asked him if he wanted to buy her a drink. He said yes and told Albert to bring this lady a Coke. Albert guffawed and walked on down the bar while Apache explained the system to him: he could buy her a "beer," which was a bottle of champagne that cost twenty-one bucks, or he could buy her a "drink," which cost seven bucks. The guy smiled at her, rustled around in his poncho, pulled out his wallet again, opened it, and showed it to her like some kind of rare treasure. It had an old raggedy-assed five in it, that's all, and the guy looked just pleased as could be. Albert came back up the bar and asked them if they'd got it worked out yet, which situation embarrassed Apache. So she said to Albert to bring her another vodka martini, she'd pay for it herself. She jerked her head toward the man in the poncho and said, "This guy's lost, he don't know where the fuck he is."

But the man didn't shrivel up and die just because she insulted him. He grinned at her and admitted that it was true, he was trying to walk back to Cambridge and took a wrong turn, he said. Apache was starting to get up and walk away because it ruins your reputation to sit with somebody who isn't spending money on you. But it was this rainy, dead-assed night, and it made sense to her right then just to keep her badelias parked on that bar stool where at least she was safe and out of trouble. The guy asked her her name, and she told him Apache; but she didn't look at him any more. Who the fuck needed to look at some lost son of a bitch with a ponytail who was dripping all over the bar and who couldn't buy her a drink, who was walking around with nothing but a five in his pocket? She damn sure didn't ask him his name, but he told her then anyway, it was John Chapman. Apache hardly ever asked anybody their name; even if they told her, she forgot it. Then John Chapman told her that bullshit about the Osage Indians in Kansas and Missouri.

Apache didn't listen. She was in a trance.

"Apache, you about to nod off there," said Lola, walking behind her putting a bony hand on Apache's shoulder. "Somebody slip you some shit, honey?" she murmured close to Apache's ear. And when Apache blinked at her, Lola smiled and sauntered on down the bar a few places, Lola in her spike heels and fishnet stockings.

John Chapman pulled the poncho up over his head in a grand crinkling of heavy plastic, bashed that thing into a semi-folded state, and dropped it on the floor between himself and Apache. "I also have an Osage name," he told her, leaning in her direction to get her attention. The man obviously intended to carry on a conversation as long as she sat there.

"Hey, Apache!" Albert shouted at her from way down at the other end of the bar. "Paulie wants to know if you're going on welfare tomorrow or what?"

Apache sighed and stood up and walked back to do her number.

"Another time, and maybe we'll talk," Chapman murmured, watching her when she walked past him even though she kept her eyes on the floor.

"Hell of a night to get married," said Lola when Apache walked past her, and Apache wished she could give Lola a grin, but she didn't have one available.

Sometimes Apache was pretty fabulous. It didn't have anything to do with anything. Or else it did. She could be high and happy, step out there, and then start feeling sleazy and old for no reason. Those times she hated even to look at the shitheads at the bar, gaping at her like a bunch of retards at a retard convention. Or it could happen like tonight when she felt lower than whale shit and dreaded putting a foot through that curtain, and all of a sudden she was flying. She was energy and muscles, and her body was the music, the Pointer Sisters singing, "I'm so excited . . ." Even the few men who sat around the bar seemed acceptable to Apache, and she smiled at them in sweet romance, let her body make its moves. Just before the lights went down for her to twirl in the white peignoir under the silver strobe light, she saw Mr. John Chapman in his poncho, raising a hand to wave to her before he went out the door. The strobe divided her into a thousand spinning Apaches, and one or two of them said aloud into the blast of music, "Go get rained on, Indian. Go get your ass wet."

When she was out working through the tables and around the bar, Apache wore a red velveteen jacket, a black one-piece bathing suit split down to below her navel, smoke-colored tights, and heels. She never had trouble getting somebody to buy her a drink, and she usually had more "beer" tickets to turn in at the end of the evening than any of the other girls. Trouble was, Apache did have difficulty with her vision and her footwork before the evening was over. There weren't more than a few drops of rum in each drink but she went through fifty or sixty drinks on a good night. She danced a lot of it out of her system, but even so, she usually felt pretty floaty by around midnight.

Which was about the time John Chapman came in, wearing a tie and a three-piece khaki suit. Just to wear that with a ponytail took a lot of nerve, but to wear it into the Zone and then to wear it into the Pussy Cat on a Thursday at midnight meant the son of a bitch was from another planet. Apache was sitting close enough to the door when he came in to see that the suit was brand new. He'd washed that long black hair of his and tied up his ponytail in a small silver and turquoise clip. But she was damned if she was going to talk with him. People seemed to be clearing a path for him to the one empty seat at the bar, and you could see every girl's eye on him when he took the stool, looked straight at Albert who was waiting in front of him, and ordered a Coke.

"Money just walked in and sat down over there," said the Teenage Queen, moving through the crowd behind Apache.

"Ain't gonna spend none of it on you, bitch," whispered Lola, moving briskly that way, too, just behind the Teenage Queen.

Apache had to laugh. This place was like something nobody could even dream of. Chapman was strafed in rapid succession by Tina, Erica Mahoney, Coco, Wonder Woman, Patsy Jones, the Teenage Queen, Sweet Anabel, Lola, Nurse Goodbody, and Gladys Garrett. The Teenage Queen tried to pick up one of his hands and lay it on her titty, which was one of several undignified things the Queen did all the time that Apache wouldn't stoop to. John Chapman shook off the Queen, told all of them no, he didn't want any company, and no, he wasn't lonely, and smiled at them to keep them happy and moving on down the bar away from him.

"Wants you," said Wonder Woman, circling back the other way around the bar, passing behind Apache. Apache shrugged, but Wonder Woman wasn't watching to catch her response.

"I'm up," said Apache to nobody. It wasn't even true. She had a while before she was up, but she walked back to the dressing room anyway. It was better to sit around back there than to have to watch the meat show.

Then she was up, and goddamnit, she was too sober to get anything going. Everything all around her was so ridiculous it was all she could do not to stop dancing and just stand there giving them the finger, those god damn stupid open-mouthed faces around that bar, a stink rising from the floor of thirty years of spilled draft beer half mopped up every night. "I'm so excited! I'm so excited!" She was bored with the song. The strobe light split her up while she tried to make herself spin. She wished she could just dissolve that way and when they turned up the lights there would be no more Apache.

"You auditioning for a nursing home?" asked Paulie when she came off. He was sitting on his stool just inside the door. She walked past him, the peignoir, the bathing suit, and the G-string all wadded up in one hand because she didn't give a damn.

"Fuck you, Paulie." She tried to sound friendly, but she really didn't want to talk to anybody right then.

"Man out there wants to talk to you," Paulie told her softly. Paulie was always doing isometrics, pushing one arm against another, flexing his legs, going up on the tips of his toes, and Apache didn't like to look at him, but she knew better than to ignore him.

"Nothing new about that," she murmured, standing there and waiting. "Well?" she said. She turned enough to see past Paulie through the two-way mirror, like a television screen, to where John Chapman sat with a little space around him in that crowded bar, as if everybody knew he didn't belong there.

"Lola's saving you a seat," Paulie said. Sure enough, she could see Lola sitting one seat down from Chapman, talking to somebody who hadn't bought her a drink—Apache could tell even from that far away.

"I don't need it," Apache said.

"Talk to him or hit the street," Paulie told her and sighed and stood up and stretched.

Apache walked over and threw her clothes at her locker and sat down to take off her white heels. "I was gonna talk to him anyway," she muttered.

"Can I buy you a drink, Apache?" John Chapman asked her when she was walking toward him, before she'd even reached the empty seat beside him.

Apache shrugged and sat down. "Sure you can," she said. "Buy me a beer?" She didn't look at him. She hoped he'd say no. Albert was standing right there in front of them, waiting for the definite signal from one or the other of them. When John Chapman nodded at him, Albert was setting that little bottle of champagne up in front of Apache in ten seconds flat. Chapman put a fifty on the bar, and Albert hustled to make the change.

"So how come you're so dressed up?" Apache made herself sound like a lady who could kick some ass when she wanted to.

Chapman smiled at her but wouldn't say anything. Under the knot of his tie there was a gold pin that made it stand up from his collar; Apache looked at that while she talked to him. "I thought you said you were an Indian," she said, still making a point of not giving him a smile. She tossed off the first glass of the champagne with Albert right there filling up her glass again when she set it down.

"An Indian can't dress up?" Chapman asked her.

"He teaches up at Harvard, Apache," said Albert, so polite she could have slapped his face.

"You talking to a professor, girl," said Lola on the other side of her.

Apache shook her head. What the hell do I care if he sells ice to the Eskimos? Apache started to say, but she held her tongue because she could feel Paulie watching her from back behind the mirror.

"I've been trying to talk Albert here into enrolling in some night courses," John Chapman said. "He's thinking about changing jobs."

"Yeah," Albert said, hitching up his trousers and standing up straight, "I want to get into a field where I can screw a lot of women." Chapman grinned at him appreciatively, and Albert burst out laughing.

"You got some customers up that way," Apache told Albert and watched him hustle his silly ass up the bar. "So what do you teach?" She hated asking anybody any kind of a question, but she wanted to get this over with fast.

"Parasociology."

"Para what?" she said.

"Pair o' what? Pair o' what?" echoed Patsy Jones gliding along the dark wall behind them. Apache reached back there and tried to swat her ass, but she was gone.

"It's one of the social sciences," John Chapman told her. "It's very new."

"Never heard of it," said Apache. She looked all around the bar, getting ready to move away.

"She's just moody," Lola told Chapman, leaning around Apache to catch his eye. "You got to make an impression on her."

Apache grimly tossed off the last of her champagne. "Buy me another beer?" She knew he wasn't going to. When Apache didn't want to see somebody she had a trick of putting her eyes on him but focusing behind him.

"I have a suggestion," said Chapman, folding his hands on the bar and leaning toward Apache.

She cut him off. "I don't go out with anybody."

Albert had been standing in front of them, ready to serve Apache another drink, but now he sidled back down the bar to the end where he and Paulie could talk with each other through the curtained doorway.

"This is special," Chapman told her. "I know a nice place. It's quiet. We can talk Indian to Indian, Apache to Osage. By the way, my Osage name is . . ."

Apache stood up and was starting to move away when Albert reached across the bar and caught her wrist.

"You're going out," Albert told her softly, grinning. "Paulie says for you to have a good time."

Apache let her arm go limp and wouldn't look at Albert. She stood there making her eyes blaze at Chapman. "I guess we have a date," she said.

"You don't have to go," Chapman told her. "I don't want you to make her go," he told Albert, and Albert raised his hands, palms open, smiling and shaking his head.

"Let's go," said Apache, making for the door. She could get this over with in less than half an hour, even if they were going to make it tough on her.

"Wait," said Chapman behind her.

"What's wrong?"

"Don't you need to change clothes?" He was smiling.

"You want me to wear the G-string?"

"No." He was still smiling at her. "Your regular clothes. What you wore when you came to work."

"A denim skirt?"
"That's fine."
"Christ."

A room like that, shag-carpet-two-double-beds-sliding-glass-doors-to-the-balcony, Apache didn't need to see, and she told Chapman she thought the place sucked. Speaking of which, she said, "If you've got another one of those fifties, you can get out of your clothes, lie back there and relax, and I'll stop wasting your time and mine. How much did you pay Paulie?" she asked him, letting the denim skirt drop, pulling the little cotton sweater up over her head.

Chapman made a slight waving motion with his hand. She couldn't believe him. She hadn't seen a man yet who wouldn't turn his eyes toward a woman taking off a bra, but this one here had turned into a statue. "Traditionally," he said, "the Osage and the Apache nations were never able to agree on any terms of trade. It would have seemed, since the former were farmers and the latter hunters and warriors, that . . ."

"Jesus Christ!" Apache said. She refastened the bra, put the sweater back on, and wrapped the skirt around her waist. She dug a cigarette out of her purse, lit it, plumped up the pillows on one bed, and lay back to smoke and wait him out. Chapman stood, posed, at the far end of the room, his hands in his pockets.

"I don't actually teach at Harvard," he told her, folding his arms in front of him now and staring at her, "but I don't think that ought to matter."

Apache gave him a look, a snort, a sneer, some kind of noise she meant to let him know she could give less of a rat's ass what he did. There weren't many things she hated worse than being out of the bar during working hours, and this was useless, what was going on now.

Chapman took off his glasses, breathed on them, and rubbed them carefully on his vest. "I'm a research assistant," he said, holding the glasses up to the light.

Apache let the smoke from her cigarette curl around her face while she watched him. He kept looking at her as if he expected her to ask him a favor any minute.

"I work for a guy who's writing up pieces on working people in the city," he said. "I told him I wanted you to have an interview." He made it sound like he was giving her something.

Apache let some silence fall between them before she asked him how much he would pay her.

"I don't need a great deal of information," Chapman told her. "Just the standard background kind of thing, your hometown, your family, where you went to school . . ."

Apache asked him how much he would pay her.

"Preliminary expenses were higher than I estimated," he told her, smiling and walking toward her. "I got a deal on this room, but Paulie's fee was substantial. Albert's tip, that drink I bought for Lola, the cab, this suit . . ." He turned a little, modeling the suit for her.

"How much?"

Chapman stood next to her and pulled a ten and two ones out of his wallet, then showed her it was empty. He continued to smile at her, though she could see it was costing him some effort. Digging up two quarters and a nickel, he let change, bills, and wallet fall on the bed beside her. When she laughed at him, he turned away and walked over to pull the drapes and stare through the glass doors. The more Apache looked at his silly ponytail and the back of his expensive suit, the more she had to laugh.

"Your flame burns brightly," she said, "and I need some air." She walked over to the doors, too, unlatched one of them, and slipped out onto the balcony. It was high and cool and dark out there. She liked it immediately and didn't give a damn if Chapman did come out behind her.

"Mr. Bigshot Indian," she said. She wanted to laugh out loud again, into that open space off the balcony, but it seemed like all she could do was chuckle to herself.

"Ten minutes' worth of talk," Chapman said softly. The man was still coming on like he was doing something nice for her. "Easy questions. What's your name? What are your hobbies?" He forced a laugh.

Apache glanced straight down from the balcony. She wasn't ready for all that space of darkness that fell away from the railing down to the lighted streets below. She felt her stomach go queasy. Then she shook her head and accepted Chapman's offer of his jacket—he was putting it around her shoulders before she even thought to herself that he was doing it to manipulate her. For a moment she understood what he must feel like, being too broke to make her a decent offer and too full of pride to beg her. She shook her head again, to get rid of that understanding. "Make it all up," she told him. "Use any name. What difference does it make?"

A noise swelling around her kept Apache from hearing what he said and made her look up to her left where a huge jet was coasting in across the harbor to Logan Airport. Chapman shouted something, and then he came closer to her. "I have to have some facts," he said.

Apache hated how his face looked now, his mouth shaping

the words so carefully and then drawing down into a thin little grimace. She stepped toward the door, but he stepped in front of her. "I spent all that money," he said.

They stood staring at each other, Apache getting madder by the second. All of a sudden she pulled his jacket off her shoulders and flung it out into the air, off the balcony. She didn't know she was going to do that until she'd done it, and neither one of them watched it drop. She started toward him, meaning to scratch his face until he moved out of her way.

Chapman caught one of her hands and then the other. It wasn't that he seemed to know what he was doing, he was just protecting himself, she could tell that, but it was like a dance in which when she moved, he moved, too. Then he had her. His left arm was hooked around her neck, not choking but holding her steady, his right hand holding her right hand back up behind her shoulder blades, and there was such a pain in her right shoulder she thought she was going to black out. In spite of that, she felt herself breathing and sort of crying. She could hear him breathing hard, too, behind her.

Chapman pushed her to the railing where he bent her forward so that she had to look straight down the side of the building. "What's your name?" he rasped into her ear. Apache closed her eyes and wouldn't say a god damn word. "Do you want me to let you drop?" he asked her.

Apache felt herself pissing. She couldn't tell what she was seeing down the side of that building, but she couldn't keep her eyes closed, and her whole body hurt. She was crying, and she didn't know if she could speak a word in any kind of language. But she tried. "Yes," she squeezed out of herself. "Yes, let me drop."

Chapman let her go.

"Bitch!" he said. He turned away from her, put his hands

against the glass door and leaned against it, panting, as if he'd been the one dangled over the edge.

"I pissed in my pants," Apache said. There was one reasonable thing to do, and she did that, took her wet underwear off. She didn't even think about what to do with them, she just flung those underpants right over side where she'd sent Chapman's jacket. "Tell you what, Mr. Motherfucker Indian," she told his back. "You come with me. I'll give you a god damn interview."

In the taxi Apache told the driver, "Fourteen Ping On Street," and when Chapman raised his eyebrows at her, she told him that they were going to the Chinaman's. No need to go back to the Pussy Cat; it was past closing time. She had a plan now. She made up her mind to be a little more friendly to Chapman. "I go to fix the Chinaman his breakfast when I get off from work. He's my old man." She laughed at how startled Chapman looked.

"You're married?"

She shrugged. "The Chinaman says we are. I can't remember it. He said we did it one morning a couple of years ago when we were both shitfaced."

"Did you?"

"I don't know. I remember drinking a lot, but I don't remember any wedding. He and I both get to laughing when we talk about it. You can ask him and see what he says." Apache felt all right now that she knew what she was going to do, but tiredness was coming down on her. She leaned back in the seat and closed her eyes, hugging herself to keep warm.

The sky was lightening when the cab let them out down at the end of a dead-end street, a little pocket of Chinatown.

"Original, huh?" Apache stifled a yawn and cast her eyes up at the restaurant sign that blinked feebly, "The Golden Dragon." "The Chinaman says he's owned a dozen restaurants, and he's named every one of them 'The Golden Dragon.' " She had a key to a door at the side of the restaurant, which she opened and then locked behind them. She led Chapman down a steep, dimly lit staircase. At the bottom of the steps she used another key to open the first door in the hallway. The Chinaman was sitting, just as she knew he would be, there at his kitchen table, facing the door.

"Apache," he shouted, "where the hell have you been?" He laughed. He was a short, stocky man, wearing a plain white shirt and an old Cleveland Indians baseball cap tipped back on his head. His kitchen was so brightly lit with fluorescent tubes in the ceiling that even Apache, who was used to it, blinked at the light. Chapman took off his glasses and rubbed his eyes. "You gonna make me sit here and starve, woman?" said the Chinaman.

"The little shit-ass would sit here all day if I didn't come and fry up his breakfast for him," Apache said proudly. She knew the Chinaman was showing off for Chapman. He liked it when she brought him somebody to talk to. "Bill Po, this is John Chapman. Mr. Chapman is a . . . ?" She let it trail off just to see what Chapman would say.

"I do research," said Chapman. Apache could tell he was using his dignified tones. He and the Chinaman shook hands across the kitchen table, Bill Po rising slightly from his chair. "I work up at Harvard."

Apache watched Bill Po give a little bow of his head to express his reverence for Harvard, and it was all she could do to keep from laughing out loud. There were no windows in the Chinaman's kitchen, the walls were bare, and the door that led to the other rooms of the apartment was shut. But Apache still found the place comfortable. She hummed while she set out eggs and bacon and butter on the counter, keeping one eye on the men.

She savored the dignity with which Chapman accepted the chair the Chinaman scooted out for him with his foot. "So you're Apache's husband," he said. "I've heard a lot about you."

Apache couldn't help but snort, and Bill Po grinned at Chapman. "That god damn Apache," he said, shaking his head. "I don't think she knows anything about me. She don't ask me questions, and if I tell her something, she forgets it the next day. Wish somebody would tell me why I married that woman." He laughed up toward the kitchen ceiling.

"Blonde hair," Apache said and smacked the Chinaman's hat off with her spatula. "Come on, Bill," she said. "I told him about all your 'Golden Dragons.' " She turned back to her cooking, poking at the strips of bacon to make them lie evenly in the frying pan. "Why don't you tell Mr. Chapman about our wedding, Bill."

The Chinaman guffawed. Apache saw Chapman start to set his elbows on the blue-and-white-checked tablecloth, then pull back when he noticed jelly drippings on it. "We had champagne," said the Chinaman. "And everybody sang." He and Apache broke up. Apache held on to Bill Po's shoulder. She could tell Chapman was trying to look casual while he sat there, but he wasn't succeeding at all.

She had to pay attention to the bacon because she liked to cook it at a high heat. The Chinaman claimed she wanted to set the kitchen on fire, but Apache knew he didn't really care. She did things the way she wanted to, not like a god damn housewife, and she knew he liked that. "Oh, Bill! I gotta tell you this," she said. "Look at this," she said, turning to face him, pulling up her apron and skirt to her waist and holding them while Bill Po took a look. He raised his eyebrows at the sight and turned to Chapman. Apache saw Chapman glance back at the door, as if measuring the distance to it from where he sat.

"She, ah . . . ," said Chapman.

"See, he doesn't have a jacket on," explained Apache. She broke eggs into the sputtering grease.

"Yes?" said Bill Po.

"Apache is the subject of an interview I've been commissioned to conduct," Chapman said. He was straining for poise. She was going to fix his ass.

"Yes?" said Bill Po, looking from one to the other of them.

"We were up in his hotel room," Apache said, setting two slices of bread into the Chinaman's toaster and slapping the handle down. "And Mr. Chapman here offered me twelve dollars to tell him about my life. I walked out onto the balcony, and Mr. Chapman followed me out there and gave me his jacket, the gentleman, you know, trying to keep me warm and get me to answer his questions. I wouldn't talk, and he wouldn't let me leave. So I threw his jacket over the side. He grabbed me and held me over the edge, asked me if I wanted him to drop me off the side of that building. He scared me so bad I pissed in my pants, then he let me go and called me a bitch. I threw my underwear over the side, too." She and Bill Po both stared at Chapman.

"These interviews will be published . . ." Chapman began, but he trailed off, and Apache was satisfied to see him squirming in his chair, facing the Chinaman with nothing to say for himself. She turned and scooped the eggs out of the skillet, laid the bacon on the plate beside the eggs and nudged the toaster handle until it popped. This was the one moment she liked best at the Chinaman's every morning, when she produced that breakfast like a magic trick and set the plate down in front of Bill Po.

"Thanks, Apache." Bill took off his hat and set it beside his plate. Then he reached behind him to a drawer in a kitchen cabinet. She watched him shuffle a batch of tools out of the way before he got hold of what he was looking for, his army-issue forty-five. It looked huge in his thin hands. He kept groping around in the drawer, tossing aside a screwdriver and some pliers and some wire and wrenches. "Apache, have you seen my . . . ," he said. But then he dug out the clip and whispered to himself as if he were alone in the room, "Here you are." He checked the cartridges, popped the clip into the handle, chambered a round and pointed that thing across the table at Chapman's face.

"Bill," said Apache softly. She knew she had to be careful not to provoke him too much.

"All right," Bill told her. He held the pistol steady, while Chapman eased himself back down into his chair. Apache watched him open and then close his mouth. The forty-five was two feet from Chapman's forehead. "Mr. Chapman," Bill said, "Apache has left all that shit behind." Bill Po's diction was very precise. "She don't have a background anymore. If she did, it would cost you more than twelve dollars. Do you understand?"

"Yes sir," said Chapman, except he said it with just his mouth, so that you could see what he was saying, but you couldn't hear it.

The Chinaman raised the barrel and squeezed off a round into the transom behind Chapman, shattering glass down onto the floor outside in the hallway.

"Jesus fucking God, Bill!" said Apache, holding both hands over her ringing ears. "Did you have to pull the god damn trigger? Now you're gonna have the cops over here."

Bill Po gave her a quick grin and brought the pistol down. Chapman sat shivering. Apache went over beside him and shouted at him. "You haven't been shot, John! You're all right!" She patted him on the shoulder, but she couldn't get him to look at her.

The Chinaman dropped the clip out of the forty-five and cleared the chamber. He reached behind him and tossed both the clip and the pistol into the tool drawer. He shoved the drawer closed, turned, and picked up his fork. "Nobody in the whole building but us," he said. He took a couple of quick bites of his breakfast, while Chapman and Apache watched him. "Check him out, Apache," he said. "See if he pissed in his pants."

Apache peered into Chapman's lap. "Don't think so," she said. She put a hand lightly on his crotch. "Nope."

"Too bad," said the Chinaman. He ate with astonishing speed. Then he put his cap back on and pushed his chair away from the table. He reached behind him into another drawer, and this time, without looking, he pulled out a toothpick. "Do you have any questions?" he asked Chapman.

"No sir," said Chapman with just his lips.

"Apache, you going over to your place now?" Bill Po asked her. Apache nodded and gave him enough of a smile to let him know she appreciated what he'd done for her. Bill Po examined the results of the preliminary pickings of his teeth. "Why don't you walk the man back upstairs?"

Apache took off her apron, retrieved her purse, and with her hands on his arms and back, she directed Chapman back out into the hallway. She couldn't hate him anymore now, but she did want to get him on his way. She waved to Bill Po, who had a leg up on the table, digging with the toothpick at a molar far back in his jaw. He winked at Apache just as she closed the door.

Apache steered Chapman up the steps. He seemed willing enough to move as she directed him. "Wasn't that the loudest god damn thing you ever heard in your life?" she asked, giving his elbow a little shake.

Chapman tried to say something, but she couldn't understand him.

Apache rattled the key in the door at the top of the steps. The damn lock was half-busted, but the Chinaman had refused to do anything about it when she complained to him. And when she finally did get the door open, Chapman just stood still, looking at the street and the people walking along in the sunshine, but he didn't look like he was planning to go out there any time soon.

"What's wrong?" she asked him.

"I don't know . . ." His voice was feeble, but she could hear him now.

Apache stared at him. "Move out, John," she said softly.

Chapman just stared at the floor, his hands shoved down into his pockets. His clothes drooped. His ponytail was snarled and skewed to one side. He really did look like somebody who didn't have but twelve dollars and change to his name. Apache thought for a moment, then pulled the door closed again. A little roughly she tugged him toward her and leaned back against the wall there in the hallway. "Where are you from anyway, John?" she asked him. She was untucking the little pullover from her skirt and reaching up under it behind herself and arching her back. "What's your hometown?"

"Parmalee, South Dakota," Chapman told her. She pulled

at his hands and put them where she wanted them, up under her sweater. His glasses were smudged, but it interested her to watch his eyes while she made him touch her. She undid his ponytail and impatiently combed through its snarls with her fingers. "Did you say you had an Osage name?" she asked him.

"Little Cougar," he whispered, his voice like a hypnotized man's. "I don't know if I want this," he said.

Bending, she unzipped and unbuckled him. "Go down one step, John," she instructed. She moved him down where she wanted him. "There we go," she said. It took a good bit more adjusting of how they were standing and how she leaned against the wall. Chapman wasn't making it easy for her either, but she was determined to make it work.

"Tell you what," she said, softly now that they were so close. "You just relax and tell me what your hobbies are. One at a time." She felt a little jolt of surprise run through his shoulders, but then he really did brace up, and she knew she could make it work now.

"Give me a hobby, John," she rasped into his ear.

"Hiking," he responded.

They each inhaled sharply.

"Yes," she said. "Yes, keep going."

"Horseback riding," he plunged on.

"Good, John," she urged him. "That's good."

"Archery!" he blurted, as if he were running out of time.

"Oh God! Little Cougar!" Apache sang. "That's exactly right!"

Playing

BILLY HYATT IS A PRODIGY of the alto saxophone. The summer between eighth grade in Rosemary, and ninth grade in Madison, Billy's mother drives him to Madison High School so that he can practice with the band. Before practice and after practice, and during practice if it's possible, Billy talks to girls, plays games with girls, chases girls across the fields of mown grass that surround the brick school building. One day just after the morning marching session, Billy finds himself shoved up against the rough wall outside the band-room door, Bob Kerns holding him there with one hand against Billy's chest and the other held back like he means to make a fist and maybe decorate the bricks with Billy's brains.

"Frieda Goforth is my girl," Bob Kerns instructs him. "You need to know that."

Billy nods. It wouldn't be something he'd argue even if Bob Kerns didn't seem ready to snuff out the bright flame of his candle. But he understands Bob Kerns's reasons. Billy, after all, has noted the billowing curls of Frieda's reddish-brown hair and her skin which is the color of a just-peeled apple. Billy has had the nerve, once when he peeped down the collar of her blouse, to imagine the whole shape of one of Frieda's breasts, though in this moment of confronting Bob Kerns and Bob's anger, he reminds himself that he did not imagine them both, only the one most apparent to him in the instant of her bending over to pick up a dropped piece of sheet music.

Bob drops both his held-back hand and the one pushing Billy's chest. Billy guesses he's looked so afraid that Bob is ashamed of himself. He should be. Bob Kerns is a junior, a big boy who plays a sousaphone. He hasn't so much as spoken to Billy before this, and now with deep contempt he's saying, "You really like the girls, don't you, Hyatt?" Bob shakes his head and walks away before Billy has a chance to answer him.

But he wouldn't have answered anyway. What Bob Kerns says to him falls on him like prophecy. In the core of his fourteen-year-old brain he knows it's true, he's a fool for girls. This is the moment he realizes that it's O.K. to like them, but not to like them as much as he does.

God knows why any girls are interested in gangly, pimply-faced Billy anyway, though they are. Every day at these band practices they call out his name when his mother lets him out of the car. When the whole band loads up on buses and goes to band camp for ten days, Bob Kerns's sad mockery still rings in Billy's ears every time he catches himself trying to look up the skirt of one of the flute players or that sleepy-eyed eighth-grade girl in the clarinet section.

"The saxophone is the sexiest instrument," Valerie Williams tells him one day during a break, squinting her eyes against the sun to be able to look up at him, a light sweat broken out across her freckly forehead.

If somebody like Valerie Williams says something like that it must be true. She's thirteen, the new majorette. She's short, with straight black hair that's shiny as a crow's wing, and a shape like those cartoon girls he studies in his grandfather's *Esquire* magazines. She's Larry O'Dell's girlfriend, but she's been recently discussed intently by every boy Billy knows—by now he's fifteen and already the first chair tenor saxophone—with the consensus of opinion being that Valerie Williams is something else.

Something else, something else, his mind chants for him all the rest of that afternoon. It's August. They're practicing their marching routines in a dry, stubbled field. Out in front of the band the majorettes prance, twirl their batons, pitch them up at the cloudless sky, fail to catch them, grimace and say shit not quite loud enough to have Mr. Banks yell at them. They get tired. Only Valerie Williams lifts her knees almost to her chin every time they go through the show. By four-thirty the others are walking through it, Valerie is still lifting those knees, and Billy, back in the fourth rank, is still listening to his old brain chant for him, something else, something else.

Nighttime at band camp is hot, and the air smells like the sassafras leaves are cooking in the dark. "What do you think?" Valerie whispers to Billy. He's got a hand up underneath her blouse, her breast in its bra cup in his palm. Billy's in a state. If he speaks or moves, he's going to shoot off a load in his pants. They're sitting out on the steps at the back of the main building, where they can hear the music from the scratchy forty-fives somebody's playing so that kids can dance in the little social area around front. "One early morning . . . ha-ooo . . . I met a woman . . . ha-ooo . . . we started talking . . ."

"Cigarette?" Billy asks Valerie. He calmly removes his hand from her blouse at the same time he discharges enough sperm into his jockey shorts to impregnate every mildly fertile female within a radius of thirty miles. He lets his face show nothing but wonders if she'll be able to smell it. Leaning forward, unintentionally over his crotch, she's tucking her blouse back in her shorts. "Yeah, sure," she says.

He drops several smokes, shaking them up then out of the pack, but it's dark, and probably she can't see anyway, and so he lets them lie there. Hospitably he extends the pack toward her, and she takes one. He has a lighter. His hand shakes. She coughs. He cautions her against inhaling if she hasn't done it much before.

"Valerie Williams! William Hyatt!" Like a figure from the Old Testament, Mr. Banks bursts upon them. He confiscates Billy's pack of Chesterfields. He extracts a vow from Valerie that she will never, ever smoke again. He dispatches them around the building into the lighted area where Billy can't stay because he has to go change his pants.

But they are impelled toward each other. When the band comes back to town, school starts, and Billy starts riding the bus twenty miles there and twenty miles back every day. Most of the hours of the day he's got a hard-on and Valerie floating through his frontal lobe.

Valerie lives in Madison. Her mother won't let her wear shorts downtown. After school Billy finds excuses to stay in town so that he can walk home with her, drink milk and eat cookies with her in the kitchen, then go downstairs with her to play Whistle-Stop in the basement. That girl can't whistle worth a damn. Billy's fingers make it all the way up under the hem of her shorts before she so much as raises one faint note. Billy's hand goes behind her back untucking her blouse, and she gets a pensive look on her face like she's thinking about something else.

Valerie's little sisters sneak around and spy on them through the windows. Valerie plays "Peggy-Sue" on the record player again and again, Billy trying to sing along, never getting it right. In shorts Valerie walks him downtown where he catches his ride home with Walter Sawyers whom he must pay a quarter for each trip. Billy rides with his books in his lap, figuring out how to explain to his parents why he stayed in town this afternoon. Valerie's mom raises a holy ruckus when she hears Valerie was downtown in her shorts again. Valerie's dad, the manager of Piggly-Wiggly, gives Billy that look every time he sees him; they both know what the look means, but they make their manners just the same.

Billy gets into a dance band. These guys his brother knows at the radio station need a sax man. Billy can play a couple of jazzy tunes, but he hasn't tried it much. They say they'll teach him. They buy him sheet music they can't read but he can. What they can do is fake it behind him. They practice and work up a program, make a date to put it on the air on Saturday at four o'clock.

Billy tries to tell Valerie who they are. Al Kravic, the newsman, claims he's learning how to play this expensive set of drums he bought in Abingdon. Johnny Wilson, the station engineer, plays steel guitar, leans heavily toward hillbilly stuff and those Hawaiian numbers that make Billy want to puke every time he hears them; but Johnny's a virtuoso of his own kind, even Billy can discern that. And Birdy Z. Pendergast, the station's morning man: Billy can't make him clear to Valerie at all, a little rat-faced man you just know was a sissy all the time he was growing up—a moody, fastidious, mildly effeminate, high-pocketed, pot-bellied genius of the cheap piano not tuned for years.

"I'm serious," Billy tells her, liking the way she's laughing at him, "if it was a new Steinway somebody had just tuned, Birdy Z. would sound like the clunker he really is." It's Saturday afternoon and they're buying popcorn and Pepsis to take into the two o'clock movie at the Millwald Theater. It's September but hot as July. Valerie talked her mother into letting her wear Bermuda shorts to the movie. Billy'd rather she wore a skirt, but he keeps his druthers to himself.

"Birdy Z., Birdy Z.," she says and laughs loud enough to make people turn around and look at her. Valerie wants the rest of his popcorn. She's got an appetite. When the movie starts—it's a western—they slump down in their seats and hold hands and lightly rub the goosey insides of their arms together.

It's five minutes until four when they walk into the radio station together, rubbing sweaty palm to sweaty palm, Billy's ears ringing and Valerie's face crimson. Up in the studio Al Kravic and Johnny Wilson take one look at the kids and commence grinning at each other, but Birdy Z. is in a fury. When they go on the air, Billy's sticking the neck into his sax and going to have to try to get it tuned while they're playing the first number.

When they switch off the studio mike to run a couple of commercials, Birdy Z. bursts out, "God almighty, that sounded like a piece of warmed over rat shit!" He's looking straight at Billy. Billy knows Valerie is watching them all through the studio window. He blows a cute little riff she can't hear, looks up at the acoustic tiles of the ceiling, tries to act like nothing's wrong. "Don't know as I would dignify it to that extent," murmurs Johnny, giving Billy a wink and echoing

Billy's riff on the steel guitar, using it as a segue into one of his Hawaiian numbers.

Billy notices the faces of his old mom and dad bob up beside Valerie's in the studio window. Thank God they'll introduce themselves. Billy's relieved he doesn't have to perform his manners for his mother. He wails out two choruses of "O when the saints," Johnny takes his two—making it sound like something you ought to strum along to with a ukulele, Birdy harangues the studio with about thirty-thousand piano notes, and they yield to Kravic's pitiful version of a drum solo. When the program's over, Billy hauls his sax case out into the waiting room and finds Valerie and his mom, their legs crossed and leaning forward toward each other, sitting on vinyl seats by a plastic fern in the corner.

Birdy Z. comes out, all sociable and Mr. Public Personality, and makes a joke out of it, but he damn sure lets Billy's old man know Billy was late getting there for the program. Taller than Birdy by an inch or two, Billy hates him standing here in his rat-man glasses.

Billy's old man doesn't say anything to him when they're giving Valerie a ride home—country folk in town, driving slow as farmers in a field, Billy leaning forward in the back seat doing all he can to give the car forward momentum, Valerie and his mom carrying on their chatting like a little song they both make up as they go along. It's all deeply, deeply embarrassing. Billy walks her to the door but they don't touch so much as an arm hair when they say good-bye with his parents watching them from the car.

Coda for the day is the lecture Billy's old man has for him on the slow, slow drive back out into the county to their house: Billy's heritage of six known-generations of responsible and decent men on both sides of his family is what he'd better be carrying on his shoulders for the foreseeable and so on. Billy bites the inside of his jaw to keep himself from offering any smart mouth.

"So he told, did he?" she says. "The damned old queer." Valerie says she never cared for Birdy Z., even when all she knew about him was his voice on her mom's radio in the kitchen. "You can just hear it in somebody's voice, somebody like that. A thirty-five-year-old tattletale. What're you doing, Billy? Listen, let's turn him on now and spit on the radio," she says, but it's not Birdy on the air, it's Kravic stumbling through the news like it was written in a foreign language. And what Billy's doing is backing Valerie up against her mom's refrigerator. They don't know what it is about that refrigerator, but they like it against her butt bracing them pelvis to pelvis. "Let's go downstairs," Billy whispers. "What do you guess is down there?" she asks him and pulls his mouth toward hers again so that he can't answer.

Her little sisters' names are Connie and Florence, Coco and Flossie. They are eight and ten and geniuses of hiding places with an angle of vision on Billy and Valerie. They could be down there doing their homework all afternoon and never hear a peep from the siblings, but let Billy get a hand up under Valerie's sweater or let them lie down on the sofa and from somewhere there'll come a twitter. Or else one bright little girl's blue eye looking straight down on them when Billy chances a glance toward the door or the window. "What would we do without them?" Billy says, standing up trying to rearrange his pants to get some comfort.

Valerie opines she has to go outside and practice her baton routine anyway. She goes up to her room, puts on shorts and a spiffy little white T-shirt. From the porch Billy watches, torn between admiration for her physical skill and resentment of the energy she devotes to keeping that two-foot rubber-tipped aluminum rod spiking through the air.

"I gotta go," he says, finally. Valerie's out of breath anyway, talks him into staying and having some lemonade with her on the porch. She's worked up a light sweat. He marvels at the fragrance of her. They talk about how much they hate the Z. "Let's go turn him on," she says, and they go into the kitchen and snap the switch on. He isn't. "Shit," Valerie says, lacking authority in her swearing, because she's just turned fourteen. Billy likes it anyway, gets a thrill from her trash mouth. "What're you doing, Billy?" she asks, but he knows she knows what he's doing. Behind her, the refrigerator makes its barely discernable humming. "Mom's gonna come in here any minute," she whispers. "That's cool," he says.

Billy turns sixteen and gets his driver's license the very next day. The band gets a job playing for the Moose in Hillsville. "God, I didn't even know they had the Moose in Hillsville," says Birdy Z., chortling, "but the man calls me up and offers us a hundred and fifty dollars. He heard us on the air."

"I'm surprised he didn't send us a bill for a hundred and fifty dollars, if he heard us on the air Saturday," Johnny says, diddling that little chrome bar up and down the strings.

"We're getting better all the time," pipes up Kravic, but he's not. The man has reached a permanent plateau at the zero-beginner's level.

Birdy Z. and the D-Jays is the name Birdy gives them. Kravic can't argue because he has no status, Johnny doesn't argue because he doesn't give a fat rat's ass, and Billy makes a face at the name because secretly he wanted it to be Billy Hyatt and the High Notes.

Besides, Birdy is the one doing the driving. "Can you believe a Studebaker?" Billy asks Valerie. She says she wouldn't have believed anything else. It's October. She has on a sky-blue sweater that spot-welds her torso into the base of Billy's brain. Mythic, downright mythic: if he could have her both naked and in that sky-blue sweater at the same time, that's what he'd choose for his deathbed vision, for the last image his eyeballs would ever shoot to his brain.

In the Studebaker, the four D-Jays drive to Hillsville, Galax, Max Meadows, Rural Retreat, all around the county. They get a reputation, not for being good, but for being cheap and for taking short breaks. All these dances are the same, boozy old guys and dames with bottles in brown bags they set on the floor under the tables, stepping through dances that went out before Billy was born. "Trying to drink themselves back to your age," Birdy Z. tells Billy. Nowadays Billy doesn't hold back his smart mouth. "How do you know, Bird? You don't drink."

"Reason I don't is that I do," Birdy Z. tells him. "Or I did." Then he tells Billy all about it.

Through a snowstorm, Birdy Z. crawled from the street where somebody dumped him on the sidewalk around back of his house and up onto the porch where he slept, got frostbite, almost lost a couple of fingers. He takes a hand off the steering wheel now and wiggles its fingers for Billy. Lost a job somewhere, got a job somewhere else, showed up drunk, lost that one, too, and no money to get home with. His wife wouldn't let him back in the house when he did get there.

It's a long drive through those mountains from Galax to Madison. Johnny and Kravic sleep in the back with Kravic's tom-tom on the seat between them. Birdy Z. tells Billy places in the house a drunk will hide his bottles. Highway's empty; nobody's out that time of night. Talk in the front seat of a car takes on intimacy. How can you hate a man who explicates for you the three dozen ways he has been humiliated?

But Billy can't explain it to Valerie. There's something about the man she can't stand; she takes him as her personal enemy. Another night he's meeting her late, after the D-Jays get back to Madison and let him out at the bus station where he's parked his dad's car. Instead of heading straight home—it's after two now—he drives up near her house, douses the lights, parks, sneaks into her backyard, taps on her window. Her face appears, her lips move, she's gone again. In three minutes she's slipping out the screen door of the back porch. He can't hold enough of her to keep her warm. She's in shorty pajamas, without even slippers on her feet. Can't stay, can't stay, crazy whispering out by the swing set in the backyard.

He's never encountered her without her bra on, now he doesn't want to stop touching her breasts under the thin material of that pajama top ("They're free," he says, "they're so free!"); but if he lets her go to do that she gets cold immediately, the pale, almost full moon over them both the ice and fire of the moment. He holds her, wraps the sides of his dumb band-jacket around her, tells her about Birdy Z. crawling through the snowstorm to his back porch, but Valerie's feet and legs are so cold she's about to cry. The story and how cold she is, how mean it is that she has to go in, make her hate Birdy Z. even more.

Monday morning, standing by her locker at school, Billy tells her, "Valerie, he doesn't care what we do"; but she's sure he does, sure he's the one who called and told her mom she was with him downtown in her shorts that day. "He's a queer, Billy, don't you know that?" she tells him. And Billy says no, he's not, suspects immediately that maybe Birdy is; but then a queer is somebody despicable, and now that Billy carries with him these stories Birdy has told him, he holds responsibility for the man, feels he must defend him, says again no, he's not. When Valerie tells him everybody in town has known that about Birdy Z. for years, it's only because Billy's from Rosemary that he doesn't know that, Billy argues that maybe Birdy used to be queer when he was a drunk but he isn't now, he's certain of it. He isn't at all.

Birdy Z. and the D-Jays need somebody else, another horn player or something. Elliott Pugh, this big-lipped kid in Billy's classes at school, is a clarinet player the band director is trying to switch to alto sax. Birdy Z. knows the kid, lives near him, asks Billy about him. Billy says the kid knows no music but classical, which he knows is an exaggeration, but he doesn't care. He reminds Bird that Elliott has taken piano lessons since he was old enough to sit up by himself. "Beethoven is the kid's personal hero, if you can feature it," Billy says. Birdy shrugs, says all they need is somebody who can play the harmony part, a second sax. "Might be just the man for us," Birdy says, "talk to him, see what he says, see what you think." Billy's the one who makes the contact. Billy's the one who actually hires Elliott Pugh to play sax and clarinet with them.

Valerie can't believe it. "Elliott Pugh?" she says. She took ballroom dancing with Elliott from old Mrs. Tyson when she was eight and he was ten. "No one I ever met had less rhythm," she tells Billy, tossing the baton twenty yards straight over her head and catching it already spinning in her hands. Billy lugs her books, the price he pays for the milk and cookies he's got coming to him. The baton twirls in the air around Valerie, going hand to hand to hand, cutting swathes of air around her, buzz-saw, propellor, finger-bruiser if you so much as reach to touch her. Valerie doesn't like Birdy Z. Billy doesn't like the baton. Elliott Pugh they figure doesn't matter to anybody.

Elliott himself couldn't be happier. He's humbled by the invitation and gives Billy more big-lipped grins than Billy has seen on his face in a year's worth of knowing him. Elliott Pugh is the only kid in the whole school who wears unpegged—pleated, for God's sake!—pants, belt buckle riding about navel high.

"They're both high-pockets," Valerie tells Billy. "Probably queering each other every chance they get." She and Billy are riding the second of two band buses back from the Martinsville football game. Good bus to ride, Susan Sweeney and Annabell Sparks up front picking out the songs and getting them going, telling who to sing what part: "Blue Moon," "Tell Me Why," "Down By the Riverside," "Try to Remember." Sweet voices come out of even the toughest kids, Maynard Johnson and Delano Phillipi doing the doom-da-da-dooms of "Blue Moon" pretty as can be. Best bus to ride, no doubt about it. The couples kiss for long miles of highway, boys in the darkest seats getting as much bare titty as the girls will allow. Billy doesn't want to talk about Elliott Pugh and Birdy Z. Pendergast, wants instead to be carrying out an inventory of the goosebumps on the inside of Valerie's thigh.

"What do queers do, Billy?" Valerie seems struck suddenly by the intellectual aspect of the whole thing. Billy's got vague ideas, but he guesses he doesn't know. "Play Whistle-Stop?" he suggests, puts a hand on her knee. She whistles three notes, loud and clear. "I mean really," she says.

"They're not queers," Billy whispers into the curly hairs around her ear. "They're just . . ." But he doesn't know what they are.

Elliott and Bird do have this understanding. Rarely do they

have to talk. But two more disparate musicians couldn't exist. Elliott so stiff, precise, not an ounce of fudge, fake, or syncopate in his bones; and Birdy Z. who never in his life read a note and/or hit the right note on the right beat on pure intuition could fake a Mahler symphony. Rehearsing "Woodchopper's Ball," Billy witnesses at one and the same time Elliott tapping a big foot like a metronome, Birdy Z. diddling both heels and slapping randomly at the pedals with his toes.

"Stars Fell On Alabama," "Blue Hawaii," "Little Brown Jug," "Rock Around the Clock," "Your Cheating Heart," "Night and Day," "Cherry Pink and Apple Blossom White," "Stardust," "Laura," "Blue Monday": Birdy Z. and the D-Jays have no shame about what they'll play, and no matter what the tune, there's one of them in the band who can sabotage it. At the kind of dances they play, nobody cares; you could take a dishpan and a hammer in those places and somebody'd pay you to knock one against the other so they could get out there and step around the floor with their arms around somebody.

They fire Kravic and get Cecil Taylor—a kid who looks like he was put together with drinking straws—to become the rhythm section. A certain ruthlessness sets in as a result of how they improve themselves. Billy and Elliott, tenor and alto, loose and stiff, reckless and cautious; not such a bad pair on two or three numbers, but Elliott can't ad-lib, no matter what they tell him to try to help, just can't do it, would rather sit, red-faced, with the sax in his lap and study his charts than to stand up and try to make up some ditty as it goes along. Something about that failure pisses Billy off way down deep. He commences a sabotage on Elliott, making him look bad, making him sound bad, mocking him, overtly condescending. "Stand up and blow that thing, sucker!" he'll shout when he knows Elliott's going to sit there, big-lipped, hair combed like an old-timey photograph, eyes cast down like a shy girl's.

"Don't pick on him," Birdy Z. tells Billy.

"You're the one they made hire him, why don't you fire him?" Valerie asks him at lunchtime, out in Billy's dad's car, the two of them out there fooling around, sneaking cigarettes. Would be a hell of a thing, damn right it would, Billy allows, chortling to himself, slumped down in the driver's seat. "You're fired, Elliott Pugh, your ass is gone!"

"You're fired, Elliott Pugh, your ass is gone!" Billy says Wednesday afternoon in the studio where they're rehearsing. Elliott's just said he's not going to play harmony or anything else on "Burn That Candle," he's sorry. To air the words, Billy has said he's fired. Elliott blinks at him. Nobody else says a word. Johnny slides the chrome on his strings, evokes the swaying hips of Hawaiian girls in grass skirts, pays no attention to anybody. Cecil's new, keeps his mouth shut, looks into the other studio where the evening man is holding forth at the board. Birdy watches, watches, a look on his face like he's ready to start slavering at the mouth and taking bites out of somebody's arm or leg. Elliott looks around at them. Nobody's got anything to say. "Haul your ass on home, Elliott," Billy tells him and knows now he's got the power to do it, knows he is in fact doing it and getting away with it.

Elliott starts blubbering while he packs up the alto. If Billy had a gun he doesn't know whether he'd aim it at Elliott or himself, but wishes he had the choice.

Small town dances are on Billy's mind. How the women put their arms up around a man's neck and let their breasts lift up against his chest is the gesture Billy begins to dream about, again and again, fat women, thin women, all of them reaching upward in that heartbreaking willingness to give themselves over to some man and politely dance with him.

Teenage master of sneaking-around foreplay, Billy's destiny is blue-balls, sperm-spotted underwear, stained crotches of his khaki pants, wet dreams, the rightful heritage of any high-school boy. He's sixteen, Valerie's fourteen, they're so clearly too young for it that even they, had they been asked to speak responsibly, would have said of course they shouldn't do it.

They do it. On a rainy night in the spring in the front seat of Billy's dad's Dodge, they park out behind the Madison country club, so close to the clubhouse door that from its window the light from the Coke machine shines on them. It's after a concert for which Valerie has ushered. She has on crinolines, stockings, a garter belt. Billy has on a suit that six months ago fit him pretty well. They stretch across that seat, managing legs and clothes and body parts as best they can, and somehow manage a penetration. To neither one of them does it feel even as good as a dry-lipped kiss on the cheek. They talk a little and lie sweetly to each other and disguise their disappointment. The rubber he probably didn't even need Billy throws out the window for the club pro to find in the morning when he opens up the shop.

Nothing changes. Billy drives home and next morning wakes up with a hard-on and smelling lilacs from the front yard. At school, standing at her locker, talking with Annie B. Loomis, Valerie gives him a grin that tightens the muscles in Billy's thighs. He has English first period and tries to change his seat so he won't have to sit beside Elliott Pugh. It's been three days since Billy fired him, but Elliott's face, like some weepy girl's, still looks tear-stained, bruised. Miss Lancaster won't let him change. Elliott hands him an envelope with Billy's name typed on the front. He doesn't open it until lunchtime, in the car by himself now, Valerie not able to sneak past Mr. Banks who from the band room doorway keeps an eye on the parking lot. Dragging hard on his Marlboro—Billy's brand now—he makes himself read a sentence or two—*want to know what right you have . . . think you are such a . . . let me tell you what a real musician would . . . will never know*—of Elliott's typed letter to him; but he can't go on with it or he'll be crying out there himself. He'll go in and find Elliott before Algebra and apologize and hire him back—if they gave him the power to hire and fire Elliott, then he knows he has the power to rehire him. But when he sees the god damned high-pocketed, big-lipped queer-ball standing and scowling just outside the door to Miss Damron's room, just waiting for Billy to say one word to him, Billy stares him down, walks right past him without speaking, and takes his seat.

Billy's cool; he's got his collar turned up, his tightest pegged pants on slung low down on his hips, he smells like cigarette butts, and he's got money in his pockets from last week's gig, money coming to him this Friday and Saturday night from gigs in Abingdon and Fries. But what cool he's got he needs—and maybe a little more besides—when he has to face Birdy at rehearsal that night. The man has a way of beaming his eyeballs through those thick-lensed glasses of his like he means to blowtorch straight through Billy's zit-pocked forehead. "I thought Elliott might come tonight," he finally says quietly.

"You want him to come," Billy says, putting a cigarette in the corner of his mouth and pretending he's got on sunglasses, "call him up."

The Bird says nothing, nor does he move toward the door to go call Elliott. Mechanically they work through the rehearsal, hardly a sociable word among the four of them. Once running through "Till There Was You," Billy hears Elliott's harmony and for a moment thinks he's hallucinating it until he sees Johnny is playing it exactly with Elliott's play-it-by-the-numbers phrasing, grinning as he runs the chrome bar over the strings. It's tasteless of Johnny to make a joke like that, Billy feels, but he says nothing when at the end of the thing, Johnny winks at him. "Billy, you want to stay a minute?" the Bird asks him when they're packing up, and Billy dreads it.

In the studio alone with Birdy now, Billy is aware of how the place cuts off every sound from outside, and he's jumpy, trying to face down the Bird, who's just looking at him in that purse-mouthed way. "I think we need somebody else, Billy," Birdy finally says. "The sound's too thin. Don't you think so?"

In about three seconds flat, Billy has to reevaluate everything he thinks about Birdy and himself and his place in the band and the world. That Birdy would consult him, would actually talk with him as if his, Billy's, opinion were the one that determined how things would go is simply outside the territory of Billy's imaginings. He's thought they were letting him hire and fire Elliott as a joke, because he's the kid of the group and because they didn't want to take responsibility for dealing with another kid besides himself.

"What do you think of Jack Lamereaux?" Birdy asks him.

Billy thinks Jack Lamereaux probably wouldn't want the D-Jays even to play for his old cat. But what he says aloud is that he'd be surprised if Jack would be interested in becoming a D-Jay. Birdy nods slowly, holds onto his rat-man philosopher face, and assures Billy that Jack would like the chance to play with them.

Before Billy makes it out the studio door, Birdy turns half around on the piano bench, with his right hand plinks out a tacky little riff, sighs, and says he wishes he was a drinking man again, he's got a hankering for a cold one. Billy wants to get out of there and so doesn't even pause. "Yeah, well, good night, Bird," he says, already clearing his mind for the project of meeting Valerie at the Shaefers' apartment where she's baby-sitting.

"These guys think I'm better than I am," is how he explains it to Valerie. Still it doesn't add up for him. "It's true, I read music, and they can't. And it's true I'm the coolest one ever to grace the corridors of that sorry radio station," he tells her, walking toward her in mock pursuit while she backs away in mock retreat all around the kitchen.

"Oh yeah?" She parks herself against the Shaefers' refrigerator lifting her eyebrows and giving him to understand she's waiting for him there, but when he lunges toward her, quick as a single-wing tailback she's gone. Billy acts like all he meant to do was take a peek inside the fridge. He pulls out a can of Miller High Life, closes the door, rummages in a couple of drawers until he finds an opener; though he's never done it before, he punches holes in the thing, turns it up and takes a big swig.

"See?" he says, but then the foam backs up in his throat.

"Yeah, I see." Valerie points a finger at him. "The coolest one ever to grace the corridors of Anna Shaefer's kitchen can't handle a little sip of beer. Give me that," she tells him. When he hands it over, she takes two reasonable sips. "That's how you do it, young fella." She sets the can on the counter in front of him. "Want me to get you a bowl of Cheerios?" she asks. When he comes toward her again, she's out the door and down the corridor, telling him no, leave her alone, she didn't mean it. Then they're rassling around on the Shaefers' big bed, trying to stifle their giggles so as not to awaken and traumatize the sweet-dreaming little infant in the next room. With Valerie flat on the bed, Billy half on the floor and half on top of her with his head pillowed on her beskirted, beslipped, and bepantied pubic bone, he says, "Hey, Val, you think this is what queers do to each other?" He kisses her skirt right there and feels her relax, her whole body go loose.

"Don't do that," softly, dreamily, she tells the ceiling above her. "Don't you even think about doing that."

So he doesn't.

Jack Lamereaux knows a lot of good jokes to tell in the car on the way home from dance jobs. The one of Jack's that Billy likes best is about the tall, dark stranger; it takes miles and miles of highway to tell it, and the punchline is "You better cut that shit out." Johnny Wilson knows a lot of jokes, too, and with his intellect aroused by the jokes Jack tells, Johnny takes to matching Jack joke for joke. He makes it even tougher on himself by sticking only to farmer's-daughter jokes. Billy's never heard men do this before, but he recognizes that he is being included in some significant way. Birdy's jokes, mostly puns, seem to him insipid, but he snickers politely along with the others.

So Billy tells the one joke he knows himself, about this retarded guy trying to seduce an extremely seducible girl, the punchline being the retarded guy's repeating after the girl, "lower, lower," in a bass voice. If Billy begins telling his joke in the spirit of manly fellowship, as he tells it, he feels himself drifting out into intense isolation and ends it feeling deeply humiliated. He tells the joke badly, his voice won't go down to anything approaching a bass register, and he's a sixteen-year-old boy performing for grown men. They don't laugh, not even politely. Billy has the middle seat in the back, between Jack Lamereaux and Cecil Taylor. His neck and ears burn. He'd like to die. Short of that, he'd like to machine gun Birdy Z. and the other three D-Jays. They ride for a long time without saying anything. Then Jack Lamereaux tells a joke about queers, lisping and making an effeminate gesture with his hand. Billy makes a point of not laughing at that one, not saying a word to any of them all the rest of the way back to Madison.

Parked with her down by Brice Memorial Middle School he explains to Valerie his relief at having the decision-making responsibility pass on to Jack Lamereaux. Jack really does know the music, really does know what kinds of arrangements they can play, how to set up the numbers in a set, even how to use Johnny's steel guitar to the band's advantage. Billy is happy to be just one among them again, but he wonders about it a lot. "It was like for a little while I was the boss of these grown men; I didn't want to be, and they didn't want me to be, but it just came about. I don't know why."

"You're the coolest one," Valerie tells him, with an edge to her voice that Billy knows is not generous. She is smoking a Marlboro now, one of her own, and they're working on a six-pack of Schlitz that earlier tonight Birdy bought for Billy at Billy's request. Valerie and Billy have had sex again a couple of times. Tonight they could have it if they wanted to, and they're choosing not to, because it's like an appliance they've bought that just doesn't work. They've taken to just sitting in the car and talking, smoking cigarettes and drinking beer if Billy has been able to get it.

He knows something that he's not supposed to know officially, though they both know that he knows: Valerie has been out several times with Pete Ratcliffe. It stands to reason because lots of times when there are parties and dances at their school, Billy is out with Birdy Z. and the D-Jays in some godawful Odd Fellows Hall playing from nine until one and even later if the old dames and geezers can come up with the cash to keep the D-Jays going. Pete's a nice enough guy, and Billy figures Valerie's entitled to a decent time. He has no doubt that Valerie only likes Pete, while she loves him.

Later, he explains all this about Valerie to Birdy Z. while the two of them sit in Billy's dad's car after a Friday night dance job. Birdy has surprised him by joining him for a beer before Billy drives home. Billy was just joking when he invited the Bird, and he thought the Bird's saying all right, he would do that, was also just playing around. But now Billy works the church key on the little can of Country Club and hands it over. Birdy holds it, grins at it, shakes his head, and then turns the can up for a hell of a big swig. He belches, and tells Billy he ought not to be sure of anything with any woman, he's here to tell him that. Billy watches Birdy grin at the beer can again and wonders if now that he's drinking with him Birdy Z. is getting ready to propose queering him. On the contrary, Birdy tells Billy he's going to have to come home with him some night soon and meet his wife. If he's going to be having a beer every now and then with Billy, he's going to have to tell his old lady; it'll be easier if Billy is there with him.

So after the gig on Saturday night they go up to Birdy's house and Billy meets Lannie. She's a big, loose-jointed women, taller than the Bird by a good three or four inches, with blonde hair going dark at the roots, buck teeth, and blue plastic-rimmed glasses. Billy likes her a lot in her faded blue pajamas and maroon bathrobe. Lannie looked really worried when the Bird brought in this bottle and set it on the counter and asked her if she'd like to join him and Billy in a little nightcap. But then she sighed and said, "Oh God, Birdy, if you just knew how tired I was getting of drinking that Sanka with you at this time of night anyway. I guess I'll have one with you." So now they're standing in her kitchen at two-thirty on a Sunday morning, the three of them finishing off a fifth of Smirnoff's vodka, mixing it with the breakfast-juice from the refrigerator.

The house is a mess, as far as Billy can tell, at least the downstairs is, evidence of kids messing into everything, scattering toys everywhere, even into real stuff like the Pendergasts' magazines, the jars under the kitchen counter, the books, and ashtrays. Billy wonders why Lannie didn't clean some of the mess up while she was waiting to have Sanka with Birdy Z. She fires a lot of questions at him, about where they play and how the people act and dance. While he's telling her, she gets this dreamy look on her face and sighs and says she wishes she could get out and go to these things with Birdy Z. Before they had kids, she used to go with him and have a great time. She gives Billy this big horsey grin and winks at him. He can just imagine Lannie out there on the floor, dancing to a fast one, letting it all out, flinging those long arms and legs of hers every which way.

"I guess that's the last of this," Birdy says, pulling the bottle down from his mouth. Billy watches Lannie's face change when she sees what the Bird has done. It does occur to him that the bottle was at least half full when they brought it in, and he and Lannie have had just one drink apiece.

"How do you feel, Bird?" Billy asks him, swirling what's left of his ice in the Bugs Bunny glass Lannie gave him.

Birdy Z. grins at them both. "I feel fine, kids, I feel god damn terrific."

Over the next several months Billy sees a good deal of Birdy and Lannie. It's a little deal they've struck—Billy wanting to be careful not to let his parents find out he's drinking, Birdy and Lannie not wanting anybody to know they've gone back to drinking—and so they drink with each other after rehearsals, after gigs, once or twice just when Billy comes up and has supper with them and the kids. They're full of good cheer, as if they've come into money or found a secret pleasure. One night Billy takes Valerie over there, but she doesn't have a good time and doesn't change her mind about the Bird one bit. "So what if he's got kids and that goony-goony wife? So what if he's nice to you? I don't have to like him, do I?"

Well, she doesn't. And the truth is, Billy has begun to wonder if she even likes him. Nowadays, without milk and cookies, they go straight down to her basement. When he untucks her blouse and reaches a hand back there to unhook her bra, she sighs, sits up straight, and says, "Here, let me do that, for goodness sakes." Then she sits back looks at the ceiling while Billy puts his hands on her. Billy still likes her breasts, but he can feel little messages being passed from every cell of her skin to the palms of his hands, "Get away from me, get away."

"Val, have I done something to you to make you mad?" He takes back his hands to his own self.

"No, but I'll tell you what." She starts crying like she just realized she was in pain.

He's ready for her to tell him something he won't like, such as she's sick and tired of him and she's decided to accept Pete Ratcliffe's invitation to go steady. What in fact she does tell him is that she's pregnant. He feels like she's taken a sledgehammer to his forehead.

"And I'll tell you what else," she says, too, from this posture she has taken of leaning forward with her face in her hands. Billy can't imagine what else there could be after what she's just said.

"It could be your baby or Pete's, I don't know which." Until this moment, Billy has never imagined sex between Valerie and Pete; now the image of them doing it in a car seat stuns him into a long silence during which he merely gapes at Valerie. She won't look back at him.

Billy goes through the motions of asking her questions—yes, she's seen a doctor; yes, her mother knows; no, her father doesn't know yet; no, she hasn't told Pete yet, but she's going to tonight—but all his mind will do for him is chant *you're not even seventeen yet, she won't be fifteen until March, you're not even . . .*

Billy slides through a couple of days like a brain-damaged kid. In the hallways at school, his pals are constantly putting their hands on him and pushing him this way, directing him that way. His teachers are bemused. "Go sit down back there, Billy," Mrs. Lancaster, his English teacher tells him, and he does. But the next thing he knows is he's in Pete Ratcliffe's dad's car with Pete driving and Valerie sitting between them, and they're heading out to the Pendleton stone quarry after school to figure out what's to be done, all three of them smoking Valerie's cigarettes and shaking so bad it doesn't even occur to them to get nasty with each other.

Billy hears himself yelping, "A god damn coin-flip? I cannot god damn believe this!"

Valerie cries at some length while sitting between the two boys. Pete finally blurts, "If you know a better way to . . ."

He and Pete get out of the car. It's a Ford, a new one, pretty, with the sun glazing its waxed hood, shining on the chrome bumper up there where he and Pete stand to do the flip. It's Pete's quarter. They agree that Pete gets to flip it, Billy gets to call it while it's in the air; they'll let it fall in the grass beside the road. One throw will decide the whole thing. One throw, one toss, what the hell—Billy feels like he's about to float out into space. Just before Pete flips that thing up in the air, he looks Billy in the eye and asks, "Did you use rubbers?"

Billy nods, then asks, "Did you?"

"Damn straight I did!" Pete spits to the side. They shake their heads at each other and press their lips together hard. Pete tosses the quarter, Billy calls tails just before it hits, then they're both leaning down to look at it, a little metal disk in the scrubby grass. It's tails. When they get back in the car Pete is the one who has to tell Valerie that he is the one.

On the way back into town not one of the three of them has a word to say. Billy has scooted over as close to the door as he can, and Valerie has scooted over beside Pete as far as she can. Billy asks Pete to take him to Birdy Z.'s place. When he steps out and says, "See ya," it's as if he's a hitchhiker they're just dropping off. Walking up Birdy's sidewalk with his hands jammed down in his pockets, Billy's whispering, "That didn't hurt. That didn't . . ."

Inside the Pendergasts' house, Lannie sits him down at the kitchen table and tells him she should have known it, she's a fool, she's got to get the Bird on the wagon again or he's going to lose his job at the station. They smelled it on him the other morning, and they warned him. The Bird is out for a walk, mulling it over. Billy and Lannie sit there and smoke. Billy wants to tell her what he's just gone through but knows better than to put that on her shoulders. He knows she wouldn't like what he really feels about the whole thing, as if he's been accused of some crime but found innocent in court. And while he sits there with her, he knows Lannie knows the Bird would have never started drinking again if Billy hadn't gotten him going. He tries to think back over that night when he joked and asked the Bird to have a beer with him and the Bird joked and said, well all right.

When Birdy Z. comes in from his walk, he's chewing gum

and smells like Juicy Fruit. Billy and Lannie know he's loaded. While he goes to wash up, sitting there at the table like parents of a wayward kid, Billy and Lannie give each other a long look. "Stashed a bottle in the garage, I expect," Lannie murmurs.

"Do you want me to go look?" Billy offers.

Lannie tells him he won't know where to look, and Billy tells her a long time ago Birdy told him all about stashing bottles. She tells him to go find it then and pour it out and come on back in for supper. Out there, behind a can of charcoal lighter fluid, Billy finds a half-full pint of Old Mr. Boston gin. He takes a big slug of the stuff, grimaces, decides what the hell, he wasn't hungry anyway. He finishes it in three more swigs, and starts walking out to the edge of town where he can hitchhike home.

The next day Pete and Valerie are absent from school, and the day after that it's all over school about them running off to Sparta, North Carolina, to get married. Kids look at Billy funny in the hallway. He feels resentful and smug at the same time. Next week they're back. Billy and Pete manage to nod grimly at each other when their paths cross; but he goes out of his way not to see Valerie, and he expects she's doing her best, too, to keep from seeing him.

Billy feels like he's chasing his life. Jack Lamereaux raises the fee the D-Jays charge for playing a dance, and they get more jobs. He raises it again, and they get still more jobs, at higher-class places. "We are god damn much in demand," Birdy Z. says in the car on the night of the day he has received final notice from the radio station. "I can make a living on my music."

"You can't do any such god damn thing," Johnny Wilson leans forward from the back seat to tell him. They are headed to the Hotel Roanoke where they will make a hundred dollars apiece for their night's work, a little dance for the Southwest Virginia Hollins Alumni. Jack Lamereaux is the one who drives them to the jobs now, though because they all still defer to him, the Bird always rides shotgun.

The Bird turns up his bottle for a quick swig and chortles and says, "Johnny, you old fart, you just lack the guts to set yourself free."

Johnny sits back. He's not saying anything, but he's grinning at Billy and Cecil Taylor on either side of him.

By eleven-thirty, Birdy Z. can't sit up straight at the piano bench. They have been hired to play until one. Two numbers too soon Jack declares the band to be on a break and helps Billy escort the Bird outside where they walk him around in the parking lot. "Can't fire me, you fuckers," Birdy tells them, giggling, his arms pulling heavily on their shoulders. "Band's named after me."

"Yeah, Bird, yeah," Jack Lamereaux tells him. Jack's pretty disgusted. "Can you handle him, Billy?" Jack needs to go back in and stall for time before they start the next set. Billy keeps walking the Bird up and down the aisles of cars under the streetlights that make everything look bluish gray, especially the skin of Birdy's face and hands.

"Billy?" the Bird says, hauling his arm away from across Billy's shoulder.

Billy's happy to see him getting hold of himself this much. "Yeah, Bird?"

"You love me, Billy?" Bird stops suddenly and stands there in the parking lot with his eyes locked on Billy. His shirt's untucked; his tie's loose and skewed around under his collar.

"Let's keep walking, Bird." Billy reaches for him to turn him back in the right direction.

Birdy brushes his hand away. "I asked you a question, Billy." He's even put a little parental authority into his voice, so that Billy has to shake himself to get a hold of exactly what the situation is.

Billy studies the Bird and knows he's not going to get off easy here. Now is the time that Birdy Z. is going to try to queer him. He isn't afraid of it anymore. He sighs and says, "You're my pal, Bird."

"God damn it, Billy."

"Lannie loves you, Bird."

"You like Lannie, Billy?" Birdy's voice takes on a smooth, interested quality that sends shivers up Billy's back.

"Hey, Bird," Billy tells him, no-nonsense now, "Time to go back in and play the last set, man."

The Bird stands there and stares at him. Finally he does say, "You're not my pal, Billy. I don't want anything to do with you. I don't want to see you around my house any more. You understand?"

Billy's relieved. He figures it's just drunken palaver, just what came into the Bird's brain at the moment. And if it isn't that, then what the hell, he can do without the whole mess of Birdy Z. and his drinking. "You ready to go back in and play the last set, Bird?" Billy asks him.

"You're god damn right I am," Bird says and takes a step. Billy reaches toward him to steady him. "Keep your god damn hands off me, O.K.?" Birdy says and walks into the back of an Oldsmobile, falls forward onto its trunk, then slides backward onto the asphalt. Billy can't get him up and so trots back into the hotel to get help. All the D-Jays come out and have a look at Birdy Z. laid out like a dead man in the parking lot.

"You free now, Bird?" Johnny murmurs while they are lifting him into Jack's car, but of course the Bird can't respond.

They try playing out the job without a piano player, but nobody argues with Johnny Wilson when he starts packing up and says that even by his standards they sound embarrassing. Jack accepts half the fee they agreed to originally, and the D-Jays head home early. By the time they pull up in front of his house, Bird has awakened and sobered somewhat, but he has nothing to say until he's out and standing on the sidewalk, glaring down at the car full of them. "You fuckers are fired!" he shouts at them. Jack pulls away, but they can hear the Bird shouting after them, "And I don't want you using my name anymore! You understand that?"

"Set us free, too," Johnny Wilson murmurs, looking back at him, as they all are, even Jack Lamereaux, using the rear-view mirror. Billy is the only one of them who giggles, but he thinks it may be because he feels almost crazy.

Jack stops beside Billy's dad's car, parked in front of the bus terminal. The four of them sit there talking for a little while, finally agreeing that it's not worth it to try to keep the D-Jays going. "We're disbanded, man," Johnny says, laughing. Jack says, "Yeah, man, that's exactly what we are, disbanded as hell."

Before he gets on the road, Billy walks into the bus terminal to take a leak. While he's in the men's room facing the urinal, he hears a stall door slowly creak open behind him. He turns to see a man's face slowly extend toward him from one of the stalls. It is an unremarkable male face, not one Billy has ever seen before, but the sight of it scares him. He hears himself saying in a voice he hardly knows to be his own, "You son of a bitch, you fuck around with me, I'll fucking kill you!" The face recedes into the stall, the stall door creaks closed, Billy rushes his urination and leaves without washing his hands.

Driving home at three in the morning, he's wide awake now, shivering and wondering about the voice that came out of his own chest and throat in the bus terminal. When he said what he said, he knows he felt a power in his arms, hands, and fingers; whether or not he actually had it in him to kill the man who peered at him, he knows he spoke out of animal certainty that he could do it. "Would do it," he whispers to the green light of the dashboard, "would do it." He wonders what Birdy Z. would have done if Billy had spoken to him that way. Then he feels a gush of affection for the Bird, imagines himself back in the parking lot, admitting to the Bird that he did indeed love him, walking toward him and embracing him. It wouldn't have had to be queer, he thinks. He entertains the idea that if he had done that, they could have gone back in and finished the gig and ridden home telling each other jokes.

At school Valerie is absent for an entire week; Pete is out of school, too, one day, back another, then absent another. Billy's friends and acquaintances talk about Valerie and Pete so much that the hallways ring with their names, every laugh sounding to Billy as if it must be on Pete's and Valerie's account. But he himself is not included in their conversations, hears no information, asks no one about them. He's almost seventeen. His days now seem full of the grim injustice of his having been cut off from everyone.

On the day she comes back to school, before homeroom, Valerie walks straight up to Billy at his locker and hands him a note that instructs him to meet her outside the band room at lunchtime. She's so quick and definite about it that what she's done goes almost unremarked by anybody but Billy himself. She's pale and puffy-faced, doing what she can to smile and speak to kids who come up and ask her how she's doing.

She looks back over her shoulder at him when he's had a chance to read the note. He nods at her.

He knows the place she means, out by a side door where few people rarely pass by, even at lunchtime. She's waiting for him when he walks back there, but she's got no smile for him, not even a hello. It's late April, a damp day. Underneath her band jacket she's got on a new white sweater that sets off her dark hair and that he likes, but the way she's standing there she looks like a tough girl. She drags hard on her cigarette, then starts speaking to him in what he figures is a speech she's worked on for a while. "The doctor was wrong," she says. "That bastard. Sunday afternoon I started hemorrhaging. What I have—what I had—was a cyst! Can you believe that?"

Her eyes drill Billy as if she's holding him responsible for what's happened to her, but he knows it's just because she's willing herself not to cry. Or maybe she does think it's his fault. Maybe it is. He can't say anything, and so he reaches toward her to pat her shoulder or something, but she backs away from him and keeps looking at him. He can't say anything for more than a minute; then he gets some words up out of his throat: "Are you and Pete going to stay . . . ?"

"Yeah, we are," she says vehemently. "My parents don't want me to, but Pete thinks we've made fools enough of ourselves now, and he doesn't want a divorce. What he thinks is what I go by since he was the one who was man enough to—"

"Valerie, it was a coin flip!"

"Yeah, tell me about it," she says and keeps her eyes on him, waiting. Billy feels the weight of enormous injustice coming down on him, but he knows better than to complain about it to her. He tries to hold her eyes, looks away, tries again.

"I just wanted you to know," she says finally.

"Yeah," Billy says.

"Can you keep it to yourself?" she asks him, and he nods. She reaches toward him—for a second he thinks she means to punch him in the ribs—clasps his hand and squeezes it. "Take care," she says, then walks away from him fast, stretching her navy-blue skirt with every stride.

Just before marching band practice that afternoon, Elliott Pugh, like a soldier reporting for duty, walks over and stands in front of Billy. "I'm playing with Mr. Pendergast now," he says.

Billy drags on his cigarette and looks at Elliott but doesn't make an effort to meet his eyes. In the last couple of days he's had about all the hostile eye contact he can stand. Still, he can't help witnessing Elliott's presence here in front of him. Billy would still like to take back his betrayal of Elliott those months ago. He figures he has some options: one, he can warn Elliott of Birdy's drinking and tarnish the prize Elliott thinks he's won; or two, he can politely wish Elliott luck. He chooses number three and tells Elliott to go fuck himself. When he sees Elliott grin maliciously at him, he knows that number three was the best for both of them.

Billy puts his cigarette in the corner of his mouth and keeps standing off more or less by himself, comfortable with the horn at his waist hooked to his neck strap like a little attached shelf for him to rest his arms on. Elliott's down at the other end of the ranks with the clarinet section, all of them toodling like free-lance musical idiots. If for no other reason than that the big queer is a clarinet player, Billy knows he was right in what he told Elliott. He snorts to himself, drops his cigarette, and stomps it. Up front chatting with the other majorettes, Valerie has changed into shorts but she's still got on her band jacket, and Billy imagines she's feeling the wind on her legs. "Val, Val," Billy hums to himself and shakes his head and smiles.

More than a hundred kids are in this marching band with Billy. He is one among them. He thinks of Birdy, home at this moment, probably sleeping off one binge, getting ready for another, and Lannie, probably sitting at her kitchen table, smoking a cigarette and trying to figure out what she's going to do about the Bird and the kids and her life—their lives. That's the thought that comes to him just about the time Mr. Banks hollers at them that break is over, put out the cigarettes, dress right dress! Billy takes his place in ranks, still thinking about how Lannie really does have to look after her kids, how she probably figures she has to do what she can for the Bird. Elliott has just hitched himself to the Bird's fate for at least a little while. Valerie is up there in front, a married woman but bouncing her baton on her toe now like a kid.

Mr. Banks pokes the whistle into his mouth, lifts his arms and gives them a shrill blast. Billy puts his teeth to the mouthpiece of the saxophone, ready to play. He's in the center of a rank, kids in front of him, behind him, and to either side of him. Mr. Banks blasts the whistle again, plunging his arms downward, and in unison with them all Billy steps forward, releasing a huge exhalation into the horn. The sound that comes forth is an enormous, rich billowing of vibration that swells up out of the moving formation of more than a hundred musicians. He keeps perfectly square in his rank and in his file. Stepping out crisply to John Phillip Sousa's "King Cotton," Billy's exhilarated. He feels so free he can hardly stand it.

Brothers

"HELP!" I HEARD SOMEONE calling. "Help!" This was around dusk of a warm mid-October Saturday in the semester I was taking "Epic, Novel, and Romance." Because I was behind in my classwork, I had no date that evening. All afternoon I had been reading *Swann's Way*. I was feeling tired and somewhat hallucinatory because of having willed myself to read page after page in spite of my lack of comprehension. I decided that I was probably hearing things or else that someone was drunk out there and simply playing a drunkard's joke. "Help! No! Please!" I heard it again, and something in the voice jolted me upright, lifted me from my bed and sent me trotting for the door. I knew it was my rural upbringing that had made me respond to a call for help.

In that, my second year at the university, I had taken a room in Miss Betty Booker's home, almost directly across University Avenue from the rotunda. When I burst out onto Miss

Booker's front porch into the fading light, I had to pause a moment to figure out where the calls were coming from. Suddenly aware of how foolish I was likely to appear, I stuck my hands in my pockets and tried to stand calmly, as if I had merely stepped out for a breath of air. As it happened, no one out there would have been looking at me. At the corner of Mad Lane and University Avenue a woman was clinging with both arms to the signpost. She was no longer calling for help, but a man was pulling at her and yelling at her.

This was a party weekend in Charlottesville. The street in front of Miss Booker's was full of students and their dates. These couples drifted past the man and woman at the corner post, some slowing down and saying a word or two, but none stopping. Just before I reached the struggling figures, I was shocked suddenly to recognize the man as my fraternity brother Geoffrey Slade, the woman as his girlfriend Goofy. Slade was cocking back his fist as if he meant to land a knockout blow; Goofy gave out an astonishingly loud final shriek for help. I stepped up to them and said, "Hey."

The look I received from both Geoffrey Slade and Goofy stopped me from coming any closer to them. Then they recognized me. Slade lowered his fist. Goofy let go of the post and said, "Oh God, Bill." Slade turned to one side and spat. "Hyatt," he said, "you piss-ant. Why don't you get the hell out of here." But his tone was one that I had come to recognize as Slade's special irony for being friendly. Again I stuck my hands in my pockets, shuffled my feet, and said something like, "Can I be of any help to you all?"

Geoffrey and Goofy both laughed at me. I saw that in my rural neighborliness I was certainly laughable, but that they had needed me for that moment. "Let's go get a beer," I said. Slade said hell no he wasn't going to get a beer with a piss-ant like me, but then Goofy invited me to come to "the apartment" and have a beer with them. So we became a sociable threesome and strolled up Mad Lane toward Slade's place.

"Goofy" was the only name I knew for Goofy. I imagined her real name was something normal like Sandra or Lucy, but I never heard it used. She was a secretary from Washington, a tall, pale woman with stringy black hair and heavily made-up eyes. She had a nose of real consequence, her legs and arms were somewhat shapeless, and she wasn't busty. In conversations with her at TDK parties, I had found her vague and inclined toward nonsequential remarks. Only when she and Slade were together did she possess any quality that I found attractive: on those occasions when I had noticed them eating or drinking together or dancing or talking, Goofy's face and body had taken on what I can only describe as a kind of "sensuous animation." I attributed Slade's continuing interest in her to that quality.

Slade had reddish hair, freckles, and a sort of bad-boyish look; he almost always appeared to be in a pout or intending some kind of meanness. A high-school All-Washington-D.C. halfback and the son of a successful lawyer, Slade came to the university on an athletic scholarship, hurt his knee in his first year, and never played football for Virginia. But in our pick-up games of touch football and basketball, and in intramural competition, Slade was the truly exceptional athlete whose team usually won. He was also the one of us most likely to get into fights with other teams and most likely to get thrown off the court or the field. A history major at the university, Slade informed every brother, pledge, and rushee of his good grades, his athletic achievements, his father's yearly income, and his sexual exploits.

Entering Slade's third-floor apartment, I was almost overwhelmed with apprehension. There were jackets, books, beer cans, shirts, papers, shoes, dishes, ties, pillows, silverware, trousers, and upturned chairs strewn over the floor; the odor—of beer, sweat, and something else I couldn't quite name—was thick enough make me back up a step toward the door. "Come in, Piss-ant," Slade said, kicking his way through the litter toward the kitchen. Goofy cleared a place for herself to sit on the floor on a pillow with her back against the wall; her dress hiked up and displayed her pale thighs and black underpants. Sometimes just the sight of Goofy like that made me understand how little I knew about the way people lived in cities like Washington. "Catch," Slade called, tossing a can of Budweiser toward me with enough force to make me put up both hands to protect my face. Standing in the kitchen door, opening his own can, Slade asked Goofy, "One for you, bitch?"

"Here, Bill, why don't you come and sit beside me?" Goofy asked, now demurely pulling her skirt down.

Slade tossed the opener to me, again harder than necessary, and grinned at me when I couldn't hold onto the thing. "Good hands, Piss-ant," he said. Once in a pick-up touch football game among six of us, Slade was in possession of the ball and I was responsible for tagging him. He ran directly toward me so that I first thought he was simply being silly because I would so easily be able to tag him. He came to a quick stop at a point where if I had stretched out my hand I'm certain I could have brushed his shirt; but he lowered first one shoulder, then the other, and when I lurched toward him, he was instantly moving in another direction and running right past me. It was as if he'd performed a magic trick for me, but it was not simply the feat of evading me that so impressed me. There was something in his face when he had stopped there directly in front of me, something that I might imagine passing between beasts confronting each other in the jungle, a momentary locking of the eyes that communicated a message that would go something like this: "I am faster, stronger, and more deadly than you are; only because you do not threaten me do I refrain from killing you."

Just inside the apartment door I picked up the can opener and punched a hole in my can; because I was standing up with nothing to brace my beer against but my knee and because Slade had thrown the beer, of course it spewed, and I had to try to catch the spray and foam in my mouth. I turned my back to the room. Such incompetence with the simple matter of drinking a beer was clear evidence in Slade's eyes of my inferior status at the university. My ears burned. When I finally had the can under control and got the second hole punched in the top, I turned around again and saw that Slade had sat down on the floor beside Goofy. He had his arm around her and was whispering in her ear. With his free hand he had unbuttoned her blouse and had reached inside there. But Goofy's eyes were on me. "Come and sit down with us, Bill," she said, as if Slade were not there doing what he was doing.

"I guess I better get back to the books," I said. "Thanks for the beer, Geoffrey." I tried to give the sentence that tone of confidence and manly cheerfulness that we TDKs used among ourselves in social situations.

"No, come back," Goofy called as I was closing the door behind me. I kept going. I heard Slade laughing. "Come back, Bill," I heard her again, much more shrilly. Goofy might simply have intended politeness; she might have been collaborating with Slade in a joke on me; or, she might have actually been afraid for her safety. But no one could accuse me of not being a fast learner. Even in that short encounter with the two of them I had corrected that first impulse that sent me down to Miss Booker's front porch because I'd heard a woman calling for help.

I saw no more of Slade and Goofy that weekend. On Monday I flunked the test on *Swann's Way*. By keeping company with Beverly Tyler, a student nurse from Grundy, Virginia, I had gotten behind in my classwork. Beverly's background was similar to mine, which meant that I was comfortable with her but that I saw her only during the week. I didn't invite her to accompany me to football games or to our fraternity parties, which of course occurred on weekends. Beverly was very cheerful about our system, and I suspected that she subscribed to the same values that I held on these matters, though we never discussed them. She had short, curly, dark hair and very light skin with rosy cheeks. Aside from her extremely pleasant disposition, the quality of Beverly that intrigued me most was the way she disguised her full figure with loose clothes and sweaters. I could almost imagine the clean, modest house in which she grew up and her pious, hard-working parents.

The initial stages of our dates were like sessions of sitting in the living room of that house and showing each other family photo albums. We walked to the Virginian Café to have chocolate pie and draft beer, to have some laughs, hold hands, and plug quarters into the miniature jukebox on the table of our booth. The middle stage began when I suggested to Beverly that we take a walk, upon which occasions Beverly never failed to give me a look that designated me a bad boy she was humoring against her better judgment.

Fall evenings in those serpentine-walled gardens between the lawns and the ranges of the university grounds Beverly and I said very little to each other; we simply walked in a kind of erotic spell and let our shoulders, arms, or hands graze each other. I led her on a slow, roundabout stroll until we arrived at the campus chapel, a miniature gothic castle stuck incongruously at the edge of the grounds. The chapel was never locked, and I never asked Beverly what she wanted to do in those moments. In silence I opened the door for her, let her pass before me, then followed her inside. I was not able to see her facial expression well enough to understand Beverly's attitude toward that final stage of our dates.

Before the door of the chapel swung shut behind us, Beverly and I slipped through the deep dark of the narthex into the main part of the church; there we stood for a while in the back, waiting for our eyes to adjust. Only a little light seeped into the chapel by way of the small stained-glass windows, and after a while we could see the outline of those windows and of each other. If Beverly had worn light-colored clothes, they then took on a feeble glow. Even her skin shimmered a little in the dark, but I had to stay within a couple of paces of her to be able to see her.

Always I was the first one of us to lie down back there. It was carpeted, and there was sufficient space between the back pew and the back wall of the chapel. Sometimes Beverly stood for a while, but whether she looked down at me or around the dark chapel, I do not know. Sometimes when I got impatient I tugged a little at her skirt to signal my eagerness to her, but usually I didn't have to. After a moment she knelt down and joined me there on the floor. We kissed and pushed against each other and panted heavily; eventually we carried out what I had heard Slade derisively call "dry humping," which is to say that we imitated sexual intercourse without removing our clothes. Whenever I tried to unbutton her blouse or put a hand inside her underwear, Beverly stopped me; and so we had set limits that both our sets of parents would have expected of us. But within those limits, we proceeded uninhibitedly, snorting and moaning and rolling on the floor.

Thrilling as I found that chapel experience with Beverly, it was nevertheless scary in there. The building creaked, and there were noises for which there was no accounting. It had taken quite a number of visits for Beverly and me to read the sounds the chapel made and to disregard the ones we recognized to be least threatening. There were nights when the sounds indicated that there were others in there with us, and then we left quickly. Once we were certain we heard footsteps approaching us, and we got up from the floor and ran outside then. Still, this ritual was what we came to almost every weekday evening. Later on, outside the student nurses' dormitory, when we said good night, it was almost always close to Beverly's curfew. We were both barely able to stay awake in our classes, and she was even further behind in her classwork than I was.

At our meeting Monday night in the Virginian Café Beverly surprised me by inviting herself to our fraternity party as my date for the coming weekend. Her voice and her facial expression instructed me that this was no light matter with her. I valued my relationship with Beverly because she kept me in touch with my origins—I often thought that, had I grown up in Grundy or she in Rosemary, our parents would have been friends. I had been somewhat curious to know what Beverly would make of my fraternity house—I expected she would be impressed—and so I told her that I already had in mind asking her. The truth was that I had a date for that weekend with a Hollins girl I didn't much like; it didn't particularly bother me to call this girl up Tuesday afternoon and tell her that I had come down with mono. On the phone the Hollins girl made it clear that she knew I was lying, but throughout the conversation we remained cordial with each other.

It was a warm, sunny Saturday afternoon for a football game. That the university had established a record for a major college, twenty-nine consecutive losses, merely heightened my fraternity brothers' responses to the clear air, the flamboyant reds and yellows of the leaves, the animated faces and rosy complexions of our kilted and sweatered dates. Before this Saturday I had never noticed the elegant wisps of hair around Beverly's ear, the almost invisible pale blue vein at her temple. Because I was so touched by Beverly's dear face and her way of taking my arm and leaning on me when she laughed at my fraternity brothers' antics, I did not join them in their customary drink-till-you-puke-in-the-stands competition. As Slade had explained the theory behind this game, the idea was to attain one's drinking second-wind as quickly as possible, because then one's limits were expanded, and one could dispense with one's inhibitions.

Beverly loved Slade's theory when I explained it to her; she leaned on me and laughed and laughed. I discouraged her from joining the game because, in this wide open space of Scott Stadium with the sunshine and the grass and the cheerleaders and the players running up and down the field and the stands full of screaming, drunken young men in coats and ties, I felt this intense tenderness toward Beverly. I didn't want to see her puke.

Slade and Goofy were sitting down at the lower corner of our fraternity's block of seats; they were often visible, Slade standing up and yelling at the football team, shaking his fist at them, and pulling Goofy up to stand beside him. U. Va. lost to Maryland, 35 to 7; but it was an appropriate loss, Maryland being a "jock school," and U. Va. of course having too much integrity to lower its academic standards for the sake of recruiting superior athletes. Walking with our dates from the stadium to the house, we fraternity men sang the good old song of "Wa Hoo Wa"—"for we all came to college, but we didn't come for knowledge"—pukers and nonpukers alike bawling out those words we loved.

Beverly walked unsteadily, but I braced her up, and enjoyed her giddy laughter. I didn't even mind so much that her blouse had come untucked from her plaid skirt. "Your date having a good time, Hyatt?" Slade asked me as he and Goofy, arms around each other's waists, strode past us.

"My name is Beverly!" she called after them. "And I certainly am having a good time," she said when Slade turned to look at her. He winked and kept going. I was so embarrassed that I had to turn my face away from Beverly. Each syllable of her voice had articulated her public-school, Sunday-school-and-youth-group, nice-girl background; I was certain that from her two sentences, Slade had been able to envision her parents' little ranch-style home in Grundy, Virginia, as clearly as I had come to imagine it. In my mind at that moment, Slade even had the power to see me, a year or two earlier, sitting between my parents in a Methodist Church, my hair slicked down and wearing a clip-on tie. I felt Slade's contempt for me deepen.

As we approached it on Jefferson Park Avenue, our fraternity house—up on a little hill above Jefferson Place, with its verandah and whitewashed columns and little second-story balcony—had a grand look to it. We were lucky that weekend in having procured the services of "The Nine Screamers," an all-black band that was so popular in Charlottesville they had to be booked a year in advance. They were set up and ready to go. Just as Beverly and I entered the house, they set forth with a blasting crash of drum and cymbal, guitar, trumpet, and saxophone that literally knocked Beverly back against my chest.

We TDKs had been forbidden to have toga parties since the

night Mike Henderson ripped Hog Holland's toga off his body while he was making small talk with the chaperone and it turned out the Hog was naked under his sheet. That moment cost us the privilege of "theme" parties for the entire academic year. This afternoon and evening was your basic dance-drink-and-try-to-get-your-date-drunk fraternity party. The Nine Screamers perfectly understood our needs; they were starting out with a comfortable version of "The Twist." They would keep a steady pace of unthreatening rhythm-and-blues dance numbers for a couple of hours, there would be a break for dinner, and then they'd start back up for the serious partying of the evening. When they got everybody dancing and beginning to sweat, they'd work up to "What'd I Say?", "Shout!", and that kind of thing. Then the last hour, they'd do soul numbers that had those poetic recitations in them ("Darling, I *need* you . . .") that inspired most of the Sweet Briar and Mary Baldwin and Randolph-Macon girls to snuggle in close to their dates and undulate with them standing up on the floor.

Because I knew that she needed to work some of the alcohol out of her system, I asked Beverly to dance. She stepped out onto the floor most enthusiastically. At first I thought her clumsiness was a result of her state of inebriation. I tried to balance the grossness of her moves and steps with restraint and subtlety in my own movements. When she shouted, "Come on, Bill Hyatt, move it!" I understood that she was much less drunk than I thought she was and that she really didn't know the first thing about dancing.

At the very moment of this realization, I got a nudge in the back and turned to find Goofy in her sunglasses grinning frighteningly at me, while she and Slade carried out their intricate and perfectly synchronized steps. Somehow I was able to see her through my grandmother's eyes, and I felt as if I had suddenly stepped off the edge of the planet. "Yeah, Bill, shake it out," Goofy said and gave a little shimmy of her hips to demonstrate what she meant. When she did that, Slade stopped dancing, stood still for a moment glaring at her as if she had insulted him, then stalked off the dance floor and out of the room. "Oh, shit!" Goofy said, gave me an inscrutable glance, and followed after Slade.

"Are we dancing, or what?" Beverly asked me. I made myself take up the movements of the dance again. But I was preoccupied with trying to sort out my perceptions. It took more than a few seconds for it to become clear to me that what had irked Slade was Goofy's flirting with me. This fact made me uneasy because I suspected it would give Slade an excuse for picking a fight with me, which he would certainly win. But Slade's jealousy also granted me a status I had not heretofore imagined I would ever have; I was thrilled to know that in truth I was more than a piss-ant to Geoffrey Slade. The ambivalence of my feeling was further complicated by my having observed Goofy at such close range: I had seen that beneath a thick layer of make-up her cheek was bruised and her lower lip on that side was swollen. Seeing the bruise affected me almost the same way that seeing her underwear in Slade's apartment had.

"I swear to goodness, Bill, from what you told me, I thought you knew how to have a good time at these parties," Beverly said. In her naïveté she was laughing at me, and I humored her. "Don't want to let it loose all at once," I told her. "Let's go downstairs," I suggested. If Slade came looking for me in the next minute or so, I preferred to be hard to find.

Our basement was a large, low-ceilinged, badly lighted, and only partially sanitary room. About a dozen brothers lived in the house throughout the school year, and they took pride in letting the place stay filthy. Tonight they were playing Thumper down here, a drinking game with four or five of the dateless brothers sitting around a table, pounding on the table with their open palms as if it were a huge drum.

For a moment I didn't even notice that Beverly was shouting at me that she wanted to play. Of course I told her no, but one of the players at the table had heard her and began to point at her and shout, "She wants to play! Hyatt's date wants to play!" I hoped the bad lighting down here had prevented my deep blush from being visible to all my brothers. The only dignified course of action was for me to join the game with Beverly; the brothers obtained chairs and made room for us around the table.

My suspicion was that Beverly must have played Thumper somewhere before that, or else she would not have caught on to the game as quickly as she did. I had had to chug-a-lug four cups of beer before she made her first mistake, and even then the brothers wanted to make her drink only half her cup. She downed the whole thing, turned the cup over on top of her head like a dunce's cap, burped, and said, "Golly, this is so much fun!" In towns like the ones in which Beverly and I grew up, ladies said things like that at bridal showers and Tupperware parties. I excused myself.

Experience had taught me the miracles of rejuvenation that could be accomplished with a finger down the throat over a toilet bowl. When I came downstairs I was a new man. Not only had I purged myself of the poisons of the Thumper game, I had also decided no longer to carry the burden of preventing Beverly from disgracing herself at that party. Meaning just to glance in on the dancers, I witnessed a drama I was helpless to stop. Hog Holland, who was always up to something, had gotten Beverly to leave the Thumper game and dance with him. While she and the Hog were out there doing something that vaguely resembled the U.T., Peter Nickle had sneaked up behind her, and he was just about to sink his teeth into Beverly's backside.

Pete made his move; Beverly jumped, turned, and smacked him straight in the face with her open palm. I couldn't tell if she meant to strike him or if sheer instinct caused her to fend him off that way. At any rate when Pete stood, his hands were to his face, and blood was trickling down from his nose. "Oh, I'm sorry," I heard Beverly say to him, as Hog Holland guided Pete from the room. "That was terrible, what I just did," she said to me, coming up to me as if we'd arranged to meet exactly in that place. I was relieved that she wasn't crying, and I suggested to her that we go out to get something to eat.

Not having a car that year had been an embarrassment to me—I still recalled my father sarcastically asking me who I thought I was that past summer when I had suggested the idea to him—but that night, with Beverly, I was almost grateful to be walking. That way I could talk with her alone and give her hints about appropriate behavior for that evening's party. We walked all the way to the corner; then, kidding about it being an old custom of mine, I steered her to The White Spot for dinner.

All through the meal I told her about this brother and that one, their majors, family backgrounds, prep schools, and dating histories. Speaking about them and about TDK customs, I was hoping to educate Beverly without insulting her.

The walk back to the house tired me considerably. Beverly had so little to say that I began hoping she would want to leave the party early. But when we were coming up the walk toward the verandah, Beverly stopped and announced, "I want you to know I'm going to have fun at this party." Of course I denied any intention of stifling her.

Almost immediately after we entered the house, I lost track of Beverly. The Nine Screamers had set forth on their first set of the evening with uncommon energy and volume. "Little Alamo," the lead Screamer was performing his acrobatic dances out on the floor in front of the band, waving his hand-held microphone like some kind of voodoo wand. So much chaos had been unleashed inside the house that even moving through the crowded front hallway had an erotic content. When I glanced into the main room, I saw Slade standing in the middle of the floor, twisting his pelvis and making conductor-like gestures toward the band; his face was contorted so that it took me a moment to understand that he intended to be urging The Nine Screamers to greater heights of performance. Goofy was nowhere in sight.

The Nine Screamers, apparently fed up with Slade's leadership, stopped playing abruptly and declared themselves to be taking a break. When Slade understood that they weren't going to listen to him, he screamed for everyone to hear, "Roots out!" and began leading a "Roots Out Parade" through the house. Only he and Philip Memler and Dick Wohl actually exposed themselves, but a number of the brothers were sort of cruising along with them just to see how the dates would react. Indeed they were receiving reactions of various sorts—some dates turning away with their faces flushed, others simply laughing, others screaming in mock horror.

I then noticed, right beside me, just inside the front door and still in her sunglasses, Goofy leaning against the wall, smoking a cigarette and looking up toward the ceiling. On his second trip around the house, Slade halted the parade right there in the main hallway so that he was facing her. "Look here, bitch," he said. A hush came over all of us standing there watching them. For a moment Goofy pretended not to have heard him, then in slow motion she turned her dark lenses toward him and down his body.

"Looks like a penis," she said and paused, exhaling a stream of smoke toward the ceiling before adding, "except smaller."

In my opinion, she probably should not have provoked him in public with a line like that, yet I must also say that Slade's response was excessive. He calmly removed the subject of their discussion from view, zipped himself back up, then swung from the waist, a powerful roundhouse right aimed for Goofy's temple. In spite of her relaxed posture, she must have known what he would do, because she slipped the punch, and Slade knocked a head-size sheet of plaster off the wall right beside the front door. He crouched over, whimpering and holding his fist to his chest, while Goofy walked toward the coatroom.

If I had not thought her incapable of such calculated behavior, I could have sworn that Beverly had planned to appear at my side right at that very moment. But she didn't seem to have moved at all, it was just that I suddenly realized that she was there, standing *with me.*

"I think he deserved that, don't you?" she twanged into the silence that still hung over us in the main hallway where we stood witnessing Slade's pain. He could hardly help hearing her, and he turned in our direction, holding up his hand a little for Beverly to see. She didn't flinch from the sight of it, swollen and discolored as it was. "Get some ice on it," Beverly told him.

But it wasn't Beverly at whom Slade was staring through those slitted eyelids. His gaze was directed toward me, and I knew he meant to be telling me that he held me responsible for what Beverly had said. God knows, he might have held me responsible for what had happened to him in that horrible accident in the hallway. As he looked at me, we all heard the back door slam, and I saw his lips shape the name Goofy. Phil Memler told Slade he'd drive him to the emergency room, but Slade shook his head. Then others began speaking to him, explaining to him that he'd probably broken some bones and that he needed treatment immediately. When the voices built to a certain point, Slade screamed "No!" He got silence in response. Still clutching his hand to his chest, he looked around the circle of us surrounding him and screamed, "Somebody get me a drink, goddamnit!"

Slade paid no more attention to me or to Beverly. He took off his trousers and spent the rest of the evening drinking and dancing, mostly by himself, in his jockey shorts, always clutching his hand to his chest. Walking Beverly back to her dormitory in the early morning hours, I attempted to explain to her why I admired Slade for refusing medical assistance and enduring his pain for the entire evening.

Approaching McKim Hall, it suddenly came to me that Beverly was obviously just as eager to gain experience as I was and that up until now I had been naive to think her a prude. I understood then that half-knowingly she was using me to help her cast off the burden of having grown up in Grundy, Virginia. This insight pleased me a great deal. When I kissed her good night, among the various other couples also kissing good night there outside the dormitory doorway, I let my hands slide down her buttocks. Her playful slap of my shoulders assured me that I was right in my changed estimation of Beverly.

The next afternoon when I walked out to the house for our customary post-party touch football game, I almost wished Beverly were with me. The weather was still balmy. I had slept well and didn't arrive until after two o'clock. Someone's hi-fi was playing an Isley Brothers album turned up almost as loud as The Nine Screamers had played the previous evening, but now the sound echoed through a sparsely populated house. A few brothers were roaming through the rooms, all of them red-eyed, disheveled, and carrying drinks. Slade, with his trousers back on, greeted me with special intensity. "Hello, Pissant," he said in such a menacing voice that I knew he still held a grudge. When I asked how his hand was, he held it up for me to see. It was swollen to almost twice its original size, the meaty part of the hand reddish-purple and each of his knuckles a blotch of white. While I examined the hand solicitously, Dick Wohl explained to me that since Slade wouldn't go to the doctor, they had stayed up with him drinking through the night. "Feeling no pain, are you, Geoffrey, old buddy?" said Wohl, clapping Slade on the back. It was then that I realized Slade was on the verge of passing out in front of us he was so drunk. "Time for the game," he announced. "Pissant's here, 's time for the game."

And so Memler fetched the old pigskin and we trooped down to the little field between apartment houses on Jefferson Place that we used for our games. Slade and Mike Henderson were the captains; there were five of us on Mike's side, four on Slade's. The play was fairly even and lighthearted for the first fifteen or twenty minutes. The exercise seemed to sober Slade. He called no attention to his damaged hand, so that we all quickly forgot about it. Only when I was covering him, and he was running for a field-long pass flung high in the air by Memler did I remember that if he were going to make that catch it would have to be with only his left hand. Nevertheless, even drunk as he was, he was quicker than I; he gained a couple of steps on me; he was extending his left arm and would certainly score the touchdown unless I stopped him.

It wasn't really something I planned when I reached out and

slapped his right hand; things like that just happen. Of course Geoffrey shrieked with pain, and when he got up from the ground where he had fallen in his futile dive for the bobbled catch, he was furious. He came toward me, frightening-looking and cursing. My brothers were not going to stop him; they were interested in what he would do to me. They stood where they were, waiting. Though my strong preference was to run for the house, my upbringing nevertheless required me to stand my ground. Having done so, I suddenly understood that my position was not such a bad one. After all, I had thought that Slade would come after me sometime. Better it be then, when he had only one good hand and he had been drinking for more than twenty-four hours straight. As he came closer I held up my open palms. "I'm really sorry, Geoffrey," I told him in my most congenial voice. "Take it easy, big fellow," I crooned.

Slade's face remained hostile, and his posture was one of being just about to take a swing at me. I had seen him stand like that on the basketball court working himself up to take a punch at an opposing intramural player. But somehow I was able to read the thoughts that passed through his mind at that moment, was able to feel how his swollen hand must have been signaling him to do nothing further to inflict pain on it. When he raised his left fist, I made a slight ducking motion. He let loose a rather hideous laugh, and then he put his arm around my shoulder, hugged me to him, and said, for everyone to hear, "You know, Piss-ant, I ought to kick your ass."

"I know, I know," I told him and circled his waist with my arm and hugged him to me. It was a powerfully emotional moment for me, and I sensed that my brothers on the football field felt some of the same closeness I was now experiencing with Geoffrey. We were interrupted by a car tooting its horn as it swung into Jefferson Place. We all turned toward the street and saw that it was Goofy in her new Plymouth convertible with the top down, waving to us as she drove up to the fraternity house to turn around. She had on her sunglasses and a yellow scarf, and her hair was streaming out behind her. "You god damn bitch, you!" Slade hollered as he released me and ran toward the street, holding his damaged fist like an infant he was carrying to her. "You god damn son-of-a-bitch bitch!" he yelled. Now I stood with the others on our little football field, waiting to see what would happen.

When Goofy pulled up beside the field, Slade was standing there waiting for her, and he leaned his whole body into the car to hug her. They kissed and murmured to each other until we were embarrassed to watch them and so started passing the football back and forth among us. After a while Goofy tooted the horn again, and she waved to us as she started the car moving back toward Jefferson Park Avenue and Route 29 North that would take her to Washington. Slade stood on the street waving until she was out of sight, then he rejoined us, shaking his head. "What a god damn bitch!" he said just before we started playing again.

At the Virginian Café that evening I recounted these events to Beverly. She was having a draft beer, but she had not joined me in our customary chocolate pie, and her mood was not nearly as upbeat as I expected it to be. "Beverly, what do you imagine your parents are doing right this minute?" I asked her, meaning to remind her of the values that were at issue here.

Her eyes flicked up toward the clock and then down at her beer mug. I watched her face darken. "My parents have been in bed for half an hour, Billy. You know that," she murmured.

"Mine have, too!" I told her. I lightly smacked the table of our booth just to emphasize my point. "And I'm not looking for a life like that. Are you?"

I wanted her to look me in the eye, but she shook her head and kept her face turned down. I didn't know what she meant. And she was not enthusiastic when I signaled to her that it was time for our nightly stroll through the grounds. For a while she hung back sulkily. The evening sky was clear, with all those stars and a moon that seemed to be hovering over Charlottesville. Of course at this time of year there were no flowers to give the air fragrance; nevertheless, the warmth of the evening had a fragility to it that was almost like some rare scent.

"Weather's turned," I said and Beverly nodded; then it came to me that the reason Beverly and I both knew about the weather was because we grew up in families that depended on backyard gardens. I was embarrassed at that understanding, but Beverly's spirits seemed to lift as we walked.

When we came to the chapel door and I stood holding it open for her, Beverly said, "I don't know, Bill," as if she, too, understood that the evening held some special promise. I said nothing but simply continued to hold the door. After a moment or two Beverly sighed and said, "Oh I guess it won't hurt anything. Just for a little while." She passed inward, and I followed her, the hair prickling on the back of my neck.

Instead of stopping at the back of the chapel as she usually did, Beverly kept pacing, very slowly up the center aisle. Because of the bright moon outside, the chapel seemed not nearly as dim as it usually was during our nightly visits. I caught up with Beverly and enjoyed the stately pace she set for our walk up the aisle. My senses were acute in these moments as if they had been sharpened by my recent understanding of her.

When we came to the end of the pews, Beverly stopped and

stood there in front of what we could make out to be two steps up into the area directly at the front of the chapel. Since neither of us had been there in daylight, and since at night it had always been too dark for us to see, that territory in front of us was equally unknown. Tonight it was almost the only truly dark part of the chapel. I took Beverly's hand and stepped up one level. "Come on, let's see what's up here," I whispered to her. She paused a moment, then stepped up with me.

It was so dark there that even with my heightened senses I could tell very little about the area, but one thing I sensed was that the carpet there was much softer than that in the back of the chapel where we usually lay down. I stooped to touch it and found it tickled the palms of my hands most deliciously. "Feel this," I told Beverly, and she, too, stooped down. "Isn't it wonderful?" I asked her and I stretched out there, feeling that the gift of that softness was appropriate for the evening.

Beverly did not join me right away, but when I touched her arm, she sighed and sat down beside me. I had come to know that just by being there with me Beverly was acknowledging something entirely at odds with her upbringing, her own capacity for desire. I was gentle in pulling her toward me, reaching to untuck her blouse. A certain amount of resistance on her part was to be expected; after all, she had been raised in such a way as to produce almost permanent sexual inhibition. It would take patience and understanding to help her. I let her push my hands away when I attempted to caress her thighs under her skirt and again when she didn't want me to unbutton her blouse. I was very excited, but I saw that the approach that would be easiest for her to accept was one of playfulness; and so I sat up, lightly hooked a finger at the top of her blouse and made as if to yank downward. My intention was only to pretend to open her blouse so crudely, but because Beverly jerked away from me at the same time I yanked, a ripping noise indicated that apparently I had pulled loose several of her buttons.

I laughed and started to apologize—I couldn't see a thing—when all of a sudden my cheek was stung hard by a slap from her open hand. In my surprise the image that flashed before me was that of Goofy in her sunglasses, grinning at me on the dance floor, mocking me as if she had the power to see both my past and my future. That vision unsettled me, and in the dark I was helpless to fend off other images that plunged into my mind, Slade sitting in the floor beside Goofy with his hand inside her blouse, Slade's eyes locking onto mine with that contemptuous smile coming onto his face. I gulped air to calm myself, kneeling now, and reached out to touch Beverly, to help both of us regain our sanity. It was not my fault that what I touched when I reached for her was Beverly's breast. I immediately realized my mistake, feeling welled up in me, and I was about to admit how terribly wrong I had been, but at that instant her second slap cracked across my other cheek. I felt this noise ripping up out of my chest at the same moment I was pulling my right fist back. I let it fly toward the place where I knew Beverly's face resided in the darkness.

It has never been clear to me how I managed not to knock her senseless, in fact not to hit her at all. My lunge carried me forward, so that my body seemed to me to be following my fist. I let myself collapse facedown on the carpet. For a moment it was as if Beverly had disappeared, had dissolved into the black air or else had never come there in the first place, and I was in the dark chapel alone. My breath rasped into me and back out again; I sounded to myself like some kind of momentarily stunned animal. While I lay there the knowledge pounded at my temples: if I had hit Beverly Tyler with my fist, I would have become someone else, I would have had another life than the one I was going to have.

I became aware of Beverly's hand on my shoulder. I knew that she must have put it there very softly at first, but it was almost as if she had suddenly reappeared. After a while my breathing eased, and Beverly whispered, "Let's go, Bill. Let's get out of here." I couldn't tell whether or not she knew that I had swung at her. For a crazy instant I even doubted that I had tried to hit her. We picked ourselves up and turned toward the faint window light falling on ranks of empty pews; walking down the center of the chapel I felt Beverly's fingertips at my elbow. I offered her my arm in the formal manner that seemed appropriate for the moment. Picking up pace as we went, we almost burst into the narthex and then out through the main door into the clear night air.

Once outside we simply stood looking not at each other but at the serpentine wall winding down the hill from the rotunda toward Alderman Library. "I need your jacket, Bill," Beverly finally said, somewhat grimly. Though it was a new Harris Tweed I cared about immensely, I took it off with no hesitation and set it around her shoulders. That was the last night I ever walked Beverly Tyler back to her dormitory, the last night we spent in each other's company. We had nothing to say to each other, but I was grateful for the reverie that seemed to have come to her. She was in no more of a hurry than I was. Not touching, we paced slowly along those walkways of the university grounds, passing beneath lamps on high posts so that always the light on us was brightening, diminishing, brightening again.

My jacket, which she wore over her damaged blouse, seemed to me some part of myself that she carried, whether or not either of us wished her to. As we walked, the silence we held became like something the two of us were constructing. Outside the doorway of McKim Hall, Beverly accepted my kiss on her forehead. It surprised me that she kept the jacket around her shoulders as she walked into the door and out of my sight around a corner of her dormitory hallway. But the next day at Miss Booker's when I came downstairs on my way to Monday morning classes, there was my tweed jacket, neatly folded on the hallway table, good as new.

The High Spirits

RICHARD KOHLER WAS DRIVING maybe thirty or thirty-five miles an hour with four of us in the car. It must have been after two in the morning when he turned the headlights out, and we began yelling at him. In the sudden dark of this country road he slowed down a little, but he also laughed at us. Then when our eyes adjusted, and it was evident that there was enough moonlight to see where we were going, he said, "I'm gonna give you gentlemen a tour," and picked up the speed again. Richard was a lot older than the rest of us, plus he was married and a French teacher; but sometimes he acted crazy. He had the top of his convertible down. If anything he was driving faster than he had with the lights on.

This was in early May, and the air smelled like freshly plowed fields with intermittent gusts of lilac and wisteria. We were on the back roads of Albemarle County, heading eventually into Charlottesville after having played for the junior-senior prom of Woodridge High School, where Richard taught. After a while we were so used to the moonlight that it seemed amazing we had ever needed the headlights in the first place. The moon cast its light all across those rolling fields; only when we passed houses and barns did the shadows around them give the darkness any power. It became lighter the farther out toward the horizon we looked. Behind the car we were pursued by a pewter-tinged cloud of billowing dust.

Richard slowed down as we passed one of those pretentious restored antebellum farmhouses that are all over Albemarle County. He gave the horn a couple of gentle taps, and he chuckled as he drove, letting the car lose speed around a long curve until we came to a gate on our right that marked the end of a sloping field and the beginning of a section of woods. "This is where I always met her," Richard said, stopping the car so that as we stared at the gate we could imagine just how she'd be there waiting for him, whoever she was. "God, she was sweet," Richard was telling Marshall, his pal, our floor leader, vocalist, and guitar player. They went on murmuring about this woman.

I was in the back seat, I was tired, and I'd had maybe four or five beers through the course of the evening. My fellow band-members and our manager were less than fascinating personalities. It was my second year at the university. The drummer and the piano player in the back with me both worked in stores in downtown Charlottesville, a place I visited infrequently. Marshall was doing graduate work in history, but he was such a weenie—goofy clothes from back home in Arkansas, red hair, freckles, a toothy grin—that I was embarrassed every time I had to introduce him to one of my fraternity brothers.

Richard was our manager. He had his master's in French

from the university, and he wasn't exactly a weenie—he was a big, blond-haired fellow who looked like he ought to be a scoutmaster or a Sunday school superintendent—but he wasn't like other men his age. Shaking his head about that woman who met him by the gate, he put the car in gear and started it rolling. Marshall asked him a couple of times, "Is that really true?" and Richard replied, "I swear to God. I swear to God."

I'd really have preferred to sleep all the way back to Charlottesville, but the night air, all that open space around the car, and the springtime smells were keeping me suspended pleasantly between sleep and wakefulness. Jack, the piano player, was pissed, though. He had to go to work early in the morning. "Kohler, you son of a bitch, you're driving in circles," he said all of a sudden, leaning forward. Richard began chuckling again. He pulled off the road onto a little parking area at the top of the hill, even though Jack asked him what the hell he thought he was doing. "Let me tell you all about this one," he said. "Jack knows her. You all saw her there tonight. She used to ride her horse up here and meet me on Sunday afternoons."

Jack began cursing quietly, curled his arms against the front seat, and put his head down on his arms. "Kohler, I'm not interested in your god damn love-life." Jack was a small man with dark, slicked-down hair and an effeminate edge to his diction. He was usually angry or upset about something, usually tired and in need of a shower and a shave. He was the kind of piano player who can't read a note of music but can play just about anything he's heard once and can even fake what he hasn't heard. He had one of those killer smiles. Most places we worked, some woman would come over and drape herself over the piano asking Jack to play something she could sing along to. Jack'd give her one flash of that smile and then ignore her the rest of the night.

"Jack, you take that girl out into an open field," Richard said, twisting around in the driver's seat of his stopped car, "and you watch her slowly take her clothes off for you—"

Jack bolted upright in the seat. "God damn it, Kohler," he shouted. "I don't want to hear it!"

We were all quiet then, knowing that Jack had reached the edge of his temper. I was surprised Jack was so worked up. Dormitory and fraternity house life had dulled my response to what Richard was saying. I was used to hearing men talk about women that way, though of course my university acquaintances were much younger men than Richard, and they made more of a joke of it than he was. But it meant nothing, and it was certainly nothing to get upset about. Richard sighed, put the car in gear, and started it rolling down the hill. He kept the headlights turned off. Freddy Gates, the drummer, and I scooted farther over into our respective corners to make room for Jack when he leaned back into his seat, letting his head loll loosely on his shoulders as if he were so pissed off he'd even lost consciousness. Keeping their tones low, Richard and Marshall kept on talking in the front seat.

I was wide awake then and gazing out at the countryside like somebody who'd never seen a field full of fresh alfalfa. I got this freaky sensation of being submerged in the silvery light, as if we were moving underneath some tropical ocean. And that image Richard was going to describe for Jack had anchored in my mind. I was pretty sure the girl Richard mentioned was the one who had caught my attention, a tall, lanky one with long, light brown hair, a strapless blue gown, and elegant shoulders; early in the evening this girl stood talking and laughing with him right beside my stand for quite a while. I didn't know her name. But I found it easy to help her tie her horse to the gate, take a stroll with her up that little knoll beside our last stopping place, sit down in the broom sage there, and watch her begin unbuttoning her blouse. I could sure do that. I was almost disappointed when Richard turned on his headlights. We'd reached an intersection with Route 29. In another five minutes we were at the edge of Charlottesville, and Jack was saying, even though his eyes were closed, "Thank God, thank God."

We were a band of very low quality. When we'd first gotten together, we'd rehearsed twice, and that was it. All of us had other things to do, and we understood that those other commitments were more important than the band. The High Spirits, Richard had named us, but that was a laugh. As I said, Jack Denton was usually mad about something, and Freddy Gates, one of the six guys in all of Charlottesville who had his hair cut in a flattop, had no emotional life whatsoever—Freddy played drums like a human metronome. Marshall Borland was so anxious about all the work he had to get done for his graduate courses that in any conversation he had with you, he could do very little more than give you one of those big-gummed Arkansas grins and giggle. Me? I guess I would have said that I was embarrassed about hanging around with these guys. Aside from playing my horn with them, I didn't contribute much to the High Spirits.

But the High Spirits did seem to matter to Richard. "I had this name for a band, before I even met you all," he had told me once when I asked him about the name. "I dreamed it," he'd said in a serious tone of voice, but he didn't go into any details about the dream. Richard didn't take a real cut of whatever we were paid—just enough to cover his gas money. He was not even a real manager in the sense of telling us what to do, he was just the one who always drove to wherever we were playing. As far as I could tell he had no real aptitude for music; he couldn't play an instrument, couldn't sing, and didn't seem to know much about any kind of music. He couldn't have been in it for the friendship because my saxophone was friendlier than Freddy Gates, and Jack Denton directed a major portion of his anger toward Richard. I made a real effort to preserve the distance between Richard and me.

We dropped Jack and Freddy off at their respective houses, then we headed up toward the University Corner where I lived. I was surprised at myself for still being so alert at that time of the night. It was that tall girl taking her clothes off in the field who was keeping me awake. I figured I'd better do something if I wanted to hold on to even a made-up vision of her. "Hey, Richard," I said, when I was standing behind the car waiting for him to open the trunk and hand me my saxophone case. "What's that girl's name? The one in the blue dress."

He looked puzzled.

"The one in the field," I told him.

"Oh, *that* girl," he said. He smiled and looked down at his feet. "Yeah, that girl. That's Louise. Louise Morris. Yeah, she's something, isn't she?"

I agreed that Louise Morris was something. I was already thinking ahead to looking up all the Morrises in the phone book and trying to figure out which would be the right number for Louise.

"You want to meet Louise?" Richard asked, looking at me then with a kind of shrewd expression on his face, as if he were measuring my social acumen. With Kohler, if you didn't know him, you wondered if he was a stupid guy who now and then got smart ideas or a smart guy who only occasionally let his looks reveal his intelligence. "Tell you what. Let me see what I can do. I don't blame you for being interested."

Richard pulled a roll of bills from his jacket pocket and with his big hands peeled off a twenty and a ten for me. This was his custom, to pay each one of us when he let us off. "I'm sorry it's not more," he said, his usual observation before stuffing the roll back into his pocket again. Back in the car, just before he pulled away, he gave me that shrewd look again.

I didn't give it a lot of thought. Sunday when I woke up I knew I had a lot of studying to do, and it was a natural process for the events of a Saturday night gig to become only distant memory. Maybe if the High Spirits had played a higher caliber of music, I'd have thought more about driving home from the Woodridge prom. But my instinct was to forget as much of my experience with the band as I could, and I was happy enough on Sunday afternoon to let Saturday night fade to the dimmest shadow. That evening, when the phone was for me, I went down, picked up the receiver and heard an unfamiliar girl's voice saying, "Bill? Bill Hyatt? This is Louise Morris." I had to stand there in the hallway and press my temples with thumb and fingers to remember who this girl was.

In that phone conversation I quickly learned that Louise Morris was eighteen and that she had a car—her daddy had given her her graduation present early. When I suggested that we ought to go out sometime, she said, "How about tonight?" It turned out she was in town, calling from a filling station pay-phone. In five minutes she was in front of Miss Booker's rooming house, tooting her horn; in another five minutes she and I were pulling into the parking lot of Patton's Grocery Store where she waited in the car for me to go in and buy a six-pack. She had on a dress, a white sweater and penny loafers; her hair was clean and curled. She had a smile like somebody's pretty little sister. When I walked out of the store, she'd turned the radio up high and was smoking a Marlboro. At my suggestion that we take a drive upon the Skyline Drive, she nodded.

"What did Richard tell you about me?" I asked her as she headed the car out of town.

She dodged my question with one of her own. "How well do you know Mr. Kohler?" Louise asked me. Her expression had clouded ever so slightly.

I told her that I'd known him for a while, but that I didn't feel I knew him very well. That seemed to me an excellent answer, one that gave me some flexibility no matter what Louise's opinion of Richard was.

"He's a special man," she said, tossing her cigarette out the window and then looking over directly at me. "Very special," she said.

I told her that I needed more detailed information than that, and she laughed at me. "What are you doing, building a case against him?" she asked. Of course I denied that, but to myself I took her remark as further evidence that fate had in mind for me to become a trial lawyer. "Tell me about the band," she said, "I thought you guys were just great."

It took me a while to straighten her out on this matter. I had to be diplomatic about it because after all we were the band that had played for her senior prom, the band that came with her French teacher's recommendation. "Richard loves the High Spirits," she said. "He says he'd be lost without you guys." Louise had found a parking place at one of the scenic outlooks, and we were sitting in the dark, halfway through our second beers by the time I had said all I had to say about each individual in the band. When she sighed and brushed one finger down my forearm, I shut up and pulled her toward me.

Louise Morris was the most advanced high-school girl I'd ever met. When I unbuttoned the first button of her dress, she helped me with the others. When I pushed the skirt of the dress up, she lifted her hips so that I could push it all the way up. When I was trying to negotiate her slip and her bra, she said, "Wait a minute," and she took everything off except her underpants and tossed it all in the back seat. I was getting tangled in my own clothes from trying take them off so quickly, when Louise smiled at me and helped me with the stuck sleeve of my shirt. "Do you have rubbers?" she asked me, and I heard myself almost wailing "No!" She smiled at me again. "Too bad," she said.

"Does that mean we can't . . . ?"

"Not unless you want to get me pregnant," she said, and the way she said it at first made me think she was really offering me that option. "Don't worry," she said, reaching for me, "this will work all right."

It did indeed work, though I was embarrassed at my yelp and at the mess I discharged onto Louise's new car seat. She, however, was as kind and considerate as a nurse helping a patient through a difficult procedure. She even apologized to me for having to step out of the car to put her clothes back on. I got out, too, mostly because I wanted to watch her dress. She went slowly, both of us listening to Ray Charles on the radio singing "Georgia on My Mind." She understood that I liked seeing her there in the cool shadows. When we were both leaning up against the car fender, finishing our beers, she finally broke the silence by whispering to ask if I thought we should go.

Back at Miss Booker's I asked Louise if she'd like to go out again. I didn't expect her to accept, because I couldn't see how the evening had been any pleasure to her. I was used to Sweet

Briar and Mary Baldwin girls who expected to be fed and entertained and introduced to my fraternity brothers. If sex were involved, those girls expected their fair share of satisfaction. Louise surprised me by saying, "Sure!" as if she'd just had a fabulous evening. "What about tomorrow night?"

I told her that tomorrow wasn't good for me because I really did have to get some studying done in the next couple of days, but what about Wednesday night? She actually looked disappointed but agreed to come for me around eight on Wednesday. "Make a purchase," she said just as she was about to pull away from the curb. When I looked puzzled, she shook her head, flipped her hair around her face, and pointed down toward the corner. "The drugstore is right down there." She wriggled her fingers at me.

I did some hard thinking when I got back in my room. Louise was a pretty girl, she was sure of herself even if she hadn't yet finished high school, she was likable, and she had her own car. But this was not even the kind of sexual encounter I felt like bragging about, because there had been something too *friendly* about it. I felt as if I had witnessed something that happened to me instead of participating in it. The whole time I was considering all this, I tried to hold the image of Louise in my mind, but I couldn't. It was like not being able to remember something I'd studied for an exam. And I felt as if somehow Richard must be aware of my difficulty. I could almost see his bemused half-smile if I'd told him what was bothering me.

The opportunity for me to do exactly that arrived entirely unexpectedly the next evening. There was a knock at my door, I hollered "Come in!" and Richard Kohler, unshaven and in sloppy old clothes, was standing there grinning at me, offering me a cold beer from a paper bag. Richard probably offered the beer because he didn't know if I'd welcome his visit, and I took it because I needed something to help me get used to his being there in my room where he'd never been before. I popped the top and sat down on the bed.

Inside my room, Richard seemed huge. His hair was disheveled, his shirt was untucked. He lurched around, looking at the bookshelf, my bullfight posters that I had bought at Mincer's Pipe Shop down on the corner, my I PISS ON IT ALL FROM CONSIDERABLE HEIGHT sign that I had spent a whole afternoon lettering. He chuckled a moment, then turned to me and asked, "She call you?"

I could have asked him who he was talking about and stalled a little bit, or I could have denied that Louise ever got in touch with me. All of a sudden Louise, in her penny loafers and emroiderered white sweater, seemed almost palpably present in the room with us. "Yeah, Richard," I said and felt as if I were betraying her. "She called me."

Richard flinched, then looked around the room as if he were trying to remember where he was. "Mind if I sit down?" he asked. I pointed to the two chairs that were available. He took the one at the desk and pulled it some distance across the room away from me, sat down, leaned back, then straightened when he heard the chair give a warning creak. He held the can of beer on his knee. It was then that I remembered Richard didn't even drink. He was holding the beer just to be polite to me.

"Great girl," he told me. "She's a hell of a fine girl, Bill," he said. He gazed out into the middle of the room as if he might also have been envisioning Lousie standing there with us.

I nodded and waited to see what else he'd say. It troubled me to have him so uneasy there. In every other circumstance of my knowing him, Richard had seemed relaxed in that devil-may-care way of his.

"Ah, Bill, Louise may . . . She might . . ." He stalled out in whatever he was trying to say. Then he blurted, "She's the smartest kid who ever set foot in the door of Woodridge. Parents both doctors. Let her do whatever she wants to do. Learned all the French I could teach her in about a month." Then as if he couldn't stand sitting down any more, he stood up and started his tour of the art works in my room again. At least that way, he didn't have to be looking straight at me. Studying one of the bullfight posters as if it were a Goya or a Velázquez, he began talking again. "Bill, you've seen Woodridge, you know what kind of a place it is, Bill, a little country town with these rich, precocious kids growing up and going nuts out on the farm just because the parents took a notion to live in the country. And you've got to figure what kinds of students would be the ones who take the French classes. Five or six girls for every boy. Nice kids. So damn smart. Kind of kids you can't help but be drawn to. If you've got anything vaguely resembling intelligence, they're going to respond to you."

When he turned to me, I knew he wanted only a nod from me. I ducked my head maybe a quarter of an inch.

"First couple of years I was scared to death. I mean, I'd walk into a classroom, and I'd almost be knocked back out the door by the energy that was in there revving up, waiting for me to come in and direct it somewhere. High-school girls," he said and shook his head and smiled.

"The boys are there," he went on, "but they might as well not be. They feel that energy, but they know it's too much for them to handle. They do their work, they keep their mouths shut, and they stay away from the teacher."

Richard walked to another poster, gazed at it, then came

back to the chair again. He was carrying his can of beer, but he had yet to take a sip of it. He sat down, sighed, and seemed to force himself to look straight at me. "One afternoon, driving home from school, after I'd had a long talk with Louise—it was her sophomore year—I asked myself if I wanted to spend the rest of my life being scared, or if I wanted to do something about it." He kept looking at me, but I didn't hold the stare. I took a long swig of beer, kept the can turned up longer than I had to.

"That's what it comes down to, Bill," he said. "Simple as that. I decided to stop being scared." He paused. It was clear he meant not to say anything else until I had given him some sort of signal.

I began, "So you and Louise—"

"It's not just Louise, Bill," Richard blurted, as if that were the great secret he had come there to deliver to me. "It's a whole different life I'm living now. A different world. Do you understand what I'm telling you?" His voice was urgent, but I didn't really feel like helping him out. The man was old enough not to need my understanding.

"Gee, Richard, I don't know," I said. He plunged up out of his chair, turning his back to me.

"Yeah, you're right," he said. "All the pieces don't fit. I know that. I haven't got it worked out yet, and I know I've got to do that. It's exciting, but I'm a little too involved. You're exactly right to remind me of that, Bill." He turned to me. "I want you to know I'm working on it," he said. He set his beer can on my desk and strode to the door. "I want you to know that I'm going to keep on working on it," he said. He started to leave, but then turned again to me. "Louise is a hell of good kid, Bill."

I nodded to him, he raised his hand, and I raised mine just

as he made his exit. I picked up the beer he'd left on my desk. The can felt full, but it held so much warmth from his hands that I didn't want to drink it. The paper bag he had brought in with him was sitting on the top row of books of my shelf, and when I checked that I found four more cans of beer, cool ones. I took one of those and opened it.

It wasn't easy to study with Richard's voice lingering in the room and Louise again avoiding my mind's eye. Wednesday night when I heard Louise tapping her horn out in front of Miss Booker's, I was eager to get a good look at her. When I opened her car door and let myself down into the passenger seat beside her, I leaned over to kiss her cheek but found her lips waiting for me. I closed my eyes for the kiss. "You smell wonderful," I told her. Again she was dressed like a girl going to her church's youth-group meeting, but in the back seat she had a cooler with a six-pack in it. When I glanced back there and lifted my eyebrows at her, she said, "There's a place outside of Woodridge where they don't ask me how old I am." I studied her while she drove, and noticed that she preferred to hold a lit Marlboro between her fingers though she rarely brought it to her lips.

"Back to the mountain?" she asked me, laughing. Then she looked at me accusingly. "Did you make that purchase?" she asked.

Given how much I'd had her on my mind, I couldn't even understand how I forgot to do it. At the moment it came to me that my lapse of memory had something to do with not being able to hold her in mind, but I couldn't exactly tell her that I forgot the rubbers because I couldn't remember her face. I felt terrible and told her so. My embarrassment caused me to lose my poise for several moments, but finally I tried to pretend that my forgetfulness must have been a reflection of my desire to carry out cultural activities with her. I suggested going to the University Theater, where the only things they showed were foreign movies with subtitles and movies that nobody but professors and graduate students wanted to see. Louise was amused by the idea, but in her cheerful way said yeah, sure, her parents used to take her there all the time when she was a kid. I knew she was just being kind to me.

When I was with her, the effect Louise had on me was to make me intensely aware of her and not to notice much about anything else. We were already inside the theater, sitting off to the side by ourselves, and the movie had already started when all of a sudden I sat up straight and asked her, "Do you know what the name of this movie is?" I got shushed from three or four directions, but that's just the way it was at the University Theater: there were professors who went to those movies for no other reason than to shush the undergraduates who came there with dates.

Louise didn't know, but she leaned close to me to whisper in my ear, "It doesn't matter." Her lips brushing my ear, her hand on my arm like that, made me lose most of my interest in the movie. It had Anthony Perkins and Melina Mercouri in it, and it was in black and white, but that was about all that registered with me. There was a scene where Anthony Perkins and Melina Mercouri made love by an open fireplace and the music built to this tremendous crescendo. Louise and I were strongly affected by that even though we didn't see much of it. There was another scene where Anthony Perkins was driving really fast on this narrow mountain road, he had the radio turned up loud, and he was shouting crazy stuff until he drove over the side of the mountain. I did watch that part of it, and at the end, with Anthony Perkins dead, I felt like something significant had passed between Louise and me.

When the lights went up, we had to kind of hang back behind the rest of the crowd. Louise needed to fix her make-up and comb her hair; I needed to get my shirt tucked in. In the lobby we were the only customers except for some guy standing at the candy counter. I felt great, walking out with my arm around Louise's shoulder, her arm around my waist. Our steps matched. I didn't even notice the first time my name was called, but then the guy said it again, "Hey, Bill."

Louise recognized him before I did. "Hey, Jack," she said. She and I unhooked our arms from around each other as Jack came up to us, but I kept hold of Louise's hand. "How you doing, kids?" Jack said. Maybe he was speaking to both of us, but his eyes were on me, twinkling, as if he could hardly wait for me to try to explain to him what I was doing there with Louise. I wasn't intimidated by Jack—as I said, he was a working-class guy, nice enough in his own pissed-off way but not somebody who was ever really going anywhere in life. God knows what he was doing at a movie like that. I put him on the defensive as quickly as I could. "You two know each other?" I asked him, looking first directly at him, then at Louise. I liked it that she was almost as tall as I was, that we could lock eyes with each other like that. Louise squeezed my hand ever so slightly, but she didn't say anything. Sure enough Jack did get a little flustered. "Yeah, sure," he said. He made a little gesture as if he were tossing salt behind his back. "Louise and I have met. Richard introduced us," he said emphasizing Richard's name. His saying it that way made me remember how pissed off he was when Richard was talking about Louise in the car the other night.

"Yeah, us, too," I told him. We were standing there in the empty lobby, the three of us sort of stuck with each other. When you're in a band with somebody, even as incompetent a band as the High Spirits, you have this relationship. So there was really nothing for me to do except to invite Jack to join Louise and me for a beer at the Virginian.

Louise softly reminded me that they wouldn't serve her beer, and Jack suggested coffee next door at the College Inn. I was having trouble reading the way Jack and Louise spoke to each other.

Under the fluorescent lights of the College Inn, in a vinyl covered booth with a formica covered table in front of us, we all three looked overexposed. Jack's sallow complexion highlighted his need for a shave; his slicked-back hair, which seemed at least half stylish when he was sitting at the piano at a dance, now looked merely greasy. Louise's eyeliner and eye shadow, lipstick, and blush-on were a little more visible than I wished them to be. But her brown hair shone in that light as if each strand had a gold center. I rubbed a hand over my chin, wondering what I looked like to them. For a while we busied ourselves with menus, deciding what to order, and making room for the waitress to set down our silverware and napkins and glasses of water. After the lady had brought Jack and me our pie and coffee and Louise her Pepsi, it was clear we were going to have to tackle a topic of conversation.

"Well, my friends," I said in my mock movie-scene voice, "our manager is not with us tonight." Jack looked uncomfortable. Louise gave me a smile, but it had only a fraction of the force of her ordinary smiles. Then Louise and Jack caught each other's eye, Louise looked away quickly, and Jack tightened his lips momentarily. "Look," I heard myself saying, "I get the distinct impression that the two of you have some things to say that you're not saying."

I wasn't sure what had gotten into me except that I didn't like Jack and Louise having this understanding between them.

Under the table Louise took my hand and set her fingernails against my palm. Above the table she was concentrating on her Pepsi, while Jack kept his mouth stuffed with pie. Maybe they meant to be giving me a chance to cool down.

"Hey," I said, pulling out my wallet and putting a couple of bucks on the table, "I can get all the silence I want in my room. I'll just leave you two here and go hit the books for a while." I made as if to stand up from the booth, but Louise took a firm grip on my wrist.

Again Louise and Jack let their eyes meet, then looked away. "It's just that—" Jack began, and at the same time Louise said, "You don't under—" Instead of laughing the way people usually do when they both start talking at once, Louise and Jack had to negotiate it out very seriously. Finally when they agreed that Louise would speak first, it was clear she didn't want to because she looked only at the table and kept her voice low. "You don't understand everything that's involved in Richard's life. Jack doesn't either, but I know Jack disapproves of Richard. He and I have had this discussion before. I don't like to hear anything bad about Richard. That's all," she said.

Jack cleared his throat and blurted his words as if he'd had to use all his willpower to hold them back to now. "It's just that he's got a wife and kids. That's not saying anything bad about Richard to state the facts. He used to be my friend, too, and so did his wife."

Richard's having a family was not news to me, but it occurred to me then that Richard would probably have been much less mysterious to me if I had ever let myself really think about everything I knew about him.

"Your good friend," Louise murmured.

"Yeah, that's right," Jack answered crisply. "Janey Kohler used to be my good friend. I used to go out there all the time.

She was somebody I could talk to, somebody . . . Look, Louise is right, we've been over this before, Bill. It's no use in doing it again. If Richard hadn't changed, I'd still be his buddy."

"He has a philosophy," Louise offered. There was an edge to her voice.

"Yeah," Jack said, "right. He's got what he calls the Principles." He took on a bored expression. "He's got a new girlfriend, too."

Now Louise was the one whose lips tightened. She said nothing, and so after a moment I offered a soft "Yes?" I figured I was about to find out something useful.

"This new one is something else," Jack said. Though he pretended to be speaking to me, his eyes were on Louise. "This one came down here from Philadelphia. She wasn't even at that prom the other night. She makes all these Woodridge girls look like little hillbillies."

"That's not true, Jack," Louise said, her eyes on him now, an expression on her face that I hadn't seen before.

"You know what he thinks of jealousy, Louise," Jack said. He was looking directly at her.

"It's not jealousy. It's just that she's not that exceptional. I have math and English with her, and I can tell you that she's a very average student. You're the one who insists on getting the facts right."

"She's a dancer. She danced in New York before she came down here. Anybody from Woodridge ever dance in New York?" Jack asked her.

"Why don't you just shut up, Jack!" Louise pushed against me to signal that she wanted out of the booth. She walked to the ladies' room with her back straight and anger in every step.

When I turned my eyes back to Jack, he was leaning forward

waiting for me to listen to what he had to say, now that we were alone. "I'll tell you, Bill, in case you haven't figured it out for yourself. Kohler has seduced every halfway decent-looking girl in that high school, from seniors down to freshmen. If they had eighth grade out there, he'd be getting it from the eighth-graders, too. The man is disturbed. I've seen him with one or two of those girls, smiling and talking and wiping the sweat off his face. He gives them this bullshit philosophy about freedom and giving affection freely and how you can't take possession of another human being but you can share—"

"You're making too much of it, Jack," I said, though the fact was that I didn't doubt much of what he was saying. "A lot of guys like to talk the way Richard was in the car the other night."

Jack leaned still farther toward me and spoke very carefully. "I'm giving you just the minimum of what I know. I'm not trying to make it worse than it is."

Louise came back to the table then. Her face was red, but her make-up had been applied with precision. "Ask Jack how he knows all this stuff about Richard," Louise said grimly. She was staring straight at Jack.

"Kohler likes to tease me. He likes to taunt me," Jack said. And now he was the one speaking quietly. He leaned back in his seat.

"And why does he like to tease you, Jack?" Louise asked him.

Jack didn't say anything to her. He studied his empty coffee cup for a while. Then he pulled out his wallet and threw a couple of dollar bills on the table just as I did a while back. "I guess you're going to tell him, aren't you?" he said to her as he got up.

"And why shouldn't I tell him?" Louise asked Jack's retreating back.

At the door, Jack turned. "Tell him," he said loudly enough for us and a number of other people in the Inn to hear him. "I should give a shit."

Then Jack was gone, and Louise and I were the objects of attention of most of the other employees and customers of the College Inn. Her face was crimson, and mine was, too; though mine was pure embarrassment, and hers was at least fifty percent anger. "I guess you might as well tell me, whatever it is," I said.

"Jack's queer," Louise murmured. "What really bothers him is that Richard wasn't attracted to him."

I was at least smart enough to keep my mouth shut while I got used to the fact of Jack's being homosexual. It made so much sense that I didn't know why the possibility hadn't occurred to me before. We sat there for long enough to make people lose interest in us. Then without saying anything we both got up to leave. Outside I told Louise that I was sorry I had started that whole thing, and she told me that it was all right, it was all bound to come out sooner or later. We'd passed through this very difficult experience and now we were closer than ever. Our arms were around each other as we made our way to the parking lot behind the theater. We couldn't get into the car before we were kissing again. "We're drunk or something," I told her, leaning back against the car door.

"I can't even get the key in," Louise said, her hair falling around her face as she bent toward the car. I put my hand on hers to try to help. Together we were clumsy, but then we hit the spot.

"God, Louise," I said.

We both got in on the driver's side, then we were pulling at each other's clothes.

"We can't do this," I told her, but I was moving toward doing it anyway.

"No, we sure can't," Louise said, but she was on the same track I was. "Let me have your hand," she said, but in another minute she was laughing. "You don't know a thing, do you?" she said. When I told her that I was willing to learn, she leaned back in the seat and whispered directions to me. It took only a minute or two. "I'm a good student, aren't I?" I asked her. Louise sighed and reached for me. "If I could just teach you how to walk into that drugstore," she said. "We got boys out in the country who know how to do that," she said, but by then she could have said whatever she wanted to and I'd have been only half listening.

While we were saying good night in front of Miss Booker's, she asked, "So when are we going to see each other?" I reminded her that the High Spirits were playing a dance at the Wilsons' house on Friday night. The Wilsons were horse breeders whose farm was just outside Woodridge; Alicia Wilson was a classmate of Louise's at Woodridge High. Louise surprised me then by bowing her head and telling me that for the Wilsons' party she had a date.

Louise very earnestly requested that I not be jealous when I saw her there with her date. I told her that I had faith in her feelings for me and that I thought she should go to the party and have a fine time. Sitting there with her in the car with the cool night air coming through the open windows, I felt sure it wouldn't be long before Louise and I meant a great deal to each other. She gave me a small smile but a very tender good night kiss.

Louise told me her date's name was Tommy Spence. I felt

sorry for him. He had probably been looking forward for a long time to taking Louise to the Wilsons' party. Friday night, I'd been standing out in front of Miss Booker's for half an hour before Richard came for me. The top was up on his convertible, and I couldn't see who he already had in there; I hoped I was the last one. He double-parked, jammed on his emergency brake, bailed out of the driver's seat, and trotted back to open the trunk for me to stash my saxophone. Richard was in his shirt-sleeves, with a tie on that he hadn't knotted yet, and he was sweating like a ditchdigger. When I opened the door on the passenger side, I was greeted by the quick glance of a skinny, dark-haired girl with high cheekbones in an unnaturally expressive face. That flicker of her eyes over me seemed to be saying she was doing me the favor of not enchanting me. She said nothing aloud. Over the car roof, Richard said, "That's Cathy there, man. Let's go."

I looked in the back seat to see if that was where I was supposed to sit, but Freddy Gates and Marshall and a snare drum and a guitar were back there. "Come on, get in, Bill!" Richard shouted. I squeezed in beside Cathy, who continued to have no words for me.

She was wearing a sleeveless orange dress without a corsage, but the perfume she had on was what I thought crushed orchids would smell like. She had long, thin hands and fingers and arms, thin shoulders, and a chest that was so flat I'd have grinned to myself about it except that it was exactly right for the rest of her. Her face was very narrow, she had huge, dark eyes and straight black hair pulled back into a ponytail. The way she held her head made me square up my own shoulders.

I wasn't attracted to her. She was like one of those models in women's magazines who wear clothes you never see on anybody in real life. But I could appreciate her. I admired how she'd set that distance between us. The girl knew she had the power to affect me, and she had honored me by choosing not to use it. Even skootched up in the middle of the seat, with her knees pushed up almost to her chin, she had a careless grace.

Nobody had anything much to say. When Richard headed out of town, I asked where Jack was, and Marshall leaned up from the back to say that Jack was getting his own ride to the Wilsons' place. On the highway Cathy leaned over toward Richard, put a fragile hand on his knee, and murmured something. Richard leaned toward her head and made a noise that sounded the way I imagine bears rumble to themselves and to each other in their caves. Snuggling in still closer to him, Cathy let one of her feet slide over into my area of the floorboard, so that her right leg could straighten out a little. Her dress pulled up to a few inches above that knee. It was a thin knee, but the calf beneath it was substantial—and the long, angled line that leg made, from her hip down to her white shoe, held my attention for most of the drive.

The Wilsons lived in one of those outrageously huge houses that were built back when they figured there would always be black servants to run the errands and keep the place clean. Mr. and Mrs. Wilson must have been defeated by it years ago, because everything was dusty, soiled, and stained. The furniture was randomly dispersed throughout the place. Every room we walked through was cluttered with clothes, bridles, cans, trophies, harnesses, toys, boxes, tools, boots, books, and knick-knacks.

It was the Wilson daughter who was having this party, Alicia, a small, pale girl with a weasel face and shining blonde hair. She wore a strapless black dress. This Alicia led us into what she called "the ballroom," told us where to set up the band, what she wanted us to play, how long our breaks were supposed to be, and when we could quit. Her mother and father, boozy-complexioned and dressed up in that rumpled-tweed horse-farmer kind of way, stood a few feet behind her, keeping their mouths shut and looking apologetic.

While Richard and Marshall and Freddy and I were hauling in the stuff from the car, Cathy strolled around, examining one thing and another. She wasn't acknowledged by Alicia or Mr. or Mrs. Wilson, but she didn't seem troubled by that. She carried her body in a way that made you want to watch her, but she didn't seem to care whether you did or not. I could see both Alicia and her mother letting their eyes slide over in Cathy's direction, then exchanging glances as if to say, "What's *she* doing here?" and "*I* didn't invite her." Old man Wilson openly gawked at her. I could also see that Richard was trying to be restrained in his attention to Cathy but that he couldn't keep himself from looking at her. She glided around "the ballroom," gazing at the pictures on the wall, paying none of us any mind.

"Where's our piano player?" I heard Marshall ask Richard while we were tuning up, but I didn't hear Richard's response. One thing about having a four-person combo was that if one of the four didn't show up, the other three were going to sound like a Salvation Army band on a cold night. Freddy Gates and I were warming up softly, practicing a little riff I wanted him to learn to play with me. People were starting to arrive at the front door. Richard and Marshall had started sweating.

"Mr. High Spirits himself, ladies and gentlemen, I give you Jack Denton!" came a voice from one of the side rooms. Sure enough, Jack, in a white dinner jacket, strode into the room, bowing slightly one way, then another, stepping to the middle of the floor and raising his arms like a celebrity at a prizefight.

"Look out, gentlemen!" said Richard. Marshall told me he'd never seen Jack act like that; I told Marshall I didn't think Jack had it in him. Jack walked over to us in the company of the apparent owner of the voice that announced his entrance, a wiry little guy with gray hair, a moustache, and a tuxedo. "This is Julian Taylor," Jack told us. Then he introduced us one by one. Julian had small hands, even for a man his size, but when he shook hands he tried to make up for that by clamping the hell out of your fingers. The two of them walked over to the piano where Jack gave a real show of trying out the thing, rippling his fingers up and down the keyboard, giving us the Jack Denton version of a concert pianist. "My God, this boy is talented!" said Julian, looking pop-eyed around at us, then around the room and the party guests. "A Liberace of the provinces," he pronounced, setting his hands on Jack's shoulders as if he had just given Jack his proper title.

"Where the hell did Jack pick up this screwball?" Richard growled behind me. "Where's Cathy?"

I started to ask him which question he wanted answered first when I noticed Louise enter the room, followed by a kid who was half a foot taller than I was, baby-faced, with blond hair and rosy cheeks, one of those boys who would probably get into Princeton just on the basis of his looks. Tommy Spence had a paw on Louise's back, right at the waist—she had on this fitted dark-green satin dress that shimmered with every move she made—and as they moved into the room, people stepped aside for them.

Marshall began twanging out the guitar introduction for "The Theme from Peter Gunn," a nonarrangement that we High Spirits ad-libbed our way through so often that Richard had suggested our motto should be "If in doubt, play 'Peter Gunn.' "

"Hooo-eee!" some music-hater out there hollered. A fat boy pulled a skinny girl out onto the floor, and we were off to an above-average start. The kind of parties we played for were usually ones where nobody danced for the first two sets. When people finally did start dancing it was often because they didn't want to have sit there defenselessly while we slaughtered their favorite tunes.

"Where's Cathy?" I heard Richard holler at Marshall. I saw Marshall shrug and jerk his head toward one of the side rooms. Richard strode off in that direction just about the time I launched myself into what I figured would be the solo that would reveal to Louise such a depth of character that her commitment to me would be absolute. I closed my eyes and let my sax wail out the profound groans of my soul's anguish. I lost track of time and didn't open my eyes again until Jack rasped out loud enough for me to hear him, "Let's not make a god damn career of this thing."

I understood Jack's point of view on the issue: "The Theme from Peter Gunn" was not a tune that showcased the piano. Marshall caught my eye, giving me the signal to wrap it up, which we accomplished with unusual efficiency. Only then did I allow myself to glance out at Louise and Tommy Spence. They were laughing and leaning against each other, apparently having exerted themselves vigorously under the influence of my extended solo. Louise gave me a little wave, but she didn't come over and speak to me. I reminded myself that after all she was merely a high-school girl, and I forgave her those bad manners of the moment. I hoped she was planning to slip away from Tommy to see me during our break; I set my mind to considering the best place for us to rendezvous.

Richard walked quickly across the floor, wild-eyed, mouthing, "Where the hell is she?"

Marshall shrugged, a grimace on his face as if he were personally responsible to Richard for keeping track of Cathy. Then Marshall jerked his head over toward the door on the other side of the room through which there was a main hallway and a huge, curving staircase. Richard trotted across the room in that direction. Just as he charged out of the room, I noticed Louise, her face away from me, twisting her whole upper body away from Tommy Spence to watch Richard; Tommy was holding her arm and speaking rapidly to her.

"Love Letters in the Sand," Marshall announced. It was one of the tunes I brought to the High Spirits, a solo I had learned in my previous experience with a real dance band. I knew that Marshall didn't care for it—I had had to ask him to restrain his guitar accompaniment to my solo—but he nevertheless thought it gave us a little class. Personally, I'd have preferred to save "Love Letters" for later in the evening when couples were winding down and wanting to dance to slow, romantic numbers, but Marshall was the floor leader—"the highest spirit," as Richard called him. Jack played the lead in, and I focused my concentration on that old ballad: "On a day . . . like today . . ."

"Marshall! Marshall!" Richard's rasping whisper caught my ear, even when I had closed my eyes and set myself into the trance of my solo. He was clutching Cathy by the wrist, as if he'd dragged her into the room and up to the bandstand. The way she stood with him there made her appear even thinner and more waiflike. Richard was whispering in Marshall's ear as Marshall was struggling to listen to him and at the same time play the right chords for "Love Letters." Richard finished what he had to say, he and Marshall exchanged these intense looks, then Marshall nodded and stepped over to me. "One more chorus and then cut it," he told me softly. I lifted my eyebrows at him, but he shrugged and then walked back to his place. He might have been the highest spirit, but right then I was the most pissed off spirit. "Love Letters" was one of my special solos, and he and Richard were trashing it.

Richard was over by the piano whispering with Jack even before we finished, so that Jack sort of dribbled out a few more notes even after I'd brought the thing to a close. I thought one of the advantages of getting a liberal arts education was that it gave you some inner resources for those times when an uneducated person would start throwing chairs and kicking music stands out onto the dance floor. While Richard and Jack were still huddled in their urgent discussion, I was sitting there with my sax on my lap comforting myself by mentally reciting my motto, "I piss on it all from considerable height. I piss on it all . . ."

Jack clanged out a couple of Beethoven-type chords, and Richard stepped up in front of the band to announce that the High Spirits were presenting a special treat tonight, a brief performance of classical dancing by the gifted young artist, Miss Cathy Yates. Jack clanged the piano twice more. Cathy, in her regular party dress but barefooted and in a peculiar way, stepped out into the middle of the dance floor, and struck this pose, on tiptoe, with her hands lifted above her head and her fingers almost touching.

I scanned the crowd of people watching to try to catch Louise's eye. It crossed my mind that quitting the band right that instant and making a real scene would have been worth doing if Louise could see me do it. But she had her eyes on Cathy, as did Tommy, standing behind Louise with his arms around her waist. "From considerable height, from considerable height . . ." I chanted to myself, certain that I could get through those moments, however difficult they might be.

Jack began plinking out a little minuet of a thing, Cathy took mincing tiptoe steps, bending this way and that, letting her arms float out to the sides. Like everybody else I was struck by the sight of a thin girl dancing, imitating a weeping willow or a colt in springtime or a daisy in a field or somebody's ridiculous idea of the meaning of young womanhood. I seemed to be the only one who understood how silly the whole performance was. Jack Denton was sitting up straight and performing as if he had just flipped his tuxedo tails over the back of the piano bench. Richard had taken this German concertmaster stance out in front of the band, and Julian, with his eyes closed, was weaving his fingers in the air in a restrained version of conducting Jack's piano concerto. Marshall was just sitting on his guitar's amplifier, gawking out toward the center of the floor.

Certain there was somebody in this room who understood how absurd all this was, I glanced back at Freddy Gates, but even the stupid flattopped drummer was hypnotized. Cathy had begun a butterfly pattern of moving around the circle of people watching her, letting her arms make these graceful lilting motions. The one positive observation I had to make about that routine was that Jack had the good sense to end it quickly. He finished with his hands held two feet above the keyboard, Cathy did a swooning split out in the middle of the floor, while Julian and Richard burst into finger-to-palm applause.

"It's all I can do not to puke right here on my music stand," I enunciated clearly into the hand-clapping coming from all around the room. But of course no one heard me. Richard strode onto the dance floor, took Cathy's hand, let her make a final curtsy, and led her off to the side. Jack was standing up beside Julian, the two of them applauding fiercely. "Pompous, self-deluding philistines," I went on lecturing into the noise. Then Richard gave Marshall a signal, Marshall shouted, "Peter Gunn," and began twanging out the guitar part. Jack sat down and banged the keyboard with both elbows about the same time Freddy Gates started diddling his cymbals with his sticks. I had no choice but to stand up and wail out a few more choruses of our retarded version of that retarded piece of music. The first set was over.

The great thing about a saxophone case is that there is enough room in it to stash your grandmother if you want to. For a year I'd had an unopened pint of Hiram Walker in mine just in case of an emergency. If I had any doubt as to whether or not that situation called for it, it disappeared when I saw Tommy Spence and Louise holding hands and chatting with Richard and Cathy, along with other admiring fans. I just stuck the bottle up under the bottom edge of my jacket, held it there, and slipped out through the back door.

A little meditation and refreshment in the clear, cool air was what I needed. Richard's car was parked by one of the small outbuildings. I made my way over there through the rows of parked cars, climbed onto the front fender of his old convertible, twisted the top off my pint and turned Mr. Walker up to the moon. Perspective is the real issue of any difficult circumstance; with the benign flame of the bourbon warming my esophagus, I began to achieve it. I took another deep swig and knew then that serenity was possible for me exactly in that place: perched on the fender of Richard Kohler's battered 1959 Ford, I perceived a connection between the starry sky and myself.

My concentration on those matters was so intense that it was both irksome and saddening to be distracted by Jack and Julian emerging from the back door of the Wilsons' house. They strolled toward me so that at first I thought they had seen me and meant to include me in their conversation. But, speaking very softly to each other, they approached what must have been Julian's car, a new Continental, and climbed into its front seat. Through the windshield, which was facing me, I saw a match flare; then I watched the red dots that were their cigarettes brighten and dim, fall and rise.

I had no wish to witness Jack and Julian in the Lincoln. I was about to scoot off Richard's car when another couple slipped out the back door; Tommy Spence led Louise out through the rows of parked cars to a station wagon his mother had probably used for hauling groceries home that very afternoon.

Two more couples slipped out into the parking lot, giggling as they opened car doors, climbed in and slammed the doors shut. Even though I had braced myself with Mr. Walker, my soul was exploring the limits of despair. Yet another couple appeared. It was Richard, like some huge dog on a leash, pulling Cathy toward the car where I was sitting. I reminded myself that what I came out there for was meditation, and that what I had achieved in my few moments of solitude had an austerity and a purity to it that had been increasingly soiled by these parking lot copulators and sodomites.

What I had to do occurred to me. I hopped off the fender of Richard's Ford and strode toward Richard and Cathy who only then saw me and stopped and stood waiting. "Richard. Cathy," I enunciated pleasantly as I squeezed between them and the car beside which they'd paused. I kept going, not taking any trouble to hide my three-quarters finished pint bottle even when I re-entered the house. Almost no one in the silly "ballroom" noticed my going up to the bandstand to take my saxophone off its stand-up rack, hooking it to my neck strap, and walking back outside with it.

From its appearance you would have thought that backyard parking lot was void of human presence, moonlight shining on the car roofs, strips of chrome gleaming here and there in the dark. I walked to what I took to be the approximate center of the area and stood for a while, looking up at the stars, holding the reed in my mouth to moisten it and cupping my right hand around the mouthpiece to warm it. The night was quiet, but I thought that I was probably the only one out there whose ears were alert enough to pick up a murmuring voice from one direction, the slight squeaking of a car seat from somewhere else.

First I played "The Church's One Foundation." Then I played "A Walk in the Garden." Then "A Mighty Fortress Is Our God" and "Bringing in the Sheaves." Finally I settled on "Rock of Ages." That was the kind of irony I was given to in those days. I intended it as a piece of instructional drama. Of course I kept my eyes closed while I played, but I heard car doors opening and closing, heard voices speaking to each other loud enough to override my saxophone. A few times the back door of the house opened and closed. When I came to the last note and opened my eyes, Richard Kohler was standing in front of me, his expression that of a man straining to hold his temper.

"Hand me the horn please," he told me. It was a voice that I would not have considered disobeying even though I was certain he was going to crack my saxophone across his knee. I unhooked it and handed it to him. Richard carefully set the horn on the hood of a car beside us. As he released the horn, without a pause in his motion, he slapped me hard across the teeth.

I reeled away from him, feeling over my mouth and jaw to determine how badly he had damaged me. Pain was not exactly what I registered at first, but my hand came away with blood on it.

"She was raised a Presbyterian. You made her cry," Richard said. He walked out of my sight, then some distance away I heard him comforting Cathy.

My injury was merely a split lip, but that meant that the High Spirits had to carry on without their sax man, which was like trying to get a plane to fly without a propeller. Though I had no allegiance to that band, I *was* the necessary element of the thing. I wasn't speaking to Richard, he was not speaking to me, and so it was Marshall I conferred with to demand a ride home. Marshall approached several people to ask for a ride for me, but apparently no one wanted to help me. What hurt my feelings more than anything was that when Marshall walked up to Tommy Spence and Louise, I saw Louise look up at Tommy, Tommy shake his head, and then Louise look back at Marshall and shake her head. Not once did she glance over at me, though I was holding a handkerchief to my bloody mouth.

Marshall managed to persuade Julian to drive me back to Charlottesville, an arrangement both Julian and I found only barely tolerable. Julian blasted that Lincoln through the countryside, I pretended to sleep with my head against the car window, and we said nothing to each other the entire trip back. When he let me out in front of Miss Booker's and I pulled my saxophone case out of the back seat, Julian said, "Hope you sleep well, Mr. Hyatt." No response occurred to me; I simply turned my back on him and walked up to the porch. His tires squealed as he pulled out. I knew he was in a hurry to get back to the Wilsons' house to give Jack a ride home.

Several times that night I woke up with my lip stinging, my

mouth dry and foul tasting. A dream kept playing through my mind, so that whenever I dropped back into sleep, I re-entered the same journey. Richard was again driving the High Spirits through the countryside at night with the lights of his convertible turned off. Louise had joined us and sat in the back seat squeezed between Jack Denton and me, very close, now and then whispering phrases into my ear. As before, the illuminating moonlight allowed us to see across the fields for miles in any direction we looked. But as we proceeded, the light became gradually dimmer, the road and the countryside swelled ominously. Instead of slowing down, Richard accelerated. Louise whispered into my ear, but I couldn't make out what she was saying. Trees flew past the car, and I saw Richard's shoulders hunch forward in his concentration on his driving. "Poor Bill," Louise said, brushing her cool hand across my forehead. "Poor Bill."

"My God, Louise," I yelled at her, sitting up in bed. It was eerie, waking to the reality of Louise's face exactly the same distance from mine as it had been in my dream; even her fragrance was the same—soap, I think it was, rather than perfume. For a moment I felt dizzy and only tentatively present in the world, let alone in my own bed in Miss Booker's rooming house.

"The front door wasn't locked," she said, smiling at me. "Nobody was down there. You showed me where the windows of your room were, remember? And you didn't come to the door when I tapped on it. I was afraid to knock too loudly." She brushed the tips of her fingers down the side of my face.

Louise followed my glance over at the clock, which read eight-thirty; none of the other boarders would be up that early on a Saturday morning. "If Miss Booker finds out you're here, I'll be out of a place to live," I told her, but that was just petulance on my part. Miss Booker was well into her eighties, half blind and half deaf, a formidable lady but not a major threat to someone as resourceful as I was.

"So, let's keep quiet." Louise took a cigarette from her purse, lit it, exhaled toward the ceiling and grinned at me. She was dressed in jeans and a loose flannel shirt; but her hair had been freshly shampooed, and her face had such perfect coloring you'd have thought she spent the night getting her beauty sleep. "God, I'm sorry that happened last night," she said in a husky voice.

"What in particular are you sorry about?" I asked her. I meant to keep her on the defensive, but as I looked at her and thought about what it must mean for her to be there, my anger was dissolving. Also, I was increasingly aware of my bad breath and my usual morning need to empty my bladder.

"That Richard slapped you." Louise put a hand on my bare shoulder, moved it down a couple of inches so that her fingers were on my chest and under the cover.

"Louise, you'll have to excuse me a second," I told her. "Do you mind turning your back?"

"You're modest? Bill Hyatt, I'm surprised at you." Louise's laugh was a gentle one; she did in fact turn her back while I climbed, in my drawers, out of bed.

"Tommy Spence cancels out whatever intimacy we've established," I told her on my way out the door. I didn't pause to hear what she had to say in reply. While I was peeing, washing my hands and face, brushing my teeth, and combing my hair, I carried on a lecture in my head in which I instructed Louise on the relationship between carnal knowledge and binding loyalty. "It is what distinguishes us from animals" was my concluding phrase, and I repeated it in time to my footsteps as I walked back to the room.

The chair at my desk held Louise's clothes: blue jeans, shirt, bra, and underpants, stacked in that order, with a pair of red, gray, and white argyle socks hanging side by side across the chair back. Louise had taken my place in the bed, under the covers; she'd been paging through my poetry anthology, but now she set it carefully on the floor beside the bed. She said nothing. Her eyes followed me as I came toward her. I was certain she'd laugh at the increasing evidence of my interest in her, but she didn't. Her eyes stayed locked to mine even when I was immediately beside the bed.

When I moved the covers aside so that I could sit down, it seemed logical to move them down from Louise's shoulders so that her breasts were exposed to the cool air. It was my way of regaining control of what was going on between us. Still she looked only at my face. I moved the covers farther down to her hips. Then I had to lean far down to push them all the way to the foot of the bed. Her breasts and pelvis were pale against the slightly darker shade of the rest of her skin.

"This is right now," she told me. When I lifted my eyebrows, she said, "This isn't last night, and it isn't tomorrow." She looked at me steadily.

The circumstance was not one in which I was inclined toward metaphysical debate. My dilemma was whether to nod that I did understand, thereby canceling out my entire peeing-and-tooth-brushing lecture, or to shake my head and chance her swinging her legs out of my bed and putting her clothes back on. I tried to paralyze myself so that I wouldn't make a commitment, but my eyes were greedy and wouldn't stop feasting. The gesture I made, of agreeing with her, was not what I intended, but who in his right mind would resist such arms as she opened to me?

"I made a purchase," I told Louise.

We stifled each other's giggles and struggled to keep the bed from knocking against the wall. The project of not awakening or alarming Miss Booker with our noises sweetened the time Louise and I spent together that Saturday morning in my room. When we had pulled the covers back up over us and while she was smoking a cigarette and occasionally leaning across my chest to shake her ashes in my trash can, I confessed to Louise that she had won a commitment from me. The intellectual gap between us was more than compensated for, I told her, by the harmony we had achieved. I told her that I felt I could give up the other women in my life without regret.

Louise leaned on an elbow and studied me while I studied the way her right breast took a completely different shape in this sideways posture, while the left was stretched and pushed almost flat against the bed. "I wonder if you'll ever understand," she murmured to me, smiling.

"Surely you're not all that complicated," I said, scooting down so that I could touch her nipple with the tip of my tongue.

Louise waited a moment, stroking my shoulder. "You don't always have to be thinking about the future—giving up your girlfriends because you like it here in bed with me, or whatever. I mean I'm flattered, of course, but I'd rather feel like *right now* I had your 'whole attention.' "

I was about to tell her that if I heard any more of the sayings of Richard Kohler, I was going to go buy a submachine gun and go looking for him just to get him out of my bed. But before I got my phrasing exactly set, Louise and I both became aware of the front door downstairs opening, footsteps sounding in the hallway, then coming briskly up the stairs. I knew whose footsteps those were, and she did, too. We stared into each other's faces.

We were wondering what we would do when Richard knocked at my door. He didn't. There had never been a latch or a lock on that door; it hardly caught when you slammed it shut. Richard swung into the room as if he lived there and fully expected to find Louise and me naked under the sheets. He had on the same clothes he had worn last night, but now they looked like he had fought a war in them. Without actually turning his eyes toward us, he walked straight to the desk chair, lifted the stack of Louise's clothes off it, laid her argyle socks on top of the stack, and set the whole thing on the foot of the bed with us. Then he turned the chair so as to straddle it backward and speak to us. "Bill, I have to tell you, I couldn't be any sorrier over what happened last night."

He still wasn't looking directly at us, though we were decently covered; both of us turned to face him, Louise's body lightly warming my back. Language was slow coming to me because I was still trying to find the way to tell him I was less concerned about last night than I was about the immediate present. Then he seemed to force his eyes to meet Louise's and mine and began blurting sentences.

"I'm in desperate shape, boys and girls, no joke. You're looking at a man who took charge of his own destiny, then had his destiny snatched right out of his hands. I've lost control. The only reason I'm sitting here in this room is that Cathy finally said she had to get a little rest. If she hadn't brought it to my attention that now and then she needed sleep, I'd still be driving around with her out there in the county. I'd be better off if somebody'd put a bullet right here." Richard tapped his right temple with his fingers. His face had gotten redder as he'd talked. Though I didn't see him sweating, I caught a whiff of him.

"That's not like you," Louise said. Then she did the oddest

thing, she snaked a hand down over my hip and circled my shriveled-up cock with her thumb and forefinger. It was a friendly gesture, I think, like an advanced form of holding hands, but I was pretty certain she didn't want Richard to notice it. I didn't move, and she didn't either. Richard was gesturing with his big hands. "Louise, honey, I tell you, I'd go to a doctor and ask for a cure, except that I don't think I could make myself tell him my disease is a ninety-six pound girl with a Yankee accent."

"I thought that performance last night was pretentious as hell," I said. I meant to be helping Richard with his cure, but I saw immediately, from the way he ducked his head and pressed his lips together, that I should have kept my criticism to myself.

"Have you gone through the steps?" Louise asked him.

Richard straightened up and faced us again. "Honey, I have gone through the steps backward, forward, and sideways. I'm all stepped out. I couldn't give her up for a minute. The steps don't work in this case. And Janey thinks I've gone crazy."

"What are 'the steps'?" I asked, but the two of them just kept staring at each other. If Louise hadn't had a hold of me the way she did, I'd have begun to doubt that I was even there in the room with them.

"What are you going to do?" Louise asked him.

"That's what I wanted to talk to you about." Richard rubbed one big hand through his blond hair—then he said, "Of course the main thing was that I wanted to apologize to you, Bill." I knew he was lying about that, but I didn't say anything. Richard sighed and hung his arms across the chair back, loosely clasping his hands together. I took special note of the gouge my tooth had made in one of his knuckles.

"I don't think I have a lot of options," he said quietly. It was clear he was speaking just to Louise. "Before I met Cathy, I knew the way I was living was dangerous, but it made some kind of sense. You know that. Most people wouldn't have liked what I was doing, but at least I had principles, and I went by them. Both of you watched me last night; I made a fool out of myself, didn't I? I don't have a philosophy any more. I'm helpless."

"What about *her*?" Louise murmured. "Can't she help you?"

"You've met her, Louise," Richard said. "What do you think?"

"She seems sort of—" Louise's pause came out of genuine bafflement, I thought, though it occurred to me that she might also be trying not to hurt Richard's feelings.

"It looks like she's here with us," Richard said, "but she isn't. She's closer to me than she ever has been to anybody. And if I disappeared off the face of the planet tomorrow, she'd hardly know the difference."

"That can't be true," Louise told him.

Richard snorted. "Louise, girl, you're the one who's always understood me. I wish it was you I felt this way about, because you would help me. You always know what I want you to do before I even ask. You're way ahead of me and everybody else. But Cathy Yates is another species altogether. You'll have to excuse me for telling you this, but I can be making love to her, it can be the sweetest thing I ever imagined, and I'll look at her and see her eyes kind of filmed over. It's scary."

"So why—"

Richard waved both hands at us like a referee in a basketball game. "I keep thinking I'm going to break through. She's going to blink at me and actually see me. She's going to kiss me or make love to me, and it's really going to be *me*."

"You're going to wait for that to happen, for her to 'see you'?" Louise asked him. I couldn't understand why she was being so patient with him.

"No," Richard said. "I'm not going to wait."

He paused quite a long while, then went on.

"I have to do something. It won't happen just on its own."

Again he paused, but neither Louise nor I said anything.

"Fear is the only thing that can ever really change a person like Cathy," he said. "You think about it. It's terrible, but it's true. And I can't just do something to her that would scare the hell out of her. I have to go through whatever she goes through. She and I have to experience the same thing at the same time."

"What do you have in mind, Richard?" Louise asked him. He must have had her whole attention, because even though she still held onto me, she had become absolutely still.

He sighed again, but then he looked directly at us and grinned. "I know those roads back in that part of the county pretty well. Bill can tell you, the other night after your prom, Louise, I drove the boys for twenty or thirty miles back in there without the lights on. I figure Cathy and I need to take a little midnight drive."

"Why are you telling us about this?" I blurted. I had this feeling Kohler was trying to put some kind of responsibility on me that I never asked for.

He stood up. "Two reasons, Bill. The first is that I want to ask Louise if I can borrow her car. Mine's too old and slow to do what I want it to. And the second is that I want somebody in the world to understand what I'm doing."

Louise let me go. She shifted just slightly away from me in bed.

"This isn't fair, Richard," I said.

"You can handle it, Bill," he said, smiling at me. I knew he couldn't have cared less what I thought about what he was doing. He came here to tell those things to Louise.

"You want the car tonight, don't you?" Louise asked Richard, and he nodded. "I'll park it out there by the gate and leave the keys in the ashtray," she told him. *Don't do this,* I started to tell her; but even with my back to her, I could sense her determination to give Richard what he wanted.

Richard nodded again, lifted a hand to both of us, and winked just before he walked out the door. He shut it carefully, as if he'd left us sleeping and was taking care not to wake us.

Louise turned to the wall. When I turned with her and put my hand on her hip to comfort her, she whispered, "He's going to kill himself."

I couldn't apprehend the tone of her voice, but I knew she was wrong about Richard. The man was indestructible. "No, he won't," I murmured into the nape of her neck and upper shoulders. "No he won't." I found comforting Louise to be particularly erotic. Since she was turned away from me, I couldn't really tell what her mood was, but she didn't resist me. At first I thought her compliance was intended to be a form of tenderness toward me. Later on it occurred to me that her mind might have been elsewhere. However it was, we moved quietly, and when we were finished, she lay quietly with me until I fell asleep.

When I woke, Louise was gone. I was immediately concerned that Miss Booker would have seen her coming down the steps. Then I realized that if Miss Booker had seen her, she'd have come straight to my door to accuse me of bringing a woman upstairs. She lived for such moments of confrontation, according to the other boarders.

All through showering and getting dressed I reviewed the

morning's conversations, but by the time I'd finished walking down to the Corner to eat, walking back, and packing my books to study at Alderman Library, I had put the whole experience behind me. It troubled me somewhat that when I wasn't with Louise, I couldn't bring her face clearly to mind. But if there was one thing I'd learned in my two years at the university, it was the necessity of going forward. That afternoon I found myself doing what I often did, spending long minutes studying the statue outside the library—Icarus about to launch himself out over the gymnasium.

Another thing I had learned there was the value of concentration. Inside the library, that afternoon and early evening passed quickly because I was able to use my time efficiently. It was no small irritation to me, then, when Marshall, in his usual weird clothes and greasy hair falling over his eyes, panting and sweating, came to my table in the main reading room and signaled me.

"What is it?" I rasped out loudly enough to make the students around me look up from their books. Whether from exhaustion or reticence, Marshall shook his head and wouldn't reply. Gathering my things quickly, I followed him outside.

"What the hell is it?" I shouted when we were trotting down the front steps of the library. He didn't stop or turn to me, but he did shout back, "Kohler!"

"Damn it to hell!" I yelled. I knew Marshall took it that I was expressing concern for Richard, but the truth was that I was expressing my outrage that my studying had to suffer because no one understood that Richard Kohler was perfectly capable of looking out for himself.

Julian's Lincoln was double-parked and waiting for us right by the library. Inside were Julian at the wheel, Jack in the middle, and Louise on the passenger side. Marshall held the back door open for me; Freddy Gates scooted over to make room for Marshall and me back there. Louise turned to me briefly, a light film of perspiration visible on her face. The look she gave me was one that I couldn't really read, and I couldn't shake off my irritation enough to speak to her with a proper warmth. As Julian pulled out, she spoke steadily to him, urging him to go faster.

"If the police stop me in Charlottesville, we won't even make it out to the country," Julian snapped at her; but Louise quietly kept exhorting him for more speed.

"What are we going to do?" I asked Marshall.

"Try to stop him," Marshall said.

"Six of us in a car are going to catch him and pull up beside him at ninety miles an hour on a country road and try to talk him into slowing down?" I shouted.

Marshall looked at me as if he were too upset to speak and shrugged. Freddy Gates, who I realized had almost never addressed me directly, said, "Shut up, Bill."

I was about to deliver a word or two to old flattop Freddy, but Louise turned around just then. "You guys are like Richard's brothers. He thinks the world of you. It's not much of a chance, but I think it's worth trying. If we can get him to see the four of you together, and you can talk to him, maybe he'll—"

"Maybe he'll what?" I asked Louise. Julian had the car heading toward the edge of town in the direction of Monticello and Woodridge. Louise, too, looked like she might start crying, and so I did the talking for a minute or two to let her get hold of herself. "Louise, you heard him this morning. He's got his mind made up. You didn't argue with him a minute when he asked to borrow your car."

Then Jack turned around and told me, "That's one of his

Principles: never ask a friend for something unless you really have to have it, and never refuse a friend what he asked for. She couldn't tell him no."

"I could tell him no now," Louise said, her voice choked.

No one said anything for a moment. I couldn't resist breaking the silence. "I still don't see what we can do to stop him."

"Probably nothing," Freddy Gates said, looking out the window at the shabby little country houses along the main road to Woodridge. "But your ass belongs here with the Spirits and not in that library tonight."

"God, Freddy, I didn't know you had this loyalty to the band," I said. Everyone in the car stared out the windows away from me.

Finally Marshall spoke up. "We all have it, Bill." He then said very softly, after a significant pause, "Except you."

My immediate impulse was to respond with a remark about the High Spirits not being exactly the kind of group that inspired loyalty, but what Marshall said struck me very hard. I was just then realizing that my acquaintances, among themselves, had been discussing my shortcomings for a long time. I leaned back into the seat and kept quiet.

Following Louise's directions, Julian drove out onto country roads that looked familiar to me, though of course I hardly knew one from another. Except for Louise we were all quiet. She pointed to a wide place in the road some distance ahead, at the top of a hill. "Right there," she said. Julian braked the big car hard and managed to pull over far enough to keep from blocking the road. "You should turn off your lights," Louise advised him. She opened her door, shedding unwelcome light on all of us, and climbed out.

For a moment or two we sat there, the band members and Julian, who whispered to Jack, "I can't stand taking orders from a high-school girl." Jack didn't reply. "I'd like to get out, too," I said, looking at Marshall to imply that he should open his door and let me escape.

"We might as well all get out," Freddy Gates announced. I was still having trouble accepting Freddy as our leader for the evening, but I no longer had it in me to make a fuss.

"Shall I leave the car running?" Julian asked him. Freddy told him he thought he should, to save time if we needed to take off fast.

Out of the car the six of us stood apart from each other as if acknowledging the night sky over us, brilliant with stars from horizon to horizon. The season was turning toward summer, but this night was cooler than the one in which Richard had driven us through the same landscape a week or so ago. There was a quarter-moon bright enough to singe your eyes.

Louise had opened a gate and walked some distance up into a grassy field. When we had followed her up there, I saw that it was the highest spot for many miles. The air was so clear that it made the space above and all around us seem unnaturally vast. The smell was of alfalfa, manure, and dirt, with only a light tinge of locust blossom in the air. Lights from houses and barns dotted the gray darkness miles from us in every direction. Far over toward the dark mountain range of the western horizon, car lights moved steadily toward and away from each other. "That's Cathy's house," Louise said, pointing to a light. Out there in the field her voice was soft and clear. "What I'm betting is that Richard is parked over there." She moved her arm only slightly toward a patch of darkness that could have been a building or some trees. "I know that's where he waits for her sometimes."

I didn't ask her how she knew. I stood beside her imagining

Cathy Yates, in dark slacks and sweater, carrying her shoes, slipping through her dark house with its porch light on.

"There, see!" Louise said suddenly, still pointing. A set of car lights had switched on down there. They began moving away from the house light. Jack and Marshall started trotting toward Julian's car, but Louise said, "Wait, let's see which way he turns." We stood there in the starlit pasture, even Julian in his fancy clothes, watching that set of car lights moving in a straight line almost two miles away from us. I stepped up closer to Louise and set my hand on her shoulder. What I meant to convey didn't come to me. Right then it seemed to me that something significant should have been passing between us; since no such thing was occurring, I had the unsettling sensation of being this stranger standing beside another stranger in an open field at night.

The car lights we were watching came to a stop, then took a turn in our direction. From where I stood beside her, I thought I could actually feel Louise's sighing, the tension in her body slightly easing. "He's coming this way," she said.

The six of us jogged down toward Julian's car which was still running so softly we could hear it only when we came right up beside it.

"I think we should stand out here by the car where he can see us as he comes up that hill," Freddy Gates said. He was posed like a squad leader giving orders to his soldiers. "We need to line up so that he can see every one of us. Julian, you should stay in the car, ready to take off if we have to chase him."

An earlier version of Bill Hyatt would have asked why we had to do what Freddy said; but now I simply took my place, lined up at the side of the dirt road with Louise and the band members. It occurred to me that we were like some kind of white, rural version of Gladys Knight and the Pips.

Once we were positioned beside the road, we stood there uneasily. It was very quiet at first, but then we could hear the car approaching, its engine winding higher than I would have thought possible for those roads. The noise built quickly. Suddenly the lights appeared around the curve at the foot of the hill, the car slewing off into the ditch, then bouncing back up onto the hump of the middle of the road, rumbling toward us. "Jesus Christ," Jack murmured, taking a step back toward the fence.

"Stay up here!" Louise shouted at us, raising both arms. "He has to see us all!"

In spite of our fear, we held our places and faced into the crazily approaching headlights. Like the others I lifted my arms and swung them above my head, the signal, I supposed, for Richard to stop. I had consigned myself to whatever fate was coming to me as one of the High Spirits. My state of mind was pure; without any irony whatsoever, I swung my arms to try to stop a maniac from killing himself and a girl I knew only from sitting beside her in a car.

Richard was past us so quickly that I thought he had accelerated instead of slowing down. Louise's car made a great humping grunt as it bounced into the ditch on the other side of Julian's car, then back out again. In the thick cloud of dust, we were coughing and waving our hands in front of our faces. Richard's brake lights disappeared as he flew up over the crest of the hill and down toward the curve on the other side. "Good God!" Jack said. We ran up toward the top of the hill. The car had covered an astonishing distance down that road. We watched it bounce out of the first curve, then make a complete spin around with its taillights advancing as if Richard had suddenly decided to drive in reverse. There was another heavy thump down there before the car stopped moving, its headlights beaming back up across the field toward us. Marshall began running down the dark road toward the car. The rest of us followed him.

It wasn't a real wreck. The car's front end was half across the road, its rear end was jammed into the bank of a curve. Louise and I were the last ones to reach it. Richard was hanging out the front window talking to Marshall and Freddy, spinning his rear wheels, churning up a rooster tail of dirt and dust. "Let's push him out!" Marshall hollered. I didn't even take a good look inside the car but simply walked to the rear of it and jammed myself up against the trunk and rear fenders, my feet scrabbling the roadside weeds of the bank to gain solid enough footing for me to heave against the car. Louise and I were beside each other, grunting and grinning. For the moment I felt as if I were with her in some grand adventure. Then the car lurched up of the ditch, almost toppling us in the dirt behind it, and we clutched at each other to steady ourselves.

Richard stuck his head, shoulder, and arm out the window again. "Louise, honey, ride with us back up to the top of the hill," he called in a voice that was much louder than it had to be. Immediately Louise was there at the passenger side. Before I could reach the door, she had opened it herself, slipped in, and slammed it shut. In my brief glimpse through the window, I saw that Cathy Yates had her head resting on her knees, her thin hands covering her face. I wanted to see more, but Richard pulled away from us, and Marshall, Freddy, Jack, and I trudged up the road, following the car in its dust. Like a wounded man, I dragged my feet; once I even heard myself whimpering. It was a long way back to where Julian's car was parked. He had made room in the space by the road for Richard to park there, too. Julian climbed out of the car, and murmured a plaintive, "Jack?"

"Yes?" Jack answered.

"Where are you?" Julian asked in this quavering voice. I thought of the parent-child game I had read about in my German textbook, where the parent calls out "*Wo bist du?*" and the child responds, "*Ich bin hier*"; for the pleasure and reassurance of it, they go on repeating, "Where are you?" "I am here." "Where are you?" In this case Jack said nothing, but he gave us a look that was both guilty and proud at the same time. He walked over to stand beside Julian.

In the dark, while the dust settled, we stood around the two cars, toeing the road and now and then kicking the tires of one or the other vehicle. Richard and Cathy and Louise stayed in the front seat of Louise's car, while we waited for them. From behind the car where I stood, I couldn't help watching the slight movements of their heads toward and away from each other; I found myself straining to try to figure out what they were saying.

Both doors opened; Richard and Louise climbed out of their separate sides of the car. Louise held the passenger-side door open a moment, but then she saw Cathy sliding slowly under the steering wheel, following Richard out the other side. Cathy never quite stood up straight. Even after the car doors were closed she still clung to Richard, not making a sound. I watched a tremor pass through her, then another.

"We're going to have a little gathering here, my friends," Richard told us. "The High Spirits and their good friends. Can I get a little firewood?" he called in the mock voice of a gospel preacher.

We were relieved to have some direction established for us,

some task to carry out. Julian stayed there with Richard and Cathy, but Jack, Marshall, Freddy, Louise, and I all split out in various directions. Though I no longer felt any real connection with her, I followed Louise up into the pasture toward a little copse of locust trees. I wanted to say something that would bring us close to each other again, but her mind was obviously on Richard. "What's going on?" I asked her when we had walked far enough away from the others. "He knows it wasn't going to work," she told me, and I asked her to explain what she meant. While we talked we had no difficulty gathering twigs, sticks, and even one sizable fallen tree-limb. What Louise told me was that Richard had realized that it was all too easy to scare Cathy, but that he couldn't get himself even close to a state of fear. "He knows he screwed up," Louise murmured just before we joined the others.

On the little knoll that overlooked all those miles of Albemarle County we built a fire from the trash and sticks we'd all gathered. Marshall had found a couple of rotted fence railings on the other side of the road, and so we had enough wood to last us a couple of hours.

"Now I'd like Brother Hyatt to lead us in song," Richard said, smiling at me from where he sat with his arm around a still trembling Cathy.

Probably I should have resented Richard's mocking me for having played those hymns in the parking lot the night before. I was surprised to find myself wanting to honor his request. I've never had much of a voice, but from far back in my church-camp days, I have loved the way ordinary people sing with each other. It was no trouble to begin one of those old songs: "We Are Climbing Jacob's Ladder," "Tell Me Why You Love Me," "Down by the Riverside," "I Want a Girl Just Like the Girl," and so on. Though I wasn't really one of them,

I was moved by the way my voice rose with the other band members' voices into the night air. Marshall had a clear baritone lead, Jack sang the sweetest tenor harmony you could imagine, and Richard and I struggled with the bass parts, while Louise's voice cleanly lilted in the upper register of a good church-choir soprano. Cathy's eyes swept from one to another of us as we sang, but if she sang at all, it was only to hum with her mouth closed. Between songs we let the silence hold and gazed up at the darkness and the stars above us.

Cathy sat up straight, with Richard's jacket around her shoulders, her legs crossed and knees flat to the ground, staring into the campfire. "My friends," Richard began. He paused just a moment before he went on. "You saved me tonight. Not just saved my old life, but you gave me a new one. I'd just about consigned Cathy and me to the graveyard when I came around that curve and saw you all standing there beside the road. That was the craziest damn thing I've ever seen in my life. When I figured out who you were, I broke out laughing. 'That's my band!' I said. The next thing I did was put my foot on the brake. Cathy and I were dead people until my headlights picked up the sight of you guys." He stopped and shook his head. "The High Spirits," he said softly and waited again before continuing.

"I want you to know it means something to me." He seemed to be looking into the eyes of each one of us in turn. "I'm going home tonight, and I'm going to stay home. Some of you know that lately I haven't been right." Here Richard paused and gave me a significant look. "I want you to know I'm going to get right. I'm not going to be causing anybody else the kind of trouble I've been causing." He stood up then and began tapping the fire out with the toe of his shoe. By then it was really just coals, but we stood up, too, and helped him extinguish it, as if we needed to carry out that ritual. We tapped out every last spark with our toes and heels.

Richard asked Louise to drive him back to his car and Julian to drop Cathy off at her house, since it was on his way back to Charlottesville. Both girls studied Richard carefully then, but he seemed oblivious to their scrutiny.

All of us walked slowly back to the cars, as if we were trying to think of some reason to stay out there in the dark field, but of course we couldn't. I stayed a step or two behind Louise, hoping she'd have something to say to me. She and I both watched while Richard gave Cathy a long embrace, murmuring to her, though Cathy stood stiffly, put only one of her hands to his side and said nothing in response to whatever he was telling her.

When Richard handed Louise the keys to her car, she stood for just that moment in front of him, holding her back so straight that she seemed to have grown even taller and lifting her face toward him so that her hair fell down her back almost to her shoulder blades. She was so still that I almost took a step toward her, though Richard seemed unaware of her. Then she turned and walked quickly around to the driver's side. Richard called good night to everyone. Just before Louise closed the door on the driver's side, she reached toward me. I leaned in over the steering wheel to her. She offered me her cheek to kiss, and I tried to hold onto the steady look of affection she gave me. Helping her close the car door, I was certain that we had been returned to our ordinary selves—a high-school girl and a college boy.

Cathy was quick to climb into the front seat of Julian's Lincoln when Jack opened the door for her. Julian had the Lincoln started and running; he was sitting there waiting for us, though the four of us High Spirits were dawdling. "Wait a minute," said Marshall, putting a finger to his lips.

Then we heard it, too. The engine of Louise's car was winding up just the way had it sounded earlier when Richard had been flying over those roads. But now we knew Louise was at the wheel. Not one of us spoke. Rushing and awkward, we clambered over the gate back into the pasture; we ran back up onto the knoll where we could see the car traveling out away from us across the dark landscape.

Louise had apparently reached a straightaway because the lights were steadily and quickly proceeding in a direct line across our line of vision. Marshall and Jack and Freddy and I were lined up, too, in the pasture as we were earlier on the side of the road; but of course this time no headlights fell on us.

Down the hill and across the fields, not quite a mile away, the lights of Louise's car bounced once, the engine noise rising suddenly to a high pitch, then falling to the same steady whine again. But abruptly the lights stopped, there was a house-high puff of flame, then utter darkness down there. The thump of the impact the car made against whatever it hit came to us a second or so after we had seen the fire rise and fall. We felt the noise with our bodies more than we actually heard it. The plume of flame that held Richard Kohler and Louise Morris stayed in my mind long moments after it had disappeared from sight.

Standing there in the dark with those three men, I found myself thinking about the heat I could feel still rising from the ground where our fire had burned earlier. With no lights now to be seen, I sensed myself coming alive to the air around me; I registered the night air against my flesh.

I waited to remember Louise's face in the last instant I saw it. I waited for the explosion of feeling—sorrow, outrage, hysteria—that I knew was approaching. I wanted it; it was my due. Instead, to my distress, what came into my mind was the image of Julian and Cathy down there in the car, probably listening to the radio, knowing nothing of the wreck.

Since that night, remorse of many kinds has visited me whenever I have thought about the High Spirits. I have attended the memory of that last night. Over the years my imagination has gained enough courage that I have been able to envision Louise sighting in on the landmark oak she knew would be there, fifteen yards to the side of a straight stretch of Virginia's Rural Route 129, just before she took one fast glance over at Richard and her car smacked it head-on. "Smacked it head-on," I will recite to myself, still trying to take possession of my rightful feelings. I am not one for wallowing in horror, but I have even forced myself to envision Louise's last moment of consciousness: Richard looking, not at her, but with widening eyes at the tree ripping through space toward him. Further than that I can't go. The last thing she must have seen, Richard's horrified expression, is remarkably vivid to me. But when I try to call up *her* face, I encounter a failure that I cannot correct. Always, what my memory offers me, instead of Louise's last look at me, is the sight of Cathy Yates through the side window, as Marshall, Freddy, Jack, and I came down the hill toward Julian's idling Lincoln: Cathy Yates, who meant nothing to me, just sitting there enjoying the warm air on her legs.

The Gorge

AT ABOUT FIVE O'CLOCK every morning Braxton wakes and swings his legs out of bed, taking care not to wake his wife. As if making another cover to warm her in his absence, he caresses the air an inch above her sleeping length, shoulder to hip, hip to knee. Then he stands up.

Braxton likes the clock's glowing red digital numbers in the dark, but the idea of using its alarm is appalling to him; triply appalling is the idea of waking to a suddenly switched-on radio. He has seen advertised a radio that can be installed in his shower; he'd sooner take a shower with a working police siren. Any sort of noise is a soiling of his brain that sleep has so kindly cleaned for him during the night. There is no sound, no human voice, no music that he wishes to hear in the first hour of his day. His wife and twelve-year-old daughter won't be up for another couple of hours.

If he's efficient, by 5:30 A.M. he is sitting down to take a horn out of its case. These first moments please him enormously. His studio is a soundproofed basement room with no windows. He knows he won't be disturbed by anyone for as long as he wishes to work this morning. Braxton has spent most of his adult life constructing this circumstance of exact hours available to him in an exact place where he can work with his horn. He's embarrassed that he owns half a dozen instruments, when the fact is that he always chooses the silver Olds cornet when he's working by himself, and for performances he always uses the dark gold Selmer trumpet.

He has his regular regimen to complete, a routine so habitual to him that he can let his mind wander during his first hour of scales, exercises for fingering, range, articulation, and tone. Then his morning's project is attempting to pick up the tempo in the Hummel concerto. Mostly what Braxton works on these mornings are pieces that he knows are beyond his ability to play well, compositions he will never attempt to perform.

This morning Braxton has his student Monica on his mind. She has made a tape for him, a tape of the music she thinks he needs to hear. Earlier she lent him three tapes, volumes one through three of David Bowie, but she was not able to leave them in Braxton's possession long enough for him to study them adequately. Monica has a lover in Boston named Cindy, and whenever she drives down there to see Cindy (which has been pretty often this semester), she needs her Bowie tapes to listen to in the car. Braxton uses the term "listen to" imprecisely; he knows Monica's relationship to the Bowie tapes is of a spiritual nature.

Monica cultivates a mildly punk, somewhat wasted look and punishes her body with recreational drugs, too little sleep, too much last-minute studying, and too much nonstop driving and listening to the Bowie tapes.

Monica told him she doesn't know why she chose the trumpet. She thinks everything might have been different if she'd started on guitar or drums or something like that. She admires rock and roll drummers for sitting at the crux of noise and silence, claims she's never met one yet who wasn't hyperactive. She thinks it's fabulous to sweat like that, to have your instrument require such physical energy and to offer such physical release. Monica told Braxton she threw her trumpet once, but it was in her bedroom, and when she flung it she could feel herself measuring how hard and aiming so that it would hit the bed and not be damaged.

In her own playing, Monica has a larger sound and a higher level of interpretive instinct than Braxton had at her age. Since she has little technical sophistication, it's hard for her to understand how good she is, or how good she could become with the given number of hours of work and the teaching Braxton can offer her. Monica is an economics major because her parents wish her to take care of the practical side of her life. Monica sees declaring herself a musician as an act of hostility toward her parents. For that reason she often entertains the idea.

Like many young musicians Monica is immensely vulnerable to the world; Braxton tried to explain Monica to his wife, who is a supervisor for the city's department of social welfare and has a certain expertise. He found himself saying, "She lives very deeply." His wife asked him how he could know that about a student he claims to be the second most reticent human being he's ever met.

With his wife Braxton did not discuss Monica's sexual preference. Nor has he discussed it at any length with Monica.

Once she did snap at him that it was the only part of her life with which she was at all comfortable, but he didn't know what to say to that. There are moments, Braxton understands, when Monica expects him to question her about Cindy, but he doesn't. Now, this morning, alone in his own studio, he stops playing to laugh at himself because it has come to him that Monica's lesbianism embarrasses him. "You are a fuddy-duddy," he accuses himself out loud. The insight cheers him.

At seven-thirty Braxton cleans his cornet, puts it away, and goes to the kitchen to pack his daughter's school lunch and nag her into eating a good breakfast. He pours coffee for himself and his wife, fetches the newspaper from the front door, and goes upstairs. His wife is awake and waiting for him. They read to each other from their sections of the paper, sociably half-listening to each other. In unison they call good-bye down to their daughter when she leaves for school. They chat until his wife has to get ready to go to work.

That first time when Monica came to his office to ask his permission to enroll in a tutorial with him, he said no. Instead of leaving, she sat down in the chair opposite his desk, opened her trumpet case, cupped the mouthpiece in her two hands and blew through it to warm it, then carefully set it into the instrument. She took her time, played a little muffled exercise toward the floor. Then she sat up straight and played once through "The Prince of Denmark's March." At first Braxton watched her, but then he had to look away, out his window toward the lake. All his professional life he'd witnessed incongruity between the physical appearance of musicians and the actual sound of the music they produced. But for the life of him, he didn't know how this small young woman made such effortlessly full tones come forth from that old concert model Conn. Braxton could have listened to her play any ten notes in sequence and known the same thing, that this one was a real musician.

While she was putting the horn away, he first told her that she ought to find a better audition piece than that old chestnut, and then he told her to find out what red tape they had to go through to allow her to sign up for lessons. Saying nothing, she showed him she had brought the add-drop form with her, and she slid it across his desk toward him. She was wearing stirrup pants and a loose shirt; she was a skinny, unremarkable-looking young woman except for dark circles under her eyes, which she kept averted. He signed the form. When he slid it back toward her, their eyes met just for an instant and the exchange made him uneasy.

After her first hour of lessons with him, sitting rigidly in the practice room, fiddling with the valves of her horn, Monica made him a speech. "I don't just play trumpet," she said. I'm a *girl* trumpet-player." She clamped her lips together, then went on. "I could play four times better than the first chair guy in my high-school orchestra, but the director told me the kid would quit if he had to play behind a girl. So I was second chair—from eighth grade on, I was second chair, and this greedy slob of a kid in front of me played every single solo, never once offered to let me have even the little two- and three-bar ones. I'm the one who should have quit."

In her bleakest mood one morning, Monica told him that when she was the age of Braxton's daughter, in sixth grade, she was ashamed of how awful she felt all the time and so she taught herself to put on a happy face as much as she could (which probably wasn't very much, because kids were always telling her to cheer up, and she was always trying to cheer up for them even though smiling for them made her want to get in her grave and rot). She remembered one of the plans she had in those days was to try to fall out of the swing with the swing-chain caught around her neck in such a way as to snap it, but she never could even figure out how to do it. She said that for as long as she could remember, without consciously meaning to, she'd been working out ways to die.

Braxton didn't know what to tell her that morning. She didn't seem to be telling him so that he'd try to talk her out of what she had in mind. As a matter of fact she spoke with such certainty that she almost persuaded him she had a right to choose death if that's what she wanted. He knew he shouldn't have sat there staring at her so long without saying anything. Finally he did hear himself saying, "I don't want you to do that, Monica," but he knew the sentence sounded like a feeble little whine.

When he asked her to tell him more—he wanted to try to understand—she went on in a low voice, as if she didn't mind telling him anything he wanted to know; it made no difference. "Other people's parents were nagging them to please go practice their instruments. Mine were begging me to stop, yelling upstairs to me that it was dinnertime, it was bedtime, it was time to do my homework. I must have been playing my horn to irritate them as much as for anything else. The thing is, I can't say that I've ever 'enjoyed it,' the way they say you're supposed to 'enjoy' music. Whenever I work hard to master a technique or an exercise or a composition, it's because I can't do it. When I get to the point where I can do it, I think I should have been able to do it all along."

That day after talking with Monica, at home, at the dining room table alone with his sandwich and soup, Braxton listened to his tape of the Vivaldi cello sonatas. What he wanted from those aching, sustained notes was some embodiment of the sadness he felt registering feebly in himself but clarified and shaped in Vivaldi's composition. What he wanted from Monica was for her to respond to his teaching in such a way as to want to live the intense life he wanted for himself. Staring out his dining room window with his empty soup spoon stopped in his hand, he thought about Monica's planning to kill herself and his own apparent settling for the less-than-intense and less-than-artistic life of a teacher.

On such a clear October day Braxton should walk to his office, but he chooses to drive just so he can listen to the radio. In his car he's a clandestine fan of country and western music. In the faculty parking lot, one of his favorites comes on, John Anderson's "I'm the Black Sheep of the Family." Braxton is sitting there bouncing in the seat, slapping the steering wheel, and singing along with John, when his department chairman pulls into the lot and gives him one of his I-know-you-but-I-wish-I-didn't-quick-nods-of-the-head. Braxton figures his only chance for even the illusion of dignity is to go on with the song, and he does: "My brother and his wife / just bought a yacht; / they like to sit around and talk / about all the things they've got." Braxton keeps his eye on his chairman's trench coat proceeding stiffly across the street and the sunny quadrangle toward the music building.

At his office door this morning, Monica is waiting for him. She wants him to ride to Pennington Gorge with her. When she sees his surprised look, she shrugs and mutters, "It's no big deal. The sun's out. I need to get out of here." Then she looks him straight in the eye and gives him a smile of such direct force that he wonders why he hasn't noticed before that she's pretty. "You need a break yourself," she reminds him. Braxton surprises himself by agreeing to go with her. He makes a sign to put up, OFFICE HOURS CANCELED TODAY, then follows her downstairs to her car.

Monica drives too fast. When she talks to him, she makes him nervous by not keeping her eyes on the road. To force her to concentrate on driving, he pretends to fall into a reverie and gazes out the side window at the gaudy-leaved countryside. For mile after mile he wills himself to appear relaxed.

At the gorge Monica leads him along the stony top of a ridge to the edge of the cliff where they lean forward to see the booming water. The damp air chills his face. On the other side of the chasm, the red and yellow leaves of the maple trees flame so brightly they make Monica, in her blue jeans and shapeless gray jacket, all the more vividly and precariously present before him. When he asks her to stand a little farther back from the edge, she gives him a level stare, then steps so close to the edge he's certain she's going to fall.

Saddening as he finds Monica's meditations on suicide, they nevertheless appeal to him and satisfy some need he has for such horrors to be articulated. Braxton can't say that he ever gave the idea of killing himself a great deal of attention, but he knows he has closed down a considerable part of himself. He knows what's possible for him now is only minor accomplishment. Monica has access to powerful forces within herself. He tells himself he's not jealous.

Once, in the practice room, frustrated by what he demanded of her, she slapped the horn down into her lap and yelled at him, "What do you want from me?"

He thought a moment and then said with a calmness even he would have found maddening, "If you turn out to be successful, I will be credited as your teacher." He gave the chuckle he hoped would signal to her his irony, but she just sat there giving him that stony look of hers.

"Why are you telling me that you don't give a shit about me?" she asked him.

"That's not what I mean," he said quickly.

A long silence occurred, during which Monica continued to stare at him. Finally she said, "I'm waiting for you to tell me what you do mean." He found he couldn't say anything. He reached over to pat the hand that lay open in her lap, but she moved it away from him.

Now skinny Monica, carrying her shoes in her hands in spite of the cool October weather and the still cooler air around the water, leads him across the spine of the rock to a point at the very beginning of the falls. Up ahead of them the Pennington River is nothing but a little trout stream, but here where they stand the stone has squeezed the water into such a narrow passageway that it pitches down in a crazy billowing of white froth. It's a place that makes Braxton uneasy. Monica is pointing to a small ledge down a couple of feet from where they stand. "What?" he shouts at her. She tells him she wants him to get down there on the ledge and sit down. "You'll feel like you're a part of the water," she tells him. Braxton doesn't want to, but he makes himself stand down there. The bulge of white billowing water is two yards in front of his belt buckle. "Now squat down," Monica tells him. He starts to, but he can't; he's afraid he'll pitch off into the falls and be crushed. He shakes his head. After a moment or two he clambers back up on the cliff beside her. Then Monica steps easily down onto the ledge and squats there with her head leaning toward the falls. He watches drops of water fly into her hair until she steps back up beside him.

They sit up there on the cold rock for a while, Monica hugging her knees and looking upstream away from him. He leans toward her and points toward the place where the smooth surface of the stream makes its first small break down toward the chasm. He asks her to notice the elegant curve of the rim of that miniature set of falls. After he's said it he wishes he hadn't used the word *elegant*, because he knows no one of Monica's generation would use such a word to her. But she nods her head and asks him what kind of rock this is—she waves her hand all around so that he knows she means the whole formation of the falls. "Granite, I suppose," he tells her. "And even if it's not granite, it ought to be," he says. He's trying to get used to the sight of her outdoors.

Then Monica and Braxton move below the falls, walking a precarious way along a protrusion of rock separating a higher from a lower pond of bubbling green water. She loses her footing. Jerking her arm up for balance she accidentally tosses one of her gray moccasins out into the deep part of the pond. She turns toward Braxton and watches him; he wonders what she means to be asking him. He's certainly not going to dive into that water for Monica's shoe. He shrugs and gives her what he imagines is a sheepish grin. After a moment, still studying Braxton, Monica tosses the other shoe out into the pond. She shrugs, too. "You get them at Frugal Frank's," she says, "for twelve ninety-five."

Suddenly he imagines it's getting late and they ought to be heading back to town. Today he will not be there when his daughter comes home from school, but she has her own key and is used to letting herself in. He doesn't know where this independence in contemporary children comes from. In a way that Braxton did not when he was growing up, this daughter has access to a music of her own, by way of the several top-forty radio stations of the area. In Braxton's home county of Virginia there was one daytime radio station they received well enough to listen to. There was one working radio in the house of his childhood, in the kitchen, which placement made it an instrument of family entertainment. His daughter has her own ghetto blaster. Now when Braxton goes to the stereo to turn on music he would wish her to love, his daughter's first response is to walk straight upstairs to her room, close the door, and turn on her favorite radio station, 95 Triple-X; the very designation 95 Triple-X makes him think of pornography, some triply powerful and poisonous force that has hold of a large portion of his daughter's consciousness. In his present family life, personal musical taste is one of the battlegrounds. His daughter cannot pronounce the word "opera" without a sociable sneer in her voice. One of her greatest fears is that Braxton will turn on a country and western station in the car when they are giving her friend Ashley a ride to school.

Now Monica is walking ahead of him down a steep slope, and she surprises him by turning to him suddenly. "What do you think?" she asks him. She pushes her hair up out of her eyes; her face is animated. But Braxton's footing is unsteady here, and he doesn't understand what she wants from him.

"Think of what?" he asks.

She makes that gesture that indicates the place, the rock formation, the relentless water.

"It's all right," he says. "I like it." But he knows he's failed her.

She just stands there, now and then switching her gray eyes toward him, but then quickly looking off somewhere to the side of him. "You like it," she says dully.

He thinks about it a while, and then says, "Sure I like it. I'm holding office hours here today, aren't I?" He takes the chance of laughing, and in a moment she laughs with him. Even if she's just laughing out of politeness, he's relieved. "Monica, you'll come to dinner tonight, won't you?" he asks.

"I don't ever know how to act at your house."

"You don't have to act any way. I just need for you to be there or else I'll feel like I'm trying to seduce you."

"If I liked men that way," she tells him, "I'd be interested." His eyes sting. He and Monica pat each other on the shoulder and stand there, each one looking to the side of the other.

One day while they were sitting opposite each other in the practice room at the end of her lesson, Monica handed him her horn. He lifted his eyebrows at her. She mimed lifting the instrument and moving the valves; she gave him the smallest of smiles. He shook his head; but then he accepted her trumpet, thought a moment, put the still-warm mouthpiece to his lips, and played a short, slow, middle-range exercise he had composed for himself within that past week.

Opening his eyes he found her watching him; when he handed her back the horn, she took it gingerly, packed it carefully in its case, covering it with a chamois cloth, closing the lid, and pushing down the snaps. "Thank you," she said, looking straight at him. "Thank you very much." Braxton nodded at her. She nodded back, looked as if she might be about to smile at him, but she didn't.

Up the steep trail they pick their way through the rocks from the foot of the gorge up toward the top. When they reach the top and turn toward the parking area, the noise of the gorge diminishes with every step. Braxton finds his spirits have plummeted, so much so that when he catches sight of the car he stops on the shady, dirt path. Monica walks on ahead of him. He starts to call out to her to stop, that they should turn back. Monica reaches the car and turns. She sees him standing back there. She takes a couple of steps toward him and calls out, "What's wrong?" Braxton is dizzy. When his head clears he'll be able to tell her that he isn't sure he wants to leave the gorge just yet. She takes another couple of steps toward him, almost dissolving before his eyes in the patterns of shadow and light that ripple over her. Braxton thinks his teeth are going to start chattering in the next moment. "Your feet must be cold," he says and makes himself walk forward.

Monica laughs at him and kicks up a spray of leaves from beside the path. "Not my feet, Mr. B.," she says. "My feet are just fine."

In Braxton's senior year of high school, his band director took him to hear Duke Ellington play at the armory in Bluefield, West Virginia. The place was packed, and he was one of maybe a couple of dozen white people and the only teenager there. But it was a dance, and they could move around as much as they wanted to. He and his band director walked down to stand at the foot of the stage, directly in front of the band, within touching distance of Harry Carney's right shoe. In those days Ellington's number one trumpet man was Cat Anderson, a man who looked like he'd weigh about two-seventy-five or -eighty. Cat Anderson came down in front of the band and played a long solo that set the place on fire. The man lived well up in the C, D, and E range—he was at home up there—but it wasn't his range that mattered to Braxton, it was the power. Cat Anderson was sweating so much that the spotlight made his head look like it was coated with silver, and drops of molten silver flew from around his head when he moved. Once he blinked down at the people in front of the stage, and he must have noticed this one white kid staring at him with his mouth gaping. Cat Anderson pointed that horn—one of those old-timey white-gold Oldses—straight at Braxton, plunged down to hit the low G and moved up through this incredible riff until he was up there where it sounded like bats squeaking. Braxton was certain Cat Anderson had lifted his feet off the floor. Then Cat Anderson turned the horn away and blew a last few signature notes that were just too huge for that building; the man made the walls bulge outward.

Again now Monica is driving too fast, keeping Braxton in a state of fear that ranges from mild to intense. And their conversation has him feeling that disaster is around the next curve of the road. What she tells him is that all through the spring and early summer she had planned, on July 27th, after a trip she knew she was going to take to Boston, to drive her car into one of the huge boulders between the lanes of Interstate 89 on her way back to Burlington. She says, "I spent most of the drive swinging over onto the shoulder or into the ditch, but I swerved away at the last minute every time."

Braxton tells her that her swerving away from the boulders clearly means she does not want to die. Monica snorts. They're on a little straight stretch. She flicks the wheel so that tires on Braxton's side are flinging gravel up underneath the car. There's a dead elm directly ahead. Braxton starts to scream, starts to duck down into the seat, sees her flick the wheel the other way, and feels the tires hit the hard surface again.

She tells him her most recent scheme. She has a mattress in the back of her hatchback; her plan is simply to stop along the road and go to sleep back there with the car running; she has heard that carbon monoxide leaks into sitting cars anyway, and her car's exhaust leaks pretty badly. Braxton is irked at her. He tells her he doesn't think that way she'll get enough poison into her system to do the job; some state trooper will see the car and rescue her just about the time she has suffered enough brain damage to make her spend the rest of her life wall-eyed and drooling all over everybody. Monica makes a face.

They're passing a brick farmhouse surrounded by huge red-and-yellow-leaved trees and the surprising open space of river-valley fields. The sight pleases him. He asks Monica if she ever yearns to live in a place like that. "You mean with kids and dogs and shit like that? You've got to be fucking kidding me," she says with such a grin on her face he knows she thinks he's joking.

When they reach the interstate, Braxton tells her he thinks it's generally a pretty lousy idea to do it before she's gone as far with the horn as she can go. Monica tells him she's certain she's gone that far already, and he tells her she's just now getting started. He doesn't like his wheedling tone of voice, but he thinks he knows what to tell her. He advises her that what's possible for an artist is to find satisfaction in the work, which ought to save her all the misery of trying to find satisfaction in her human circumstances. Monica still won't watch the road. She tells him he sounds like he's lecturing to a classroom full of students. She tells him that her relationships with people—and especially with Cindy—are very much to her satisfaction. She tells him it's her work that makes her miserable. "I can't get it right," she tells him. "It makes me feel worse. You don't have the slightest idea." Braxton feels as if she's winning a debate when every bit of the evidence is on his side.

They are coming off the exit ramp into the city; their ride together is coming to an end, and what Braxton is reckoning with is that Monica is damn sure going to kill herself, sometime or other.

The resident sadness that surfaced in him when they left Pennington Gorge has increased its weight in his chest. But one of the elements of his feeling is—he is ashamed to admit it even to himself—relief. A silence falls between them in which Braxton thinks they both understand that in fact she wants him to say or do something that will stop her. Then there comes to Braxton a thought he hates: maybe he wants Monica to die his own death for him. "Stop it, Monica!" he hears himself shouting at her, even though he can't remember what she's just said. Her eyes flick once at him. A smile curls at the side of her mouth.

It's getting dark when he comes into the house and goes into the kitchen to wash up the day's dishes and commence fixing dinner. He calls hello to his daughter who is upstairs in her room doing her homework, and she calls hello down to him. He's shocked at himself for feeling full of energy, exuberant. His wife will be home from work in another half hour, and Monica, who drove back to her apartment for shoes and a change of clothes, ought to be here in a few minutes. Ahead of him, he has the pleasure of making a salad and a sauce and boiling pasta an exact amount of time, and of eating a meal he's sure will be good in the company of his family and his finest student.

Through the window in front of him where he stands at the sink is the clear twilight making its progress down onto his moderately neat backyard. He feels familial and citizenly. He is the author of the little city that is this household. He can find whatever it is that Monica needs to stay alive. He turns on the radio.

What Braxton wants to hear is 95 Triple-X, the pop-rock music of the day. He makes a little speech about it to himself: *My friends, I want to hear it because it is my duty at this time of day, and especially after this particular day, while I am fixing dinner, to dance by myself in the kitchen.* He's a pretty ungraceful dancer, but he grooves, he jives, he shakes it on out there on the linoleum floor.

When his daughter slips into the kitchen with him, Braxton slyly modifies his steps to slight and subtle movements and pretends no embarrassment. She is kind to him in these circumstances because he often comes upon her in similar ones. She, too, caught dancing alone, is clever in adjusting her movements to indicate only casual involvement with the music—restrained, mincing steps of the feet, bends of the knee, sways of the hip. The logical development of these circumstances would be for one or the other of them simply to commence dancing with the other, but he and his daughter are in tacit agreement that such musical collusion between them will never come about. Braxton thinks it's disgraceful enough that he boogies by himself to the trashy stuff oozing out of 95 Triple-X.

Finally Monica shows up. When he takes her jacket from her, he lifts his eyebrows to express surprise at her wearing a dress, but she doesn't acknowledge his look. He has to switch the radio off to be able to hear what Monica and his daughter are saying. He's jealous of them both for being able to understand each other the way they do even though they've talked only a couple of times before. He's glad when his wife appears, color in her face, her cheek pleasingly cool to his lips when he kisses her. Now he has somebody who wants to talk to him while he serves up the plates. He likes his wife's height, her sturdiness, her blazer, and flannel skirt.

Braxton wonders if it might be simply the fall weather working on Monica. He knows he himself gets goosey and morbid when the leaves start changing and the air turns cool. He glances over at Monica and his daughter making gestures at each other and talking about teachers. He knows better than to tell Monica it's just the weather making her want to die.

For no good reason he winks at his wife. He feels giddy and wants to call up old family pleasures of the dinner table. Before sitting down to dinner with them all, he goes into the living room to put on the Mozart flute concertos. At the table when the moment is right he springs the question on them, What's this instrument? Monica keeps her eyes on her plate. His wife and daughter try to ignore the question and to condescend to him, as if this is an old, old question, not worthy of their attention, as if they're not going to humor him by playing this game anymore. But Braxton knows them too well. His wife is tired from her long day of work, his daughter is bolting her food so as to get to dessert as quickly as she can; but they can't resist because the answer is too obvious. The daughter says "Flute."

Braxton doesn't pause, doesn't give his daughter an ounce of credit; immediately he springs the next question, What composer is this? He knows that once they're in the game and they've got that first question answered correctly, they can't resist trying to answer the second one. And they'll certainly get it wrong, because they know his record collection well enough to remember that there are at least two Mozarts for every one of anybody else and that it's most likely Mozart they're hearing. But neither one of them will take the likely answer; they figure he's too sly for that, and so, sure enough, the daughter guesses Bach and the wife says Vivaldi, and he says Haw haw haw, it's Mozart, you dummies! The moment makes his head spin.

Monica blurts something toward him at the same time her fork falls from her hand and clatters onto her plate. He thinks what she said was "What the hell do you think you're doing?" but he knows better than to ask her to repeat it. His wife and daughter are giving him their Daddy-you-asshole looks.

"I'm sorry, Monica, I didn't hear you. What did you say?" Braxton's wife says. She is smiling politely, and Braxton is grateful to her for her effort to smooth over this moment.

"Why do you let him pick on you?" Monica asks. Braxton can tell she's so furious she'd punch a fork through his forehead if he so much as whispered the word "Mozart."

Braxton watches his wife to see if the question will fluster her. He thinks it does momentarily, because she merely looks at Monica. Then she says very quietly, "I don't think he means it as bullying."

He's recovered his wits. "It's just a game I like to play with them," Braxton says in a voice that makes him shudder with its obviously diplomatic tone.

Monica ducks her head then. "I'm sorry," she says. Braxton is afraid that she'll cry, and if she does that he'll hate her for it.

They sit in an uncomfortable silence. His wife turns to ask his daughter a question about school. While they talk quietly with each other, Braxton eats and sneaks looks at Monica, who continues to look downward, her hands in her lap, her lips moving ever so slightly. He understands that she is reassembling her poise, and he is moved by the effort he knows it is costing her.

When he comes out of the kitchen carrying the coffeepot, Monica has her jacket on with the collar turned up and her face buried down inside it. She's standing at the door waiting to say good-bye to him. She won't stay for dessert. Braxton exchanges a quick look with his wife and understands her to be instructing him not to interfere with Monica's departure. He walks with her out onto the windy front porch. "I don't know what got into me," he tells her, shaking his head. In spite of the cold out here, he means to talk with her a few minutes, but she moves down the steps.

"Will you stop by the office tomorrow, Monica?" he asks her. She gives him a look that seems calculated to cremate him where he stands. Then her face changes, and she says, "I think we've come to the end of it, Mr. B." She surprises him by chuckling and reaching back to pat him on the sleeve. "I don't think I can teach you anything more," she says.

"Maybe there's something we haven't thought of yet," he tells her.

"I don't think so," she says. She turns and heads back down the steps. From her quick pace he knows she's exhilarated to be escaping from him. "I'm gone," she says, waving, just as she opens her car door.

"Good night, Monica," he calls to her and thinks his voice must sound hatefully fatherly to her. "I'll call you tomorrow," he says; but he knows she can't hear him now. He watches her car move down the street, not stopping or even slowing down very much at the corner. He stands there a moment before he goes back inside.

With no rehearsals scheduled tonight, his bedtime comes early. In their bedroom, as he and his wife undress, it occurs to him that they are carrying out a sort of dance, moving in tandem about the room. They're chatting about their daughter's eating habits. He starts to tell his wife how much he appreciates her being with him here in this room right now, but he knows that will make her want to talk about Monica, and he doesn't want that. He can imagine his wife's stunned expression if he blurts out his new, crazy idea, that Monica's death will keep them safe. When he swings his legs up under the bed covers, his wife is tying the sash of her bathrobe. She kisses him good night and goes downstairs to help their daughter with her math homework.

When he is by himself, he turns out the light. His mind is tracking Monica speeding out on the interstate with the car radio turned up high, the steering wheel loose in her fingers.

He wants sleep, but in this before-sleep time when his brain can select any topic it wants, he finds himself making a speech to her as she drives. Briefly into the light we come out of darkness and silence, he tells Monica, and we proceed forever back into darkness and silence. There must be this intercourse between the human body and the world; our lips must touch the metal of a mouthpiece or the wood of a reed.

Braxton knows his phrasing is so pompous that his speech would do nothing but infuriate her, even if he had the nerve to say it to her; but he is powerfully swept up in the composition. He can feel her accelerating farther out into the cold night. He struggles with the effort to instruct her. *I'm gone,* you say, words hard as stone, when what is available to you is breath touching flesh, the vibration set going by human will.

The clock's red digits float in the dark and turn forward in silence. Monica is hurtling out away from him. Impelled, Braxton goes on constructing reasons for her to go on. In another moment or two, maybe he will be released from the desperation to make her this lecture, maybe he will begin his soft drop down into the vortex of sleep. In another moment or two.

In the Mean *Mud Season*

"GET A LIFE, DAD," Victoria told me last night on her way into her room. This is a thing they say at school. She shut the door but didn't slam it. She was in a good mood—the phone conversation I had just broken up must have been to her liking—and I assumed she really was going to do her homework, as I had just asked her to do. If she had slammed the door, I'd have had to go in there and start yelling at her to make her sit down at the desk. Even then she'd probably have doodled or written notes to her friends or taken up her ongoing project—the excoriation of her mother and me in her diary. (When she's especially furious, she leaves the diary open for us to see what she's written.)

The place we live in makes her the way she is. This is a northern city, and my wife and I are from Virginia. Years ago, when Marie's Uncle Bill Catledge found out that we were moving to Burlington, he told us a grim story about a Confederate raid on St. Albans, Vermont, in which the rebels robbed a bank and escaped back into Canada but never made their way back to the South. When Marie's pregnancy became general knowledge in our families, Uncle Bill advised us to come back to Leesburg for the birth of our child. He said letting that child claim Virginia as its place of birth would be something valuable we could give it.

This northern season helps me understand my daughter's personality. It's mid-March. Last weekend the temperature went up to sixty. Dirty snow rotted before our eyes. Where the ground appeared it was a soggy greenish brown; but the rivulets that ran down our driveways and street gutters sparkled, and the sunlight inspired even some old people from the neighborhood to try the treacherous sidewalks. But before daylight on Monday a wind came up, the thermometer started dropping and by ten in the morning the windchill factor was five below zero. Now the snow is a hard shell of ice; it promises to stay that way for weeks to come. At night the stars glisten meanly. In a hard place like this, you can't be surprised when your daughter turns into a rock.

Not everyone, however, has the same vision of our Victoria as I do. Twelve out of the thirteen or fourteen phone calls that come to our house every day are Prescott Rochester asking, " 'S Victoria there?"

"It's Scott Rot," I call upstairs. When she answers on the upstairs extension, she doesn't say, "Hi!" or "Hello, Scott." She says, "Got it, Dad," and waits for me to hang up the phone before beginning her conversation.

What irks me most is that these two don't want to spend time with each other in person. Once after she'd been to an afternoon basketball game—also attended by Prescott the Lout—Marie and I pried it out of Victoria that he had declined to sit beside her, that in fact he had spent most of his time with his pals stomping up and down the bleachers (I can just envision their jackass behavior!) and even failed to say a decently polite good-bye to her. When I told her that he was a wimp, she agreed, but with bemusement.

That evening, when we sat down for dinner, the kid called up just as he usually did. Victoria wanted to leave the dinner table to talk with him. When I forbade that, she machined her food down and excused herself. Marie had to go back to the office after supper, and because the Celtics and the Hawks were on TV that evening, I forgot about the telephone. Two and a half hours later I found her in the kitchen, cuddling the receiver to her ear, still talking to him. I confess that I made her hang up and yelled at her, accused her of wasting her time and keeping my phone line busy talking to a twerp who didn't even have the gumption to sit beside her at a basketball game. "Why do you hate him, Dad?" she asked me on her way out of the kitchen. "You've never even met him." Her voice was maddeningly cool.

"I don't have to meet this guy to know all about him," I told her.

Children behave this way only in the North. When I was growing up in Rosemary, Virginia, I said Sir and Ma'am to all adults, I "talked back" only in extreme circumstances, my feelings were really hurt if my parents or my teachers got mad at me, and I pitched in with the work that needed to be done around the house.

Here at home Marie and I have given Victoria elementary jobs to do—clearing the table after dinner, keeping her room straightened up, and in warm weather watering the shrubs at the front of the house. But she will do none of these unless we ask her, then order her, and finally threaten her. She assures us that Karen, Janet, Liza, Betsy, and Pauline do nothing at their houses, and that Jason, Patrick, Jerry, John, Benny, and of course Prescott the Hotshot not only do nothing but eat junk food and watch rock videos on TV all day—these boys even yell at their parents if their parents intrude to clean up their rooms for them. "At least I don't do that," Victoria reminds us.

In theory, of course, one finds such values among adolescents utterly unacceptable. In practice, one finds it just too exhausting to battle negative convictions subscribed to by an entire generation. You can't let hassling them be the only communication you have with your children. On the other hand, if your daughter in simply walking through your house leaves a wake of clothes, food wrappers and crumbs, empty cups and glasses, shoes, markers, schoolbooks and papers; if she talks relentlessly on the phone; if her room is a metaphor for nuclear destruction; and if you can smell the stink from her hamster's cage all the way at the other end of the house, then it's very difficult not to make certain requests of her.

Today began as an unusually sunny morning for March in Vermont, especially for a Friday. (Vermont schedules its most inhospitable weather for weekends.) When I looked casually out the window around seven-thirty, I thought it was probably in the high twenties. But when I stepped outside to empty the kitchen trash, I found that it was single-digit city out there and that the wind meant to slice a groove in my forehead.

At eight, when Victoria was about to leave for school, she had put on only a sweater. Marie, who had read the weather report in the *Free Press,* said, "Wear something warmer, sweetheart, it's cold out this morning." Victoria made a noise that sounded more or less like "no" and kept tugging at the door. She was eating toast, as she usually does on her way to school, clutching it in her teeth because she had her backpack in one hand and her Walkman and earphones in the other; her saying no involved spewing crumbs on the carpet. Her mother asked her please to put on a warm jacket; Victoria removed her toast from her mouth with the Walkman hand and yelled at her mother to get off her back. I yelled at Victoria to come back this instant and get the jacket on or lose telephone privileges for three days. Victoria then in a high pout yanked her jacket out of the closet, spraying coat hangers every which way, gave us each an incinerating glare on her way out, and slammed the door hard. Victoria's braces give her mouth a swollen look anyway, and when she puts on that mean expression, she's a most unattractive girl. Marie turned to me and asked, "Why do we have to fight her just to keep her warm?"

Obviously I have no affection for northern weather. For sixteen years I've lived in Vermont, teaching Beowulf and Chaucer to university students almost exclusively from the northeast. I still speak with the flat-voweled Southwest Virginia accent of my upbringing; even my voice is ready to leave a climate that's so cruel people don't have time to be polite to each other.

When Victoria came in from school, her face was fuchsia-tinted from the wind. I expected her to apologize for her behavior that morning and to thank me for persuading her to wear her warm jacket. I was a fool of course. Since the first words I had to offer her were, "Please don't eat up those cookies, Victoria; they're all we have for dessert tonight," her homecoming got off to a bad start. She jammed a final Pepperidge Farm Geneva into her mouth and banged shut the cookie-box lid. She was all set to flounce up the steps to her room and slam that door, too. But then, while she was still chewing, I saw a transformation occur in her facial expression. It was as if she instructed herself to be pleasant.

"Dad, do you think I could go to the movies tomorrow afternoon?"

I had to give her credit. Her voice was not so saccharine as to sound completely phony. "Unless you do something hideous between now and then, I imagine you can," I told her. "Why wouldn't you be able to go to the movies?"

"Oh, no reason. Just thought I'd ask, Dad."

I could see it was costing her considerably not to be able to add, "Is that all right?" She drifted by me on her way upstairs, willing even her gait and carriage to suggest sweet-tempered good-daughterhood. In the hallway I stood there waiting. Sure enough, before she reached the top of the steps, with brilliantly executed casualness, she called down, "Scott may come over after the movie."

"Scott may come over?" I murmured just loud enough for her to hear me up there.

"Yeah, sure, he's taking me to the movie."

"Oh," I said. I heard her reach her room, pause a moment, then enter and softly close the door. Grateful to Victoria for her delicacy in making her announcement, I went to the window to meditate. I was reminded again that my daughter understands me at least as well as I understand her; she knew I would need a few hours to consider this new development.

In the phraseology of her school, Victoria has "gone out with" several boys, but "going out with" someone is not to be taken literally; it's an assignment, a formal designation of who holds a romantic interest in whom. In Victoria's eighth grade one almost never goes out with the person he or she is going out with. Victoria has met boys at the movies before, but one has never "taken her" to a movie or to anything else. Why did her first real date have to be with Prescott the Not-Even-Halfway-Acceptable?

I was gazing at my front lawn, which looked enormously ugly in the freezing sunlight and wind out there. The gray shards of snow, the brownish mat of grass, and the frozen dog-droppings seemed to offer an answer: in a northern climate a daughter will make a northern choice; she'll figure out the one boy her father can't stand, and that's the one she'll go out with. Abrasion is the Yankee way. I wished my wrong-headed ancestors had won the war and declared all the land north of Gettysburg unfit for human habitation.

All the while I was cooking dinner I carried on a discussion with myself about the posture I would strike in regard to the "date" Victoria had with Prescott the Misbegot. I am the cook at our house because Marie is an accountant whose hours at her office prevent her from getting home in time to put a meal on the table before eight p.m. This, too, seems to me a peculiarly northern phenomenon; I'd bet that northern house-husbands outnumber southern house-husbands by five to one. Nevertheless, I was grateful for the salad to be made, the rice to be boiled, the chops to be fried and seasoned while I clarified my thoughts. By the time Marie came home, I had hammered out a policy: if Victoria made one wrong move, she would not be allowed to go to the movies. I was perfectly willing to stand at the door and deliver the bad news to Prescott the Damned Spot.

I was also willing to admit that there was an unfair advantage built into my policy: dinnertime at our house has customarily become a ritual of bickering. Marie and I are unable to keep ourselves from expressing concern about our daughter's diet, schoolwork, and appearance; we know we seem to be nagging her. And Victoria never fails to speak rudely to us, to insult my cooking, and to display table manners that would embarrass an orangutan (manners she has learned, practiced, and perfected with her northern friends in the school cafeteria). I figured she'd make her first wrong move within three minutes of sitting down to the table.

She didn't. Discussing her math homework with us, Victoria did assert that her teacher has been brain-dead for the past ten years, but having talked with Mrs. Phillips at PTA meetings, neither Marie nor I could readily dispute Victoria's evaluation of the lady. In the course of the meal, she went on to observe that Mr. Wilks was a jerk, Benny Olshan was a goob, Laura Johnson was a little geek, Chris Graham was a nerd, and Donald Matthews was a dink. In spite of the brutality of her vocabulary, she was cheerful. When I asked her to remove her elbow from the table, she didn't even give me one of her swollen-mouthed glares.

Had I been a nation, my government would have accused Victoria's government of having stolen state secrets. She behaved as if she knew exactly the terms of my policy on Five-Watt Prescott. Her behavior was impeccable. The three of us watched a television movie set in South Carolina; and though I called Victoria's attention to the decorous speech and behavior of the young men and women, she merely teased me with her own silly version of a southern accent. Victoria, Marie, and I enjoyed ourselves. At bedtime we exchanged such tender good nights that I almost forgot the plot to date Prescott.

I slept well, and when I woke on Saturday morning, I remained lying quietly beside Marie, entertaining the fantasies that are available to a middle-aged family man—of moving back to Virginia and constantly having the kind of pleasant life Marie, Victoria, and I had enjoyed last night. No more nagging, no more northern abrasion and chattering teeth: I rose from bed, almost whistling, planning perhaps to do my annual springtime cleaning of the yard and the flower beds.

But downstairs when I opened the living room drapes, I felt as if I were staring directly into the eyes of this monster of a place in which we live. It was snowing hard. The white layer on Marie's car roof was ten inches thick. Outside the window, a lilac branch was so weighed down with snow that I knew it would soon crack and split the main branch. It is March the eighteenth, I whimpered to myself as I trudged into the kitchen to make my morning coffee. By March the eighteenth in Virginia, lilac bushes are greening and forsythia is in full bloom.

It was all I could do to make my coffee, then to carry my cup up the steps to my third-floor study. The skylight Marie insisted we install up there was covered over with snow, and the subdued light falling on my books reminded me of my exile from my own true land. I sat at my desk, too paralyzed to work or even to think properly. In a trance I watched the assaulting flakes of snow descend past the small side window.

"I know you're brooding up here," Marie said when she brought me up a warm, buttered muffin and a fresh pot of coffee to refill my cup. I was grateful to her, but my depression weighed on me so heavily that speaking to her was out of the question. "I need you to shovel my car out of the driveway," she told me softly as she went back downstairs. "I have to meet some clients at the office this afternoon. Besides, it'll be good for your spirits." She paused at the bottom of the steps and called up to me as if I were a child, "Take a bite of your muffin, please."

I started eating the muffin and then finished it because I had started it. Time was still a glacier, and though there were no more flakes falling I remained seated, staring out the window. The footsteps on my stairway the next time were Victoria's. She put her hand on my shoulder and said, "Dad, Scott says he'll help you shovel the driveway. He'll be over in about half an hour."

I might have given Victoria a karate chop to the forehead for inviting that pimply twerp over here to interfere with my daily life. But in my condition, I could say nothing. The stimulus of her news did provoke me to rise and go down to my bedroom and dress. I had enough momentum to move myself to the closet and put on my coat, hat, gloves, and boots. That telephoning idiot Prescott was not going to shame me by doing my work for me. Victoria dressed for the outdoors, too, her manner subdued, as if I were some old geezer from a nursing home she had agreed to escort on his daily constitutional.

"Victoria, do you know how much I hate the outdoors on a day like this?" I asked her when my boots sank into a foot of wet snow.

"Come on, Dad, you've got to get Mom shoveled out." Victoria waded through the slushy stuff to the garage, fetched the snow shovel and brought it back to me. There are few things I hate more than shoveling. Just as I began, a short-haired boy walked around the house toward us.

"Hey, Tory, what's happening?" he said, as if he were just accidentally taking a walk there in my driveway. He had the face of an altar boy.

"Look, Dad, he brought his own shovel," Victoria said. Of course it was out of the question to hope that she might perform a proper introduction.

Meaning the two of them to see good manners even if they

chose not to learn them, I took off my glove, extended my hand to the boy, and enunciated my name clearly. I could see the boy wondering whether or not to take off his own glove. Finally he did so, though the hand he gave me was half the size of mine and its grip wouldn't have harmed a baby sparrow. "Your name is . . .?"

"Oh, Dad, this is Scott, you know that," Victoria told me. He had a serious look on his face, and she was worried that I was about to insult him.

Then the boy and I commenced shoveling. I was surprised at the sensation of working with someone at that job. It had long been a sore spot with me that Marie and Victoria acted as if I were the only one of us who might lift a shovelful of snow. This was the first time I had had help. My shovelfuls of snow were substantial, my pace measured. Lancelot Prescott just chopped at the stuff, but he worked so energetically that he managed to keep up with me in sheer displacement of snow. We quickly cleared the driveway, and the boy was going ahead with scraping the front steps while I took a breather.

"Hey, Dad, look at that." Victoria pointed out over the Engelses' roof where a volume of blue sky was driving the dark cloud bank away to the east.

I was still standing there, braced up with my shovel, sweating and catching my breath, when Prescott the Good Scout propped his shovel against the garage and he and Victoria left for the movies. Walking away from me, they kept their distance from each other as much as the snow-banked sidewalk would allow. My eyes stung from the sweat while I stood there watching them. The boy was an inch or two shorter and even more frail-looking than my daughter. My back pained me terrifically when I started to move. Then the sun swept down onto our street, almost blinding me, ricocheting off every plane of new snow.

Indoors, without asking me if I wanted it, Marie fixed me a cup of hot chocolate. While we sat at the dining room table, I told her that I was going to update my résumé and once again start looking for teaching positions in the South. She heard me out, both of us gazing out the window, watching the bright sun melt the snow off the shrubs by our front porch. Suddenly free, branches snapped upward and flung out sprays of water-crystals. "While I'm gone, why don't you go upstairs and take a nap," Marie suggested when I remarked how empty the house seemed without Victoria there.

I did exactly that. I read for an hour or so, but then I dropped down into a subterranean level of sleep. For a long while I was utterly without conscious life; then I heard Victoria's voice calling me from an immense height. "Hey, Dad, come up here!" As my mind rose toward waking, I momentarily thought she must have been in danger; but when I opened my eyes and began lifting my body, I realized that I was in my own bedroom and that Victoria was simply calling to me to join her upstairs in my study.

"You've got to see this, Dad," she said while I trudged stiffly up the steps.

"Close that thing!" I snapped at her when I saw that she had opened my skylight and was standing with her head poking out the roof.

"No, Dad, it's warm now. Come here, you have to see this," she said and moved over to give me room beside her. When I squeezed in, the little alcove was like a two-person cockpit. She was right, it was warm outside, or at least it wasn't cold. With no leaves on the trees now, we could see the hillside sweep of the city of Burlington down to the waterfront and

Lake Champlain and the Adirondack Mountains on the New York side. The sun was huge and red-gold. The lake was molten. The sky was so clear that I saw a gull flying high over Plattsburgh, thirty miles to the northwest.

"Remember when you had to lift me up to see out this window?" Victoria said.

"Mmmm."

"Remember when you told me you had a magic steering wheel hidden inside the wall right here and if you wanted to, you could drive the whole house down to the lake?"

"There's a steering wheel in there, I've just never learned the right words to make it appear," I told her.

"I used to worry that one night you were going to drive us away from here."

I tried to catch her eye, but she was entranced by the sunlit lake. Victoria is an uncommonly pretty girl. "I'm sorry if I worried you like that," I said. "Did you have a nice time at the movies with Prescott the Polyglot?"

"Oh, sure," she said, as if her first real date had been something that happened weeks ago. "He had to go straight home," she added. Then we stayed quiet, looking out across the city while the sun and the sky and the lake took on deeper shades of reddish-gold. When Marie first had this skylight put in for me, I used to open it and look out fairly often. The view pleased me, but I always felt detached from it, as if I were looking at a painting in a museum. Now, bumping shoulders with Victoria, I understood that this was the place she came from, that what we were seeing was hers. I was able to see every detail with affection. I remembered something Uncle Bill Catledge used to say to tease me when I first started courting Marie, "Boy, you look like they just found land on your property."

Victoria was grinning as if the city below us were a boy she was flirting with at recess. “Is it getting too chilly for you, Dad?” she asked.

“Not at all, dear,” I told her. “You’d be surprised how long I can stay up here with you.”

The Crossing

"PROBABLY WE SHOULD GET GOING," she said, reading my thoughts. I knew hers, too: she'd rather I had asked for another piece of her berry pie and more coffee—she'd have made a fresh pot—so that we could have sat there at the kitchen table and talked away another hour or two of the afternoon.

"I expect so." I'd taken her suitcases to the car right away. Ashamed of how wary I was of the house, I'd nevertheless hung back in the kitchen during the short time I'd been there. I wanted to leave, even though I knew I should have been walking slowly through each room, seeing all the changes she had made. She thought a long time before she did even a small thing like moving a school picture of a grandchild from the piano to the dining room mantel.

Out on the porch I told her, "That's a nice-looking coat." She didn't seem to hear me. I was pretty sure she'd bought it just for this trip, but she wasn't holding her shoulders straight the way she'd have done in a new coat a few years earlier. When she turned away from the door, she left her keys dangling from the lock. Though that seemed odd, I took her to mean that she wanted me to check after her to be certain the house was secure. I tried the door, then pulled the keys out, and trotted to catch up with her, opening the car door for her and closing it after her. When I got in on my side, I handed her her keys. She shook her head. "Getting absentminded, I guess," she said. Only then did I notice that she'd just had her hair done and that she'd taken special care with her make-up. I could hardly bear the history I saw in her face.

It was mid-April, one of those windy spring days that spits rain but never really lets a storm go. I made myself drive slowly because I figured she'd be looking back a lot, but I was wrong about that. She was gazing ahead and almost smiling.

I wanted my new car to please her. I hated to admit it, but its most attractive feature was its stereo. I waited until after we'd passed Roanoke, when we'd begun to settle into the tedium of the journey, to pick a tape out of my canvas carrying case and slide it into the deck. I chose the one I'd made of Mozart's horn concertos on one side, and flute concertos on the other.

She'd never heard the kind of sound that car stereo could make. Her taste for classical music was mostly Strauss waltzes or Chopin the way Liberace played it on TV in the fifties. I was glad my tape had the Horn concertos first because they're bright and brassy. I rambled on to her about how Mozart had penned these pieces for a french-horn-playing pal of his, how he had scribbled in the margin beside one particularly impossible solo passage, "How do you like that, Herr Leitgeb?" She let her head go back against the headrest, smiling as I talked.

Around Staunton we drove out from under the clouds and entered one of those Valley of Virginia twilights that move gradually through shades of lavender, pink, orange, and crimson; it lasted for mile after mile. Gliding through it, I began to sense this correspondence between the valley and mountains, still holding the blue light, and the last flute concerto, which is so transcendently sweet it can almost damage you.

We were both still. The old certainty that she shared my feelings was with me, but here in my middle age, I've come to be skeptical of such assumptions. My two daughters have taught me that because an aria from "The Marriage of Figaro" exhilarates me, I should not leap to the conclusion that they find it even partially enjoyable. My daughters have as little regard for Mozart as I have for Liberace. I had set the car's cruise control for 63 miles per hour; the highway was straight; traffic was thin. As discreetly as I could, I stole glances at her. "Are you all right?" I murmured.

Then she looked at me directly. "I'm fine," she said. "How about about you?"

I decided to tell her the truth. "Sometimes I get a little teary-eyed," I said, "but never when I expect it."

"Yes," she said and turned to look out her side window. "That's how it is with me, too." And miles later, she said, "but I don't mind it."

We spent the night in Winchester with old family friends who'd moved up there, Jake and Cassie Hawkins. When we arrived, Jake and Cassie each made a grave little speech to us, as if they'd practiced it, then cheerfully treated us like visiting royalty.

At breakfast the next morning, she and I forced ourselves to eat slowly, but we were both leaning forward in our chairs while Jake and Cassie sat back and relaxed. Our plates were clean too quickly. We had to split another sticky bun to fend off Cassie's generosity. Then at the door, she had to accept a pair of Cassie's wool slacks because, Cassie assured her, "It's cold up there even in the middle of the summer." She took the slacks as if she'd been hoping somebody would give her a pair just like that.

"Don't you dare heave a sigh," she said when we were in the car, moving off and waving back to the Hawkinses.

"Don't you," I told her; in another time we might have had a good laugh. Even so, it was a sunny morning, the Winchester homes we passed had spring bulbs coming up in little side gardens, and I knew she was as pleased as I was to be on the road. "We're a couple of country bumpkins," I said.

She said that I was right about her, but that I had gotten too much education to be any kind of a bumpkin. I said that it wasn't a matter of education; it had to do with the individual spirit. I told her that I could read poetry, listen to opera, visit every museum in Europe, and still not be somebody who could enjoy what they call a "leisurely breakfast." I told her it was the soul's configuration that determined these things.

"You shouldn't joke about that," she said. I wished I hadn't momentarily forgotten that somber side of her sensibility. We rode quietly for all of West Virginia and Maryland. Just after we passed the sign that announced, "Welcome to Pennsylvania," she said, "This is all new to me. Up here I'm an immigrant."

I laughed and started telling her about the stretch of interstate north of Harrisburg, how remote it was up in those mountains, how afraid I'd been a couple of winters ago when I'd driven through a blizzard in that part of Pennsylvania. She denied that she'd ever be afraid of mountains, regardless of the weather. The way she thought of herself as a Blue Ridge

Mountain girl tickled me, as if most of her life she'd gone barefooted and worn flour sacks.

"I want you to hear my hillbilly tape," I told her, and she grinned at me. Over their singing we gossiped about Ricky Skaggs and Johnny Cash and Merle Haggard the way we'd discuss distant family members. Coming into Scranton I had a moment of fear when Joan Baez came on singing, "Will the Circle Be Unbroken"—I'd forgotten it was on the tape, and I didn't want her to have to hear it. I started to punch the fast forward button, then changed my mind, because I thought cutting it off would be just too conspicuous. She read even that slight gesture of my hand.

"It's never been a song that meant very much to me," she said. Her face was kind, slightly bemused. "Eyes on the road," she directed me, still smiling. Then she picked up my case of tapes, set it on her lap, and started scanning the titles. "This one," she said, plucking it out. "When we get through this traffic, I want to hear this one."

"I didn't know you knew Emmylou Harris."

"I don't," she said. "I just like the name. It sounds like somebody from home."

At Newburg, New York, we took a break for lunch. There hadn't been any question where we'd eat; it had to be Howard Johnson's, even though Ho Jo's had declined considerably since the days of our family vacation trips. Back then she'd thought it the ultimate luxury stop. Sitting across from each other in a booth, we solemnly placed our orders. Then I couldn't resist. "Did you see her tooth?" I asked. Our waitress had a gold one. "I've always wanted one like that," she said. It was an old habit of ours, a favorite recreation. Now that I thought about it, she was probably the one who taught me the art of remarking strangers. "Good thing you and I didn't go to junior high school together," I told her. "We'd have been thrown out of every one of our classes."

We were still speaking lightly enough when we carried our ice cream cones out to the car; but the minute I headed the car toward Albany on the Northway, our spirits dropped. Neither of us said anything, but I felt bad, and I could tell by looking at her that she did, too. So far she had been keeping her face from showing what she'd been through, but now she gave up that effort. Her mouth sagged; wrinkles deepened around her eyes.

I tried tapes: Mozart's clarinet concerto was like an aching in the bones. Bach's cello suites were so bathetic I knew we would both be in tears if I let them go on. Linda Ronstadt was abrasive. Bruce Springsteen was a loud-mouthed hoodlum. Ben Webster and Art Tatum made witty mockery of our sadness.

"Would you please just turn it off?" she murmured. I could say nothing except that I thought she was right.

But even moving through the billboard-festooned Catskills became a form of pain. By the time we reached Albany she was rubbing her temples. I could feel her headache so intensely that it became my own—a thin wire stretched tighter and tighter behind the forehead.

"I don't know if I can stand it up here," she finally said. This was after we'd passed the last exit for Saratoga, and I realized we'd had nothing but silence for a couple of hours. "I may have to go on back home."

I knew what she meant. I was worried about the visit, too, worried that everything Marie and Victoria and Sally and I did would remind her of how alone she was now.

"I think you can manage it," I told her, hoping I believed it. "We need for you to do it."

Talking seriously has never been a talent of mine. I am typically male in this regard—afraid of strong emotion in myself or anyone else, even more afraid of expressing or hearing it expressed. But through those miles of the Northway I made myself talk and tell her how we needed her to help us register what had happened.

After Lake George, traffic diminished, and as we moved into the Adirondack region, the landscape became wilder, more natural. I pointed out the white trunks of the birches in the trees alongside the interstate; she became interested in them, calling my attention to them some miles farther on. "I know I'm really in the North now," she said.

I'm always underestimating the distance to the exit for Essex, New York; it seems always to be another thirty miles toward Canada. When we finally did reach it, somehow I took a wrong turn and ended up in Whallonsburg. We'd had plenty of time, but now I had squandered most of it. I started speeding, screeching my tires on the sharp curves of that rural highway. I was gritting my teeth, because I knew she associated my fast driving with the trouble we'd had between us in my teenage years. Still, the last ferry was at six o'clock, and we had to make it, or we'd be driving another three hours around the lake. The silence we held between us now was savage.

Several times I thought I had gotten us back onto that little road that winds its way down into the village of Essex. Then the fields and houses turned strange; I knew I was still lost, and I pressed the accelerator another notch downward. She gave me a hard look but kept her silence.

Suddenly, at five minutes till six, we were coasting down the hill into Essex. Tucked into a little bay on Lake Champlain, the town is a crossroads, some houses, a couple of stores, a few hundred people, and a ferry dock. Today the water was calm, gently lapping the rocky shore. When we pulled up to the loading point, the ferry had cut its engines and was drifting silently toward its moorings. It looked like half a filling station floating across the water toward us.

She was leaning forward to try to apprehend the northern horizon. "Look how far you can see," she said. Most often around this time of year the weather is hazy, but it must have rained there earlier in the afternoon. Now it was so clear we could almost make the details of houses on the other side of the lake. Farther back, over there, Mount Mansfield and Camel's Hump were etched against the sky.

We were the last car to drive across the ramp onto the ferry. A hefty young woman with a blonde ponytail directed us to our parking place; we craned our necks to watch her lift the ramp, unhitch the docking cables, then set up the chain-and-post barrier at the back end of the ferry. That female sailor provoked a lifting of the eyebrows and a small smile. I laughed and suggested we get out.

"It's all different now," she said when I joined her on her side of the car. I couldn't read her mood.

We walked up to the front and leaned against the railing, enjoying the wind on our faces as the ferry picked up speed. "Now where will we be landing?" she asked me, and I directed her across the expanse of silvery-blue water toward a barely visible patch of white sailing masts. "That's the bay near Charlotte," I told her.

"Out here in the middle, are we in Vermont or New York?" she asked. I laughed and told her I didn't know. I felt as if the two of us had just been allowed to set down heavy burdens. I stretched up onto my toes and extended my arms out toward the sky and the water.

"I think I miss him most when I'm happiest," she said. She

startled me so that I touched her shoulder more for my own comfort than for hers. "It's all right," she said, smiling. "I'm through the worst of it."

"He was sick for such a long time," I murmured. "I wish we could have helped you both more than we did."

"I wouldn't have let you." She was looking steadily toward Charlotte, toward which the ferry seemed almost to be coasting through space. "We'll be in Vermont in just a minute or two," she said then, as if to assure herself it was so. "Do you know what I wonder now?" she asked. She looked slowly up and down the lake and even turned to glance back at the New York side, blinking from the wind and smiling at me. "I wonder if I'm entitled to all this." The gesture she made with her hand was up ahead, where the water took the reflection of the Vermont shore and held it like a treasure.

"You're entitled," I heard myself saying. I was surprised it was mine to give. "It's all yours," I told her.

The Beautiful Gestures

AN INVITATION HAS COME to me to speak at Portland State University. While there I will see one of the first good students I taught here in Vermont. Susan Larrick has become a teacher, and my suspicion is that she's a considerably improved version of the teacher I was sixteen years ago. I'm forty-six now, and through all this time I have carried in my mind a sort of paraphrased version of the poem she wrote for my class that convinced me she had talent: it was called "Tight End," and it documented a college girl's drunken behavior on a football weekend. I loved the title's pun, and I was thrilled by the nerve of this girl who wasn't afraid of presenting to her classmates a somewhat slatternly self for the sake of a poem. When I mentioned "Tight End" on the phone to Susan last week, she said that she had long ago disowned the thing and destroyed all her copies of it.

When I was twenty-nine, I weighed 175, had gaunt cheeks,

and imagined that I would write novels that would rival *The Sound and the Fury* and *The Sun Also Rises*. I might have been a dashing figure in the eyes of a literary-minded sophomore with a lousy social life. Susan was always struggling with her weight. She had a tendency to grin in most circumstances, and toward hooting laughter—though her mirth was often on the edge of weeping. As the fall 1971 semester went on, and I came to know her, I began to understand that Susan was frighteningly well-suited to be my student. She was amused, moved, or disgusted by what amused, moved, or disgusted me.

"That's because she has a crush on you," my wife said while the two of us were eating supper and I was singing Susan Larrick's praises. I couldn't deny that, but it seemed to me that at least some of Susan's ability to apprehend what I had to teach came from natural inclination and ability. I hadn't put into Susan the gift that enabled her to write a terrific villanelle. But it was true that Susan's laughter at my little classroom jokes was loud and long. True, too, was that the grin she gave me each morning when I walked into my classroom usually got me off to a terrific start.

Intimacy is a necessary condition between teachers and students of any art. If a student is good and a teacher wishes to serve that student well, then the teacher must be prepared to be intimately connected with the student. Nineteen seventy-one was the fourth year of Marie's and my marriage. As to kids, push was coming to shove: Marie thought she wanted them, and I thought I didn't. If you're moderately constant and sociable, you can get through five years of marriage without children; ten years is another question, and it was one Marie and I were just beginning to address. Everything was relevant to it. My accord with Susan Larrick was especially relevant, though Marie and I acknowledged this only in subterranean levels of our separate and maritally bound consciousnesses. When just two of you eat dinner together night after night, your unborn children sit there at the table with you, and so does your terrifically talented student who has a crush on you.

Susan had a couple of pals who would come with her to visit me during office hours. I liked the pals, but in my office those girls made me nervous. Bea Thackston was tall, bucktoothed, and gawky-limbed, the kind of girl you think of as a genuine *gal*, and she had a laugh that echoed up and down the English department hallway. Candace Winters was lithe and silky-haired; only partially aware of it herself, I think, she generated the purest sexual energy that has ever fueled my imagination. Susan was usually in the company of only one of her pals at a time. But when I remember those fall afternoons of 1971, I place the four of us there in my mop-closet of an office—Candace's skirt riding up her thighs, Bea spouting riffs of laughter, Susan grinning at me and making nervous wisecracks while she poked around the stuff on my desk. All the while I was sweating it out, trying to act cool but hoping to hell they'd make an exit before someone walked down the hall to complain to my chairman.

Toward the end of that semester she handed in a poem that troubled me; about her father, it included a couple of lines describing his inclination to touch people and how, when he had had his evening cocktails, he was inclined to touch Susan in ways that she found offensive. She did not ask me to consider the poem privately; in fact she presented the poem routinely for discussion by the class. Students in undergraduate writing workshops are completely unpredictable: they'll devote hours of class time to arguing about capitalizing each line's first letter, but in the case of Susan's poem, not one sensitive soul brought up what it had to say about incest or child abuse. Throughout the discussion Susan squirmed in her seat, red-faced, and with sweat broken out on her forehead and upper lip, but that was how she'd appeared in discussions of all her previous work.

I knew Susan was much taken with the work of Sylvia Plath and that she had the kind of fondness for Plath's "Daddy" that her peers would have had for a Neil Young or a Van Morrison song. In my office after class, without the company of Bea or Candace, after we'd sat a moment or two without talking, I said something like, "That's pretty serious stuff you're writing about in that poem"; and she replied with something like, "Yeah, I know." I didn't know how to direct the conversation to any further illumination, and I wasn't sure I wanted to know anything more. Plath's poem is a mean-spirited fiction, and Susan's might well have been an imitation of something I had directed her toward admiring.

Among the ways in which I am responsible for Susan is my having infected her with with my taste (in those days) for a certain trembly lipped strain of literary document, Plath's poetry being high on the list of work I admired and read aloud to my classes. Faulkner's Nobel Prize Acceptance Speech, Tillie Olsen's "I Stand Here Ironing," Theodore Roethke's "Elegy for Jane," and W. C. Williams's "Dedication for a Plot of Ground" were other favorites of mine from that early period of my teaching. Nowadays I'm partial to more densely constructed and restrained work. I have come to love design at least as much as conviction. Robert Hayden's "Those Winter Sundays" is what I wish I'd directed Susan toward appreciating rather than Plath's adolescently exhibitionistic "Daddy."

There were boys she hung around with—there were a couple of bearded, raggedy-dressing literary boys who even gave her some halfhearted romantic pursuit, but throughout her four years at this university Susan's social life was generally pretty sad. She kept me informed on this subject as if I were somehow responsible for what a lousy time she was having. She didn't help matters with her inflated standards of male acceptability; a girl so basically human in her appearance couldn't afford to be as choosy as she was. Bea Thackston had a deadly handsome pre-med boyfriend with whom, according to remarks she and Susan let drop, she enjoyed such a vigorous sex-life that both their dormitory roommates had requested reassignments. And in the area of romantic success, Candace Winters had begun surprising us all.

Candace had been one of the first people I met on the first day I walked into the department office. She was the niece of our secretary, Mrs. Hansen, as well as being an English major, and so she felt at ease around that office. "Have you met Professor Puckett yet?" she asked me when I told her who I was. At the moment, she was sitting up on the belly-high counter surrounding the secretaries' desks; she was wearing a miniskirt, and I was using all my willpower to direct my eyes no lower than her chin. "Professor Puckett," she explained happily, "is the other creative writing teacher here," as if with that piece of information I had the key to a successful career. When she turned to Mrs. Hansen for confirmation of Puckett's significance, I snuck a look up her skirt and thus have never forgotten that first encounter with her.

One reason Candace didn't try to hide her adoration of Scott Puckett was that she knew it was absurd for her to hope that he would be interested in her. Everyone would have agreed with her. Puckett was just not a romantic figure. Short and muscular, a fireplug of a man, he spent every free moment in the gym playing squash and lifting weights. He was reticent around everyone and almost catatonic around women, so much so that I wondered how he ever managed to meet Sally, his wife, who was a very personable young woman. Puckett attended her as knights of the fifteenth century attended their ladies.

From the beginning, because he and I were "creative" types, we had things to talk about, business to transact. Among the department's thirty-some literature Ph.D.'s, he and I with our writing M.F.A.'s were foreigners of the same nationality. And maybe because we were both tacitly aware that our colleagues would have been delighted if we had become enemies, he and I became friends in spite of Puckett's difficulty with intimacy. He even tolerated my wretched squash-playing for so many hours that I became a decent opponent for him. After our matches and after our showers, we had many a good talk, sitting under that huge maple tree at the corner of the gym. When you've cooled off, but you're still too tired to want to do anything, you can sometimes get right to what you really want to talk about.

With Puckett and me in those days, our topic of choice sometimes was Ms. Larrick and Ms. Winters. He began it by speaking well of their writing. I'd shared Susan's poems with him, and Candace had shown me a couple of her stories from her classes with Puckett. My perception of their talents was that Susan was the real thing, but that Candace was your basic above-average undergraduate proser. When Puckett praised the two of them equally, I was surprised and a little irked. I took his high opinion of the two of them in fact to be a diminishment of Susan's value. Couldn't he see what a remarkably mature poem "Tight End" was for a college sophomore? But the subject was touchy, and I had the accidental good sense merely to question him further.

"She's made me step back and think," was his remark that signaled to me that the man was experiencing marital slippage. Which in itself was only mildly shocking. What struck me was that he was taking Candace Winters's attention seriously—that he was elevating a child to the status of a woman. Well, she wasn't a child. I have to confess that I'd carried on a flirtation with her since I'd met her that day in the office; and though her interest in me was purely casual, I had thought I understood her pretty well. I had thought she was going to pine impossibly after Puckett, all the while polishing up the nugget of her sexuality—polishing it up until around graduation when she'd haul off and marry some up-and-coming young Republican and for the rest of her life she'd hold onto this romantic past history of the silent man who had remained out of her reach.

I had it all wrong, unless Puckett anchored himself back into his marriage. He and Sally had no kids. Sally Puckett hated all forms of athletics, she loved fine clothes and restaurants, and she gave one to understand that she loved dancing, though Scott was a nondancer. Sally was from Texas, and she also gave one to understand that she'd had some high old times before she met Scott and "came north." She had a way of saying the word "north" that I thought charming. I liked her. Marie and I sometimes called them and had them over for a few drinks late in the evening. Scott would be yawning and wanting to go home, but Sally was a terrific midnight boozer. She was funny, reckless, and full of peculiar opinions in that southern way of colorful talkers. She knew I liked Faulkner, and she liked to rag me about him; she spoke about Faulkner as if he were her reprobate uncle. She knew his work almost as well as I did, though she certainly thought less well of it.

Neither Candace nor Susan had been around for the summer. When they returned to school in September, both of them seemed to have gained strength. They no longer needed each other's support to come to our offices. Walking past Puckett's office, I'd see Ms. Winters in there holding the man's total attention, even though he might have a couple of students slouched in the hallway outside his door, hoping for a chance to see him. I'd think, those students know what's going on in there, why doesn't Puckett wake up? But then when Ms. Larrick was in my office talking about a book of poetry she'd borrowed from my shelf, I'd glance up and see Puckett walking past my door, giving me a little grin or a wave, and sweat would break out across my forehead. What did students waiting outside my office door think? And there was one significant difference between us: he had tenure, and I didn't.

Bea Thackston had come back to school, too, but she didn't find her way to my office. According to Susan's hints, what kept her away was what Bea and her med-student fiancé did with every minute of their free time, in his room with a chair propped under the doorknob. I don't know if what she suggested was true. Those were peculiar times. The sexual freedom of the sixties was being joylessly translated into seventies pragmatism. Middle-class kids screwed to improve their social skills. Or if they weren't as comfortable with sex as fashion instructed them they should be, then they told their friends they were screwing a lot. I liked it when Susan, grinning and checking her watch, suggested that Bea and Kelly, right at that very moment, had sent his roommate to the library so that they could get it on during the free half hour they had between her major's seminar and his Organic lab.

But God knows what was actually true and what wasn't. The culture sent messages to all of us about what we were supposed to be doing. A female colleague in the department made overtures to Marie and me that we took to mean that she and her husband wanted to do a little spouse-swapping. At a lawn party we'd attended that summer, another colleague—a male and a rather large one at that—a specialist in the nineteenth-century American novel, had worn bright red lipstick. Except for that detail his behavior was normal and his appearance exemplary—he'd worn a blue seersucker suit, a tie, and nicely polished cordovan shoes. No one said anything to the man about his lipstick; it was almost as if it had been drawn on his mouth by someone else as a joke.

Those were the days of streaking. Naked young men or women would suddenly dash through crowds of people. Streakers usually performed alone or in pairs; men streaked with other men, women with other women. I never heard of an incident of cogender streaking, though it always seemed to me something that couples might want to do together.

The point of all this is that people did shocking things in those days, or said they did, though I have a great deal of doubt about whether such acts were really what we wanted. It was an odd time in the nation. We were pulling our troops out of Vietnam, but Nixon had mined Haiphong Harbor and stepped up the bombing of the North, and even though we were still meddling around with it, we'd begun shrugging off responsibility for that war. In the sixties there was conviction. In the early seventies there was phenomenon, but it did not necessarily reflect the truth of anyone's thoughts or feelings.

Of course, every age tests a person's sense of identity. One day when she was bemoaning Bea's efforts to fix her up with one of Kelly's pals, I remember telling Ms. Larrick, "You have to figure out who you are and proceed. If you let your pals tell you who are, you've got some sleepless dark nights to pass through." I advised Ms. Larrick that if you write, you've got something to brace you up against the outside world. I'm afraid I let her know just how talented I thought she was, which wasn't good for keeping her humble or for keeping her out of my office. One day when I told Susan that another student was waiting in the hall for an appointment with me, she said, "He can wait until I finish telling you this." She wasn't kidding, though it was to her credit that at that moment she had been telling me something she'd figured out about a Theodore Roethke poem. But right then I began worrying about how insufferable Susan would become if I kept on trying to nourish her poetic talent.

Though Ms. Larrick and Ms. Winters carried out separate visitations on our hallway, apparently they talked with each other a good deal when they were away from the English Department. They cooked up a plan for having a Halloween party—a four-person party to be held Halloween afternoon in Ms. Larrick's dormitory room. When I recall those times, I wonder just what Puckett and I were doing to let ourselves be talked into a scheme like that. I want to think that both of us acted freely and courageously, but I have my doubts. I remember that a day or two after I got the hand-drawn and lettered invitation ("to a 'spirited' party"), I stopped by Puckett's office to ask him if he was going. He shook his head, a much-used Puckett mode of communication, but then he said he wasn't sure, was I going? Without saying so, we both knew that if one or the other of us refused the invitation, there'd be no party, or worse, one of us would be going by himself to a dorm room to socialize with a female student. It would be a good deal less shocking if there were two of us. At the end of the week, when he stopped by my office to check with me, I told him I thought I was probably going; and he shook his head again but then said, yeah, he thought he probably was, too. In that very moment we must have been daring ourselves to do something improper.

Kissinger was trying to negotiate peace. Puckett and I were going to take an afternoon stroll over to the dormitory they called the Shoebox. Ms. Larrick and Ms. Winters were going to throw a little wine-and-cheese party. The nation's fate was not in our hands.

It was a day full of weather. Wind sailed battalions of clouds overhead from horizon to horizon. First the sky darkened, then a patch of light opened out over the lake and came sweeping over the city and up the hill toward the university. When the sun was out it was hot. When it clouded over, the day was brisk and chilly. Wind was the one constant. I remember that wind as one that, if it were with you, pushed you, almost pummeling at your back.

Walking with Puckett across campus that afternoon, I joked about our teacher-costumes. We both had on jackets and ties—ties the wind snarled around our necks and flapped over our shoulders as we walked, heads down, hands in our pockets, toward the Shoebox. I was wondering if I'd be feeling so foolish if I'd been by myself, and I thought he was probably wondering the same thing, though he said little. The nearer the dormitory we got, the more aware we were of students casting their eyes on us.

Entering the Shoebox and climbing its stairwell, Puckett and I were solemn as pallbearers until we'd located Ms. Larrick's room, number 307 according to our invitations. Then we exchanged grins, realizing that like responsible adults we'd both brought the cards with us, folded up in our inside jacket pockets. In unison we lifted our hands to the door; I grinned and dropped my hand while he rapped crisply three times. Instantly the door swung open. We faced two goblins in full regalia.

Susan and Candace had bought devil costumes (red face-masks and red paper-cloth capes) for Puckett and me, which of course we refused to put on. There were crackers, cheeses, and an ice chest containing beer and bottles of Chablis and Chardonnay. The beer was the one Puckett liked, the wines were ones I thought acceptable. There was a stereo, and there were records that demonstrated that Ms. Larrick and Ms. Winters had studied Puckett and me carefully enough to know our tastes in music.

Through our first hour of awkwardness, the young ladies teased us and giggled. Puckett and I slugged down beverages. It wasn't long before we were enjoying ourselves. Around three o'clock, I struggled up from the floor where I'd been sitting being entertained by Susan's tossing grapes toward my mouth. "I'm gonna try on my silly-assed costume," I announced. Puckett stood up beside me—Candace had been rubbing his shoulders—and said he was going to try his on, too. So for the rest of the afternoon we were two devils and two goblins. Though we did nothing really wrong, we nevertheless had a very comical and affectionate time of it until around four-thirty, when Puckett and I knew we had to start heading back to our houses and our wives.

Getting out of the costumes took a bit of time, as did calming ourselves down enough for us to believe we were leaving the room with some decorum. I remember that I accused Puckett of being a rowdy man and that he loudly denied it. Ms. Winters and Ms. Larrick wouldn't hear of Puckett and me going back to the English Department by ourselves, and so, stifling giggles like a pack of high-school sophomores, the four of us clattered down the staircase of the Shoebox.

The outdoors was sobering. The wind had picked up a bit, and though the huge cloud banks had broken up, small clouds still sent shadows skittering across the landscape like fast-moving ghosts. And the yellow light of that afternoon was so intense it was almost palpable. "It's like Sauterne," I told Puckett while we stood there outside the dormitory, blinking. Before us was a small quadrangle of grass, criss-crossed by sidewalks and recently planted with pear and crabapple trees, wind-whipped as in a Van Gogh painting.

"Race you!" Susan said to me. She'd been jittery ever since we'd decided to end the party. Her eyes were wide, and her grin was a grimace. I took off running the instant she did. The spectacle I was making of myself did occur to me, an English professor sprinting across campus with the wind almost ripping his jacket and tie off his body; but the running was ecstasy. The first twenty yards or so I outdistanced Susan. Then my legs felt odd, as if they were suddenly aging. She caught up with me, so that only by exerting myself far beyond what I knew was good for me did I manage to touch the door of the English Department building before she did.

Gasping for breath, grinning at each other but unable to talk, Susan and I leaned against the brick walls and waited for Ms. Winters and Professor Puckett. When they walked up to us, they were shaking their heads in disapproval that was not entirely joking. Then discretion and common sense seemed to occur to all four of us, and we said quiet thanks and restrained good-byes before the young ladies turned back toward the Shoebox and Puckett and I headed upstairs to our offices. He and I could hardly face each other. When we'd retrieved our briefcases and topcoats and come back downstairs, I knew he was just as relieved as I was to be alone for the walk home.

My dread of facing Marie was wasted energy. She'd left me a note asking me to get supper started and reminding me of a neighborhood pre-trick-or-treat meeting she had agreed to attend. I was dicing carrots and humming along with the radio when she came in, full of news about who had said what at the meeting. All evening, taking my turn to hand out expensive little candy bars to trick-or-treaters, I felt as smug as a man who's found money in the street. What remained in my mind for many days afterward was not anything that happened in the Shoebox room (which almost anyone else would have construed to be the "good stuff") but running shoulder to shoulder with Susan through the yellow light of that windy afternoon.

Puckett and I never talked about Ms. Winters and Ms. Larrick's Halloween party, but around each other I think we were both embarrassed by the memory of it. And we were both aware of having stepped back from the afternoon's intimacy among the four of us. Cold weather set in earlier than usual that year. Nixon's landslide re-election had provoked a "winter of the consciousness" in the university community. When Susan came into my office one afternoon to tell me her father had announced his plan to divorce her mother, it seemed to me news in the spirit of national events. Kissinger seemed on the verge of negotiating a peace at the same time that we were heavily bombing the North Vietnamese. The troops were coming home, but the Watergate scandal was breaking open like rotten timbers in an old house. Susan's dad had taken up residence with his receptionist; Susan's fifteen-year-old sister, whom she claimed to be "the only decent one in the whole god damn family," was expelled from school for being drunk in homeroom. On April Fools' Day, the last American prisoners of war were released in Hanoi, and Susan brought me in a letter from her mother asking her to withdraw from the university and come home "to help out."

Although Marie and I were carrying on the most quotidian lives in our little two-bedroom apartment, the world beyond our front door battered us in ways we weren't aware of; we suffered a kind of invisible damage. Like most educated men and women, we needed to make sense of our lives, needed to understand our tiny places in the larger scheme of history. Thirty hours a week Marie did social work in a nursing home, helping old people as best she could, and I taught poetry-writing to twenty-year-olds. What did our petty little jobs mean in connection with the resignation, at the end of April, of four members of the staff of the president of the United States?

Marie is a tall woman with crow black hair and such a presence that people often rudely stare at her, but back then I found myself looking straight through her, talking with her and immediately forgetting what we'd said. I had lost track of myself, too. Almost nothing I said or did interested me. I had stopped showing Marie the little bit of poetry I was writing. We were this standard American couple grabbing toast and coffee in our apartment before we went to work. If one or the other of us happened to glance at a newspaper headline, it might stall us out for ten minutes at a time, not so much reading the story in detail as trying to figure out what planet we were standing on.

Susan Larrick asked me to write her mom a note saying she should at least finish out the semester at the university. I did that, but as I composed my little argument, I kept wondering if one thing might not be as good as another—Susan going home to hand her mom Kleenexes or staying at the university to read Ezra Pound, what difference did it make?

The springtime that came to us that year was unmerciful. Here in the upper regions of the northeast, spring is usually a weatherman's notion of black humor. "Mud Season" is the polite name for three relentless months of slush, chilly rain, constant mist, and soggy gray-green ground. Not so in 1973. We might have believed we were on the coast of South Carolina, the way the balmy breezes caressed our faces when we went outside, and the tulips, daffodils, hyacinths, and lilacs turned promiscuous that summer. A university campus in that kind of weather goes "a little sweetly crazy," as I phrased it to Puckett. (I'd been composing in my mind as I walked up to the office that morning.) Puckett and I had just scurried into the building, having witnessed more than we could stand of America's upper-middle-class youth cavorting outdoors in shorts and T-shirts. "Speaking of springtime images, did you see Nixon's face on the front of your newspaper this morning?" I asked him as we walked up the steps, and he laughed much louder than the remark warranted. When we reached Puckett's office, Candace Winters, in a white sundress, was waiting for him.

The change in weather brought a hard season to Marie and me. That spring she knew she wanted to start having children—right away—and I was more certain than ever that I wasn't ready to be a parent. In fact I was wondering how much longer I was going to be able to stand being married. I wasn't romantically inclined toward anybody else, and I supposed that if I had to be married, Marie was a better wife for me than anyone else I knew. But something was driving me crazy about that apartment when I'd walk home through those gorgeous afternoons. Marie wouldn't even be there when I'd come indoors to our composed living room, our coffee table with the day's newspaper and two stacks of magazines, our wedding-gift lamps, pictures of our parents, and our combined collections of records. Something in me wanted to start pitching things through the windows.

One particularly luxurious early evening, Marie came back from a downtown shopping expedition looking as stricken as I'd ever seen her. She didn't even return my "hello, darling," or come to the kitchen counter where I was working. She stood in the kitchen doorway and studied me from that distance. "I saw Scott and some student," she told me as if accusing me of betrayal. "Yes?" I said, perfectly casually, but I knew what she'd seen and knew how it had affected her. "Something's going on," she said. When I met her eyes, she knew that I knew what she was talking about. "Tell me about it," she said.

I told her the truth, that I hadn't wanted to suspect anything but that in spite of myself I did. It was odd discussing the Pucketts and Ms. Winters with Marie, because as I realized then, I'd wanted to have her opinion all along. The talk was charged. It was my night to cook, and I didn't get dinner on the table until almost nine o'clock. By then it was dark outside. Marie lit candles, I suggested opening a bottle of Beaujolais I'd been saving, and so we picked up the flatware I'd put out and reset the table with our wedding silver. It was one of the most tender evenings we'd shared in a long while; but when I handed her her brandy, Marie shivered and said, "Frank, do you think we're celebrating the end of the Pucketts' marriage?"

"Of course we're not doing that," I told her, but I couldn't think of what else to say to reassure her.

There was a phase in which Candace and Scott were seen

frequently together in public. In the English Department hallways my colleagues and I talked ravenously about them. People assume scandalous things go on all the time in English departments, but for years, apparently, ours hadn't had so much as a stolen kiss. Now there was an associate professor holding hands at a poetry reading with a voluptuous student. That spring, Ms. Winters had become round and rosy, so sultry in her movements that I knew I wasn't the only one who'd considered running a hand down her back just the way you'd stroke a longhaired cat. As if to show the entire university they weren't hiding any longer, Professor Puckett and Ms. Winters started taking bag lunches out to the quadrangle in the noon hour. When we looked out our office windows and saw the two of them together out there, we understood the power of biology or of romance, depending on how we thought about such things.

The way Marie thought about them was with increasing anger. She visibly seethed the afternoon of the English majors' party, to which all the faculty spouses were invited and most attended. Sally Puckett's absence was conspicuous; Sally had always had a pretty good time in previous years of this party, and I know I wasn't the only one who missed the sound of that Texas accent loudly riding over the other voices in the room. You could almost tell that Scott Puckett and Candace Winters had taken vows to stay away from each other during this party but that they were finding it difficult. They stood by the hors d'oeuvres table, a yard apart, but watching each other eat little blocks of cheese. "I'll swear to God!" Marie snorted under her breath at me and strode away from me.

As Ms. Winters blossomed that spring, Ms. Larrick seemed to undergo a shriveling of the spirit. She was able to persuade her mother to let her finish the semester at the university, but she was no longer able to joke about it. She remained on speaking terms with Candace, but her own parents' divorce made her unable to take any joy in Candace's having snared the affections of Professor Puckett. Susan gained weight and took on a bad color. I didn't see her much; though a couple of times, when I went out into the hallway, I found her wandering around out there with her jacket collar turned up as if to hide her face. The second time, I made her come into my office and sit down. She requested a Kleenex and blew her nose forcefully. Then, as if she were bored and impatient, she said, "Whaddaya want?" I just looked at her; as I did so, her eyes welled up and tears began splattering her jacket front. I tried getting her to talk, but she would only stare at her lap and shake her head. I called the university counseling service, set up an appointment for her, and walked her over there.

And as Professor Puckett and Ms. Winters drew the forces of that outrageous springtime into their lives, Marie and I felt a gradual diminishing of the pleasure we took in each other's company. Our dinners were filled with uneasy silences. Marie spent many hours with Sally Puckett, and although at first she had shared her impressions of "how Sally was taking it" with me, she came to say less and less about what she and Sally had done or said. Agnew was much in the news those days; his jowly face seemed a cruel joke visited upon us in our time of personal difficulty.

Susan Larrick's therapist advised her to continue talking with me. We were both relieved that now when she came to my office, we were carrying out an officially approved task. Susan's mood was darker than I'd imagined. She gave me to understand that she had been suicidally inclined enough to persuade the university's counseling service to pass her along to a private therapist. This therapist was encouraging Susan not to sever the ties she'd established with her university friends, but Susan still wasn't able to bear the company of Candace Winters.

The last week of school Susan and I met each day for at least an hour. I felt privileged to be allowed access to so much of Susan's inner life, and in thinking that these talks were helping her, I felt the smug pleasure of a do-gooder. But a bond was being forged between us that made me somewhat uneasy. Susan and I had begun to understand each other and to communicate at a very subtle level. That intimacy made my life with Marie even more painfully absurd in those days of our barely being able to smile when we said good-bye to each other before we went to work.

I still think of that spring as having been hexed. In mid-May Susan told me that Bea Thackston had asked her to stay a couple of weeks to tend the plants in the apartment she and Kelly were renting. Though I was aware of Susan's mother's desperately wanting her to come home, I didn't question that arrangement. I knew Bea and Kelly were getting married that summer; I knew they planned to move things from both their dormitory rooms into the apartment. Then Marie informed me that the following weekend she intended to fly down to Boston with Sally Puckett. Though she told me very little about what she and Sally planned to do in Boston, I didn't question Marie because obviously, if I chose to resist the idea, she stood ready to argue with me. As I remember it, my thinking then was that Marie had taken on a kind of generalized husband-anger—I remember thinking up a German word for it, *Übermanngeraucht*, or something like that. I knew that it behooved me not to give her any cause for moving from the general sentiment to a specific fury toward me.

Marie allowed me to take her to the airport, but I gummed up the occasion of our good-bye hug by saying, "Maybe things will be better for us when you get back." Marie pushed away from me, gave me a look, and opened her mouth to speak. Though the words never came forth, I heard them anyway: "Don't count on it." Well, at least I still understood her well enough to know her unspoken sentences.

In the airport parking lot I felt like a neutralized man. Airports conspire to genericize human experience anyway; and in this case I was an exemplary victim, your basic citizen climbing into his basic car having put his basic wife on the plane to Boston with her basic friend. I felt empty of emotion or personality or consequential thought.

With Marie in the apartment, I enjoyed solitude, the kind available to me in my study with her in the living room listening to public radio or working the crossword puzzle from the *Times* Sunday magazine. With Marie out of the apartment, I felt a lonesomeness like the constant high whine of a violin note. I tried reading, listening to records and then the radio, tried every channel on the TV several times, opened a bottle of good burgundy and finally had a couple of brandies. I never was able to settle down and relax. All through the early morning hours, I kept waking, aware of Marie's absence in the bed. Late Saturday morning, when I finally did haul myself out of the sack, I felt exhausted and headachy. Then, opening the drapes, I faced one of those mean windy rains slashing at the trees and shrubs.

It takes superior inner resources to get through a rainy Saturday in a four-room apartment by yourself. The baseball games on TV were all rained out; you'd have thought rain was battering the entire United States of America. The public TV station was doing a Nixon story, showing photos of his boyhood and college years, playing the old speeches, and so on. I sat there and gawked at the image of Nixon lifting his hand to be sworn into office as Eisenhower's vice-president. I felt utterly absorbed by what I was seeing; as my personality diminished, Nixon's seemed to be swelling before my eyes.

All through the day I hung around the apartment, hoping Marie would call. By six I knew she and Sally would be heading out to eat in one of the Boston restaurants. I envisioned the two of them, dressed up and enjoying the looks they'd be getting from city men. I put on my slicker and went downtown, took a sandwich at a bar, had a glass of the house wine at one place and then another. Whenever my eyes met someone else's, the other person looked away quickly. I knew despair must have been on my face. All the more troubling was what a cheap brand of despair it was: I was no returned Vietnam vet, burdened by all the buddies he'd lost in battle and the Asians whose ears he'd cut off; I was just a husband who couldn't get through a day or two without his wife. At ten o'clock, I lost conviction and went home.

From the foyer I heard our phone ringing. I rushed unlocking the door and ran to answer it, certain that Marie was calling from a pay phone in some theater lobby. It was Susan, calling from her borrowed apartment. "I'm scared, Frank," she said. "I've been trying to get you for hours. I'm really scared. There's this noise."

I wish I could say I was disappointed that it wasn't Marie calling. The fact is I was probably happier that it was Susan—Susan calling me by my first name, something she'd never done before. I cared about her; she needed me and wanted my company in an hour in which circumstances had forced me into such a devaluation of myself that I felt almost invisible. I didn't quiz Susan. I told her I'd be there in a minute or two. I hung up, turned the light out by the phone, walked back out of the apartment, and locked the door.

Though Bea and Kelly's apartment was only five blocks up the hill, I drove the car there; and though it didn't seem unusual at the time, it does seem so now as I think back over that rainy night. As clearly as if it had been a film, a vision came to me of Scott Puckett entering an apartment where Candace Winters was living. So far as I knew, at the end of the semester Candace had gone home to her parents' house in Montgomery Center, and so this fantasy of mine was all the more untoward: Candace was in Puckett's arms before he'd even gotten the door shut behind him. He was slipping the nightgown off her pale shoulders, following it with his mouth down her chest. That was the kind of thing I was witnessing mentally—while the windshield wipers slapped the rain this way and that—and I strained to see the entrance to the parking lot behind the apartment building. I remember chiding myself to "stop it" and forcing myself out of the car and into the heavy rain so as not to sit there and carry on my lewd imaginings.

In an old bathrobe pulled tightly around her waist, Susan met me at the door and backed quickly into the shadow of the little foyer when I stepped into the apartment. She led the way to the living room where a single lamp burned on a low table. "I feel silly now that you're here," she said. The calmness of her voice made me immediately understand that on the phone she'd been exaggerating about how scared she was. I didn't mind. I smiled at her.

"Listen," she said, cocking her head. I was relieved that she wasn't lying about there being a noise. But it wasn't hard to locate the source of it—a tree branch brushing against the window of the small bedroom in which Bea and Kelly had stored boxes of their things. (Or perhaps Susan had pushed all their boxes in there to clear the other room for her living quarters.) I called Susan to come in there and look out the window. When I pointed to the waving branch, she said, "Oh yeah!" in such a forced way that I knew it wasn't a revelation to her.

"I *was* scared," she murmured.

"I believe you," I said. I did my best to make up a kind of generalized fear Susan might have experienced that she couldn't have described for me in any literal way.

I was following Susan's broad back into the living room when she turned and made a gesture with one hand that I remember with extraordinary vividness through all these years. It was a curving, ripple-fingered rise and fall of her hand that conveyed a history of her many hours spent arranging everything in the room so that I would see it in just that certain way.

A packing crate was her bedside table. She had purchased bookends that were miniatures of the "Thinker" bookends I used for special books on my desk at school. Copies I had absentmindedly given her of the little journals that had printed poems of mine were aligned with books I had recommended to her—the Williams *Selected Poems*, the Roethke *Words for the Wind*, a couple of thin volumes of Sylvia Plath's poems, and Baker's biography of Hemingway. Blotner's two-volume biography of Faulkner was on the floor as a kind of step up to the table. I knew enough of Susan's financial circumstance to know that buying such books had been no casual matter for her. The picture taped on the wall at the other side of the bed was of Marianne Moore and Muhammed Ali sitting at a restaurant table; where she'd gotten that photograph I couldn't imagine, but I clearly remembered telling her the anecdote that I'd read about somewhere, of Ali's insisting that he and Miss Moore work on a poem together when they met at Toots Shor's.

I know that I stood there with Susan for quite a while, letting my feelings evolve as they would. In a way it was devastating to be made to see what an overwhelming effect I'd had on Susan, and though it played on my vanity considerably, her arrangement of these effects also demonstrated the paltriness of my offerings to her. What she must have thought to be a grand education I now saw to be a small portion of what she'd need to get her through the years that were coming to her. What in God's name did I think Williams and Plath and Roethke and Hemingway and Faulkner had to say that would be of use to Susan? Especially in the light of that little table lamp on the crate by Susan's books, I saw what a wretched life I had made for Marie and me—how I had failed to make any happiness for us in our marriage and had instead taken us both to a point of mere sullenness with each other. What had the books that I claimed to love done for me, and what right did I have to teach anyone anything?

It seemed to me that the only thing to do was to leave Susan's apartment, go walk in the rain all night, and in the morning type up my resignation from my teaching position at the university. It came to me that what a man like myself should be doing for a vocation was deliver the mail. I needed to be functional but not to be in any position to have an influence on people. When I turned toward the dark foyer and the door, I felt Susan's hand touch my forearm. "Don't go yet," she said in a voice that in my coldest moment I wouldn't have been able to refuse.

She walked heavily into the kitchen and in a moment came back with two opened bottles of beer. She handed me one of them, went to her bed, sat down, and directed me to the one chair in the room, by the desk in the opposite corner. In silence, we both drank for a while. It amused me somewhat to observe how our postures suggested a couple of workers taking a break on a construction site. Then she put her bottle down, crossed her arms in front of her, looked at me and said, "I want you to stay here with me tonight." It was not a romantic request, she clearly conveyed that. There was in her voice something so straightforward that she might have been asking to borrow a sum of money.

"I can't" were the first words that occurred to me because they would have been appropriate on almost every previous night of my acquaintance with Susan. I sat there not saying those words, knowing that if I did say them, Susan was ready to ask me why not. In one corner of my brain I was trying to figure out how Susan knew that Marie was out of town. The only answer I could come up with was that the information had come to her by way of Candace whom Scott would have told because Sally and Marie were traveling together; that made me wonder if in fact Candace was in town somewhere and if she and Scott were carrying out carnal adventures in somebody else's apartment at that very moment. I felt a chill. I was about to stand up and say something like "I'm sorry, Susan, it's just impossible" when Susan lifted her hand and opened her palm to me. She held it like that only for an instant, but the effect on me was dizzying, as if she had lifted a shroud in my brain: I knew that I could stay with her and that there would be nothing carnal about it. "All right," I started to say. Then I understood that I didn't even have to say that. She was grinning ever so slightly, in that way of hers, and so I grinned back.

Susan left her bathrobe on, and I kept my pants and T-shirt on. It wasn't an easy night's sleep, though we curled around each other in ways that were comforting. Still, we weren't used to each other that way. I kept waking, and whenever I did, I saw that she was awake, too. But we made it all the way through until daylight, and when we climbed stiffly out of that little bed, it was as if we'd taken a long bus ride to somewhere we both wanted to go and now we had gotten there.

Susan fixed us coffee and juice. (I said I didn't want pancakes or toast.) We chatted at the kitchen table for a while, and then I said I'd better go home. At the door we kissed awkwardly as if years ago we had been lovers.

That Sunday afternoon when Marie came home (Sally having given her a ride from the airport), I heard her steps in the foyer and met her at the door. I meant only to help her with her luggage, but when I saw her face, I knew immediately that something had changed; where before she left I'd seen simmering rage, now I saw longing and regret. I still don't know if the change was in her facial expression or in my perception of it. And whatever else the results of my night with Susan meant, it seemed to have eliminated my ability to mask my feelings in the presence of Marie. We could hardly get ourselves inside the door fast enough. Even now, fifteen years distant from that afternoon, I still remember exactly how we moved from the overheated foyer into the cool shadows of our apartment, how I carried Marie's suitcase with one hand and with the other pulled her by both her hands, laughing, behind me into the bedroom.

That summer of 1973, Scott Puckett had me help him move his belongings out of his house; Sally wasn't there, and I didn't know if it was something they'd agreed on or if Scott meant to be sneaking his stuff out in her absence. At any rate he moved into an apartment on the other side of town; before he and I had got everything unloaded from the rental truck and moved indoors, Candace Winters was there with a bag of groceries, offering us cold beer from a six-pack. I think Scott was a little embarrassed at how familiar she was with him and me and the new apartment. As usual, though, he had little to say. Candace was chipper, I'll say that much, as well she should have been, knowing the future as she did: she and Scott have a real pistol of daughter, almost ten years old now.

Scott Puckett is still my good friend, but here in our middle age, we've both given up squash; so even if we wanted to, there's little occasion for us to talk. That old history that gave us what lives we have now is this undiscussed subject between us; it is what holds Puckett and me close at the same time it keeps the distance between us.

If Scott or Candace were telling this story, they'd probably be saying what a pistol of a son Marie and I have. They'd mean the fourteen year old, Steve, who in my opinion is more of punji pit than a pistol: with him it's not a shoot-out in the street, it's guerrilla warfare. Of all the difficult human beings I've known in my forty-five years, Steve is the most difficult by a factor of three or four. He's smart enough, though, that when I'm ready to kill him, he's gotten Marie on his side enough to defend him, and when she's ready to kill him, he's gotten my sympathy. If the kid ever gums up his timing and gets both of us mad at him at the same time, he'd better barricade himself in that wasteland of a room of his. Our other boy, Charles is eight, and his main project is making his older brother look bad; thus Charles maintains a pretty clean image around here, but it's clear he's taking instruction from Steve as to what he can expect to get away with as an adolescent.

I keep on receiving instruction about how kids anchor us into our lives. Just the other day, Marie got a letter from Sally Puckett, now Sally Dalton, remarried and living in Austin,

Texas. She wrote to Marie that she's finally been able to forgive Scott, because even though he didn't mean to, he let her go home. She enclosed school pictures of a kindergartner and a second-grader. "And to think," she wrote, "I used to be so certain I didn't want kids! Tell Frank I feel like I've finally been granted tenure or something."

Susan Larrick Parisi has begun learning all this, having just become the mother of a hefty little boy, one Michael Joseph Parisi. In her letter to me giving me the news, she says, "We would have named him Frank, after you, except that I never got used to calling you by your first name anyway, and I could hardly name him Professor Berry, now could I?" Susan met Paul Parisi when she moved out west, and they lived together for years, finally getting married a year or two after Susan's father died. Paul is now in his second year of coaching the football team and teaching phys. ed. at Columbia High School. Susan herself is taking a leave of absence from her job—teaching four sections of freshman English a semester at Portland State, where, as I say, I've been invited to speak.

This little topic I've worked up, "The Place of Creative Writing in the Study of Literature," turns out to be attractive to college and university English departments that like the idea of literature still being the most important item they have to offer. In it I talk at some length about how differently students come to understand what is commonly called "symbolism" once they try to engineer some symbolism of their own in their stories and poems.

The example I use is the hypothetical one of a student who would write a poem about the Vietnam War: with only a crude understanding of literature and symbolism, the student might very well use a rose, an eagle, or a sledgehammer as his or her imagery. And what a good creative writing class might teach this student would be how to look into the subject matter itself for a more natural kind of symbolism; thus, a helicopter, say a UH-1, might become an image suggesting both assault and flight. I will call to my audience's mind the last American helicopter's departure from the embassy rooftop in Saigon, will lift my hand upward in the gesture of the abandoned ones who failed to scramble aboard. If I find that audience out west especially responsive—and I hope Susan will have found a baby-sitter so that she can attend my little talk—I may go on to mention the helicopter that whisked Nixon away from Washington after his resignation in August of 1974. If I am feeling especially loquacious, I will speak of Nixon's retreat to his California mansion, Ford's pardoning him for all federal crimes that he "committed or may have committed." I will demonstrate how the helicopter might be used as a symbol for the flight from responsibility for one's actions. "What do you suppose," I will ask my audience, "the American people made of the sight of their highest elected official—the father of the nation, so to speak—boarding that aircraft?" (Actually, now that I am entertaining this scenario, I think I prefer for Susan to bring the infant Michael with her to my presentation.) "Do you remember, before he flew away, how Nixon turned and smiled and waved, as if he'd just done something marvelous for us?" I will ask, and of course I will lift my hand and wave.

THE HIGH SPIRITS

has been set in a film version of Electra by PennSet, Inc. of Bloomsburg, Pennsylvania. Designed by William Addison Dwiggins for the Mergenthaler Linotype Company and first made available in 1935, Electra is impossible to classify as either "modern" or "old-style." Not based on any historical model or reflecting any particular period or style, it is notable for its clean and elegant lines, its lack of contrast between the thick and thin elements that characterizes most modern faces, and its freedom from all idiosyncrasies that catch the eye and interfere with reading.

Printed and bound by
Maple-Vail Book Manufacturing Group,
Binghamton, New York.
Designed by David Gray